To all the souls with the inner-strength to get back up and go bang bang bang.

The small girl smiles. One eyelid flickers.
　　She whips a pistol from her knickers.
　　She aims it at the creature's head,
　　And bang bang bang, she shoots him dead.

-Roald Dahl

PROLOGUE

"When they said an FBI agent was here to see me...well, let's just say I didn't expect this to be my lucky day."

Prison has stolen pounds from Wayne Killington's physique. Hollow, gaunt cheeks give him a haunted appearance, and his once robust middle is unnoticeable. His blond hair has thinned substantially and receded. The man who once sported a perma-tan now has a pasty white complexion.

The glare on the glass separating us masks a diagonal slither of his pallid face. The air conditioning blasts and chills my skin beneath the blazer, yet my armpits are damp.

There's an inch of space between the handset and his ear. His brow creases high along his forehead. "What brings you here, Sophia?"

Curiosity? A need to face the monster? He won't tell me anything he hasn't already told the feds. No, a man like Wayne Killington won't share anything unless there's something in it for him.

"Sophia, I can sit here all day and look at you. We don't get much beauty in this place. But unfortunately, we have a time limit."

The guard standing by the door folds his hands over his belt and leans against the back wall. Out in the hall, voices carry and footsteps fall.

Wayne rubs his fingers through his remnant hair. He's not handcuffed. I wish he were. In moments of reflection, I like to think his cellmate rapes him daily.

"Stand for a minute. You're like a ray of sunshine. Let me take you in."

I sit in the plastic chair and breathe. In the academy, they teach you about your body's reaction to stressful situations. We dunk our hands in ice water and shoot targets to learn how to squeeze a trigger and aim when our hands are frozen with fear. Adrenaline has undesired physical side effects.

My eyelids close. I swallow. Inhale and exhale. When his face reappears, my control has returned.

"Mr. Killington—"

"Sophia, sweetie, there's no need for formality. Call me Wayne. You've always called me Wayne."

"There are other words I've called you." He chuckles, and his hand rubs over his stomach. It's a familiar movement, but it feels out of place on his thinner profile.

I shift, eliminating the glare from the overhead light. "Why did you do it?"

"Is that why you're here? You want an apology?"

"No." I slowly shake my head. This isn't going to work. There's no sign of remorse. There's no emotion. Given the opportunity, this man would kill me if it suited his purpose. If he doesn't have a conscience, this is a waste of time.

Those cold, dark eyes watch me with a cocky intensity. His lips are relaxed, and the corners of his eyes wrinkle in amusement.

"Did you love my mother?"

His lips tighten then relax. I wish I could send a video of his

reaction to my Aunt Alex. She's a behavioral analyst. She might see more than I do.

"I loved your mother until she didn't love me." There are no inflections in his flat tone.

I narrow my eyes and tilt my head. "Love doesn't work like that."

"You an expert on love now that you're all grown up? Have you got yourself a boy?"

"Have you ever thought about what my mother would say if she knew what you did?"

For a flash of a second, his facial features stiffen. Remorse?

"Do you want me to tell you about my relationship with your mother?"

"You were both married. It couldn't have been much of a relationship."

"We were both miserable in our marriages." His chin juts out. He shifts closer and rests his elbows on the ledge. Jagged black ink protrudes below the hem of the short sleeve of his shirt. *That's new.* "When we were together, I loved your mother very much. More than she comprehended."

So much you engineered her daughter's abduction after her death. *Bastard.*

"Sophia, why are you here?"

"Would you tell me something? As a favor to my mother, the woman you loved more than she comprehended?"

He's stone-faced. Difficult to read. My heart pounds against my breastbone. My stepmother's therapist voice comes to mind. *Listen.* So, I sit and wait.

"What do you want to know?"

"I've poured over the court case records. I study criminal enterprises."

"For your job? At the FBI?"

"Yes."

"Are they re-opening this case? I wasn't offered the chance to have a lawyer here."

"No." I give my head a quick shake and my most sincere expression. "This is just me. I'm not here for the FBI."

"'Cause this is visiting day." He lets out an exaggerated, dramatic sigh with his arms still crossed over his chest. Aunt Alex taught me that's a protective gesture, but he looks lazy and relaxed.

"Yes. My job at the FBI is as an intelligence analyst. A strategic group. I'm not here for the FBI."

"Why'd you register as an FBI agent?"

"I'm not on your friends and family list."

"Well, I'll add you. It's a short list." His lips pucker. "What do you want to know?"

"Everything doesn't add up. Others were involved. Who were they?"

"I'm pretty sure your dad cleaned house. Anyone left got the boot."

He's correct. After my abduction, and the discovery our family company, Sullivan Arms, was selling guns illegally to foreign countries, cleaning house became his mission.

"I'm not interested in the people who worked for you. I want to know who you worked for."

"You already know about Mark. You must be following his case."

"My uncle died." And Uncle Mark probably wouldn't have been convicted because he hired some of the best defense attorneys in the country and the evidence was weak. But given his health, he kept winning delays.

"Sorry to hear that. He was a good man."

"No, he wasn't."

Killington's gaze flashes upward and he smirks. "Wasn't my favorite, if I'm being honest."

"Who else did he work with? He didn't do this on his own."

"No, I helped him. I did it all. That's how it works."

"But who recruited Uncle Mark? How did this all begin?"

"Sophia." He says my name softly. Is that sadness? How would a therapist, someone like my stepmother, hear it? "Let it go. Your dad caught the bad guys. Go back to your trust fund and live the luxe life your mom wanted for you."

"I can't." I shake my head and shift in my seat. My fingers are ice. It's funny how the body works. "You see, Wayne, there are others involved. Just like I was a chess piece in your little game—"

"Little game?"

"You orchestrated my abduction, so in my dad's absence, you could resume the CEO role. Right?"

He squints, narrowing his eyes into slits.

"Uncle Mark promised it to you. Then reneged." *Show empathy, Sophia.* "I get it."

He's unmovable.

"I was a pawn in an elaborate plan for you to capture the CEO title. What happened to me... that was all," my gaze travels to the cracked, stained ceiling, "let's call it collateral damage. The smuggling operation, guns, and drugs... maybe humans... that was a chess piece in someone else's game. I've thought a lot about it."

His lips shift for the briefest of seconds, offering a glimpse of stained enamel.

"My uncle yielded to shareholder pressure for sales growth. That's why he did it." I snap my fingers. "But he wasn't the orchestra conductor. He participated, sure, but he wasn't the ringleader. He was one piece on a complex chess board. I want to know who the invisible chess players are. The queen. The king. The rook."

"Honey, if these invisible men exist, I can promise you, you don't want to find them."

CHAPTER 1
TWO YEARS LATER

"The lone fisherman returns. You catch any fish?"

"You win the lottery?" Frankie tilts his head back and laughs. He's a heavy-set man, but the thick coat and scarf around his neck adds girth. A sure sign it's a chilly day, he's wearing a dark cable-knit hat instead of his standard New York Yankees ball cap. The man's lived in Virginia for the better part of two decades, but he's still faithful to his hometown team.

A newsstand customer approaches him, and I throw a two-finger salute Frankie's way before pushing open the entrance door to the lobby of my apartment building.

My mail from the last two months fills the thick white plastic bin the United States Postal Service collected it in, so there's no need to stop at the bank of mail slots.

Back in my apartment, I flick on C-SPAN, set it to mute, and dump the mail. Other than a notification of a change in credit card terms, it's one hundred percent junk. I dump it all back in the bin for recycling.

The only items in my refrigerator are butter, ketchup, mustard, and electrolyte water bottles. Hardly appetizing. Grocery

shopping is a top priority. Thanks to the once-a-month cleaning service, there's no dust on the counters, and the sink gleams.

After I down a bottle of water, I head to the shower. Hot water pours over me. When I close my eyes, I glimpse the past. The market. The dirt paths. Smiles. The roar of a motorcycle. Gunfire. The stream of blood down the cheekbone and the collapse of knees.

That's enough of that. I turn the water off, shake my head like a dog, step out, and dry off.

First day back from an extended mission in Mexico, and I've got a load of reports to write. Technically, today is a day off, but after I buy food, there's nothing else on the agenda. Might as well login and get some HQ drivel done.

My cell rings, and the intrusive sound has me staring at the device. I rub the back of my neck, breathe deeply, and answer.

"*Hola.*"

"Fisher? It's Bauer. I know it's your day off, but can you come in? If you're up for it, I've got a quick project. Shouldn't take long. Week or two tops."

Outside the double-hung apartment window, a deceptive blue sky shines and tempts like a summer day. Deceptive visuals aside, the bone-numbing February chill forced my morning workout indoors.

I'm due time off, but if the company needs me, I'll push through. "What time?"

"You had lunch yet?"

"No."

"Will you pick something up on your way in? I'll brief you over lunch. One?"

"Sure."

There's just enough time for me to drop off laundry, fight any remnant DC traffic, pick up the requested lunch, and meet with my boss.

Ninety-two minutes later, I pass through security without a single nod of recognition. But then again, I'm part of a select crew that spends little time on-site. It's amusing that the newsstand guy on my block is the only one who acknowledges my absence.

The redheaded woman behind the desk outside Bauer's office appraises me as I approach.

"Bauer in?" I ask, holding up the grease-stained white paper bag for her to see that I bring food. "He's expecting me."

"Officer Fisher?"

"Yes."

"Go on in."

The back of the woman's monitor faces me, and she returns to her keyboard, typing away. The demure black cardigan over a white Oxford shirt underscores her youth. I suppose she's a new recruit assigned to the role of assisting the deputy. That sucks for her.

"Where'd Maggie go?"

Her fingers slow, and she peers over her monitor. "She's still with us. She moved into a different group."

"Well, welcome aboard."

"I've been with the company for eight years."

"Oh. Well, I meant—"

"Fisher, get in here." Bauer holds the door open for me. "What'd you get for lunch?"

"Cheesesteaks."

I pull the subs out of the bag and he cranes his neck to read the napkin that's pressed up against the plastic sleeve. "Tony's. This is why I love you."

"Funny. I thought you loved me because we brought down Esteban." His arrest hasn't yet made the news, but it will. It's an impressive coup and the result of a multi-year cross-agency endeavor. The highest-ranking Mexican diplomat caught taking bribes.

At the square cherry wood table that Bauer uses for meetings, we unpack the subs. Bauer takes an enormous bite, closes his eyes, and moans.

I spread out napkins and use the plastic wrapper they gave me to help protect the table.

"What'chu doing? You haven't had real food in months. Eat."

The cheese and salty, buttery, thinly sliced steak, combined with the crusty fresh-baked French bread roll, is mouthwatering. But this isn't a feel-good social call. He's about to dump another assignment on me.

Bauer flips open a file folder and shifts it on the table so it's in front of us, but far enough away it won't get splattered. There's a typical cover sheet for an op, but it's the photo in the bottom corner that has me setting down the cheesesteak and wiping my hands.

He's familiar, but only through briefings. Rafael Toro. His uncle runs the Toro cartel.

"Colombia?"

The Mexican and Colombian cartels have a symbiotic relationship. My guess is if I'm getting called in, there's a connection with the bribery case and the Colombian cartels.

"Rafael Toro," Bauer says, then chomps down, chews, swallows, and wipes the bottom half of his face with a napkin. "He's a middle-aged playboy. Extreme sports. But his father is a high-ranking diplomat."

"And his uncle is the Toro, right? Is his father taking bribes?"

"I'm sure. But that's not what this case is. Working theory is that Rafael is going to be forced to grow up and take the reins."

"Which reins? Government or cartel?"

"We're not so convinced they aren't one and the same. But he's newly married. She's young. Sources say they don't think she's too happy. We're thinking she might be accessible."

"You want me to convince his wife to be an informant?"

Typical CIA move, but I'm not sure I'm the best pick to bond with Rafael Toro's wife.

"Not you, your wife."

That comment earns a full-on belly laugh.

He rolls his eyes, but he's smiling. He gets the humor in what he just dropped. "Seriously. We need you to go in as a team. We've got a new recruit who will play your wife. She's really got the job here. You just need to pose as an older husband who brought his wife on vacation and ignores her. If our sources are right, they could bond. Become friends. Get her phone number." Bauer grins before chomping into the cheesesteak. There's a lot we can do with a phone number.

"But why me?" If I remind my boss I'm overdue for time off, I'll sound like a whiner, but it's a legitimate question. He has to have other officers he can assign to this.

He wipes his mouth again and rests his wrist against the edge of the table. There's something more. I sense it.

"This new officer. She's one we recruited from the FBI. We promised her she'd be in the field. She's green. You're the best pick to work with her. It's an easy gig. The Four Seasons in Canada. It'll be like a vacation. Good food. Wine. I wish I could go. Consider it a thank you for a job well done."

Now I'm officially suspicious as hell. I have a military background. "Easy gig" is synonymous with "fool beware."

"Why, exactly, am I the best pick to work with her?"

"You know her."

I push the sandwich away and swipe a napkin across my beard. Bureaucratic BS drives me insane. Someone got something wrong because I spend zero time in Langley.

"The age difference between the two of you and our targets is similar. His new wife is American. Emigrated to Colombia as a child. Wealthy. It's a perfect match."

"Because of my age or because I supposedly know her?" Bauer's riddles exhaust me.

"Don't be like that," he says, finishing up the first half of a foot-long sub. "You could do this in your sleep. It's the easiest op imaginable."

If he had a military background, he wouldn't keep repeating that. I lift the top of the hoagie roll, checking to see how saturated with butter the bread is. "And who is this officer I supposedly know?"

"Sophia Sullivan. Didn't I say that?"

As he digs into the second half of the greasy sub, I flip through the pages in the folder. On the back page, they stapled my headshot next to her photo. She doesn't look any different from the last time I saw her when she was twenty-two years old and a newly minted college grad. The colors are off in the black-and-white still. Her light blonde hair appears to be almost ivory, and her light blue eyes are monochromatic. But I'd recognize that classic straight nose, porcelain smooth skin, and petulant, sulky lips anywhere.

The rest of the world last saw her primarily in photos from when she was fourteen years old, as that's what her dad possessed and plastered everywhere when she was abducted. She wouldn't be immediately identifiable to anyone who remembered the missing girl from twelve years ago. But she's the daughter of a billionaire. He keeps his family out of the limelight as much as he can, but that's not to say folks from her hometowns of Houston or San Diego wouldn't recognize her.

"Why her?" When an officer is assigned to an undercover role, there are always reasons.

"She's got the background to run in affluent circles. Nothing's going to impress her or leave her speechless. She's personable. And her specialty at the FBI was money laundering and South American cartels. We gotta use her somewhere. That was the deal."

"The deal with who?"

"Her." He reaches over and punches my arm. "Weren't you listening? When we recruited her, she had terms. Now we gotta see if we can live with 'em."

"And you picked me because I know her?" I play this all back in my head as he chews a bite that would choke a smaller man. "And because, I'm what…" I glance down at her birth date. "Nearly twenty years older?"

"You spent eight years as head of her security. No one else is going to stand a chance of recognizing anyone from her former social circle. If there are any run-ins, you can steer her correctly."

I suppose the logic is sound. "Is she going to be in disguise?"

"We'll do something."

Sophia's a good kid. But she's also loaded beyond comprehension. Why would she join the CIA? We don't exactly get luxe accommodations. I live in hovels on some assignments. It's all about fitting in and living the cover.

There's a rap at the door. Bauer sets down his sandwich and wipes his pudgy fingers. "Come on in."

The door swings open. Sophia Sullivan stands in the doorway, canvassing the wood-paneled walls in the way a first-timer to the deputy's office would. She's wearing a black pantsuit, her blonde hair is pulled back tight, and her expression says she's all business. There's no trace of the young college student, although graduation day wasn't that long ago. Four, five years ago tops.

"Come join us, Sophia," Bauer says to her. "Let's get through this."

Travelers crowd the Los Angeles airport. My palms sweat but my heart rate remains steady as I scan the crowd for any anomalies. Rushing to a gate fits within expected profiles. Someone standing, watching people as opposed to a television, or phone, or airport map might warrant closer analysis.

The first-class lounge consists of three families and five business people, judging from the open laptops. One man leans against the wall of a booth, Beats headphones covering his ears and his eyes closed. He's slightly overweight and blends in.

Fisher scans the scene, then lets out a loud exhale. "Want anything from the bar?"

I shake my head in the negative. There's no justifiable reason to drink at this point. We're here on business.

He approaches the bar. Anyone would pinpoint him as a businessman, possibly on vacation. He's wearing well-fitting black jeans, a sable crewneck sweater, and black monochromatic On running shoes. My guess is he's dressed for his role, playing a part. The Fisher I remember leaned toward cargo shorts and button-down untucked shirts. My friends and I especially liked it when

he'd wear a form-fitting Lycra shirt or tee. In addition to running shoes, he wore shoes that were more like hiking boots, but with treads similar to a running shoe. I didn't understand that particular clothing choice until I entered the FBI and noticed former military personnel wear those shoes all the time.

Caramel highlights coat the ends of Fisher's wavy chocolate strands. They fall half an inch above his thick, dark eyebrows and truly help to bring out what my friend Lauren used to dreamily refer to as sapphire eyes. The longer hair suits him. The crew cut he sported back in the day didn't reveal the caramel. The thick beard is new. It gives him a rugged mountain man aesthetic. I'm on the fence if he's more attractive with the beard or without it. Either way, he's one gorgeous specimen.

It's mind-blowing to me that of all the officers in the CIA, I'm working with Fisher. All those years he oversaw my family's security, and it wasn't until I received the project brief that I learned his surname is Fisher.

Three years in the FBI, and not once did the urge to share confidential information with a friend hit. But I'd absolutely love to tell Lauren that not only am I working with Fisher, the guy she used to sneak photos of because, in her words, he qualified as an Adonis, a status reserved for very few men in this world, but Mr. Adonis is also going to be my pretend husband for a CIA mission. Every time I imagine telling her, I hear her squeal, which makes me smile like a loon.

"So, how's your first week been?" He's relaxed, lounging in the chair across from me, the long neck of a Michelob Ultra dangling between two fingers.

At any time, in any place, someone could be listening. The risks are ground into us. But at the same time, in an undercover role, you have to act natural. We pick names close to our own to minimize error risks, and our cover stories bear similarities to our

own. He's going to go by Damian, I'll go by Sophia. Our last name is Garcia. My cover's middle name is Hernandez, which is my target's maiden name. It's a potential conversation starter.

I scan the room.

"It's okay. No one's listening. Just be nondescript." He says it like it's no big deal, and of course, he's right. We haven't even met our targets yet. There's no one who would be watching us.

"Last week was actually my second week." Those deep blue irises, the sapphires Lauren once claimed were also the color of the Adriatic Sea, send me into a tailspin, which is nonsensical. I need to eject Lauren from my head. "Have you heard of gray mail?" I look quickly around, wondering if I've been too descriptive.

He chuckles. I suppose to any onlookers, we appear to be a normal couple hanging out, chatting while waiting for our flight to board.

"Fun times. Any good tales to share?"

In the last two weeks, I've read all kinds of letters. Most were absolutely insane. Suspicions of neighbors being Russian plants or working for the Chinese government to monitor Chinese citizens on U.S. soil, or truly nonsensical rantings. I try to recall a nondescript story.

"Aside from Bigfoot and UFO sightings?" He nods and takes a long swallow of his beer. "And lots of Chinese weather balloons..." I search my memory for the more fanatical claims, the ones that did not get passed on for review. "Elvis has a son and he's living in Alaska as a militant working to overthrow the U.S. government." I snap my fingers. "And Hillary really is operating a sex ring, but it's in North Dakota in a building shaped like an unfinished pyramid."

He holds his beer up in a salute. "Here's to America."

"Here's to the field," I counter, earning a slight grin. Fisher doesn't really smile. Although, I have to say, he seems more relaxed now than he did back when he patrolled the yard around my dad's

house. Back then, when my girlfriends would come over to ogle the security men my dad hired, he would never engage. Others would wink or at least smile. But not Fisher. It was like we weren't there or he was a guard in front of the Queen's castle. In all likelihood, he found us to be irritatingly silly, because we were.

Of course, that's entirely my dad's fault. He could've hired men who resembled mall cops and they would've gone unnoticed. But no, he hired former elite military men from the security firm that rescued me.

I don't want to think about that time in my life, so I ask, "What's Sheila like?"

"Met her on the same day you did."

Huh. The redheaded assistant outside of Bauer's office had been nice. She must be new if Fisher just met her.

"I've been out of the country for years." He leans forward, using a low voice.

That's right. Fisher's a legend within the CIA, as I learned when a colleague told me I could learn a lot from him. He must've been deep undercover if he didn't make it home for years. I specifically asked Bauer if Fisher is my commanding officer, but he's not. We're partners in what I've been told should be an easy operation.

In the FBI, as an analyst, I studied the cartels. The Toro cartel is one we didn't have a substantial amount of information on. Like many of the modern-day criminal organizations, they foster legitimate business enterprises, which makes it more difficult for authorities to catch them breaking the law.

My objective is to get our target's phone number. The CIA can do a lot with a phone number. Potentially gain significant intelligence or understanding of operations. If she becomes a source, even seemingly innocuous information could be useful to building our understanding.

I'd been surprised to learn our target was Rafael Toro, as I'd thought he was an athlete.

I didn't question the intel in our meeting, but at this table, when it's just me and Fisher, I broach the subject.

"Wasn't Rafael a superstar athlete?"

Fisher sets his beer down on the table and pulls the sleeves of his sweater up on his arms. He's wearing a platinum Rolex on one wrist and a faded braided leather bracelet on the other. He rests his elbows on his thighs, and his forearm muscles flex when he picks his beer back up. Forearm candy is what Lauren would call it, and he's packing enough candy to equal an insulin shot.

"In his early twenties he played professional soccer. Colombia didn't have an Olympic team when he was competitive, and he attempted to make it onto Brazil's World Cup team but didn't succeed. Tore his ACL in his late twenties. Ended his soccer career, but he went on to pursue a multitude of sports. Completed an Everest Expedition in 2016. He's a big scuba diver, base jumper."

According to our intel, he's traveling to Canada for heli-skiing with a group of friends. Bauer told us they don't expect Fisher will get to make contact. The hope is his wife, who is new to skiing, will be grounded at the resort, and she and I will bond.

"I bet you can do all those things." Fisher slowly nods confirmation. "You know, scuba dive, base jump." His lips don't smile, but I could swear there's a glimmer in his eyes and smugness behind that beard. Yeah, I bet he can do all those things and do them well.

The Toros had a private house reserved. But a water pipe conveniently burst in the rental yesterday. The hope is they will take the alternative suite the Four Seasons offers them. Of course, we can't possibly know what they will do. If they find a different resort, or choose a different place, this little op could end before it begins.

Fisher points the neck of his bottle at the monitor showing flight status. "We should leave in five minutes."

Right. We have plenty of time to make it to our gate, and we're flying first class, in case the Toro's research how we arrived in Canada as part of a background check. The nice thing about first class is we can basically stroll on board. Once we're on board, by mutual agreement, we won't say much. On a plane, you truly never know who might be listening. Even if it's an air marshal who might report us for sharing classified information on a flight.

But there's one thing that's been bugging me. I left the FBI because I ended up an analyst. It's completely possible they felt I served the agency best as an analyst. But in the back of my mind, I've always wondered if my well-connected, protective father pulled some strings. When the CIA recruited me and promised to put me in the field, I jumped at the chance. And now, here I am, on my first CIA operation, and the man who spent years in charge of my security detail is my partner.

"Do you speak to my dad much?"

I watch him closely. My Aunt Alex specializes in behavioral analysis, and she taught me the signs of someone lying. He scratches his beard. Finishes his beer and sets it against the table with a clink. He looks me straight in the eye, hands on the tops of his thighs, elbows out. An open stance.

"Nope. I owe him a visit. Haven't been great at keeping in touch. But you know, I consider him a friend."

His tells are contradictory, but I'm inclined to believe he hasn't spoken to Dad. If good ol' Dad is behind this turn of events, my gut is telling me Fisher isn't aware.

"You ready?" he asks in a way that says that line of conversation is over.

And now, I'm not so certain. Maybe Dad did pull strings. But, if he did, that's fine. Bauer said this would be one week, two tops.

I should have down time to continue doing research for my

project, which makes this an ideal assignment. Bauer doesn't seem too hopeful I'll crack Gemma Toro, as we're the third team to attempt to reach her.

The results of this op won't reflect negatively on me, or Fisher. It's in and out.

CHAPTER 3
FISHER

Years in the CIA have taught me to expect the unexpected. My current situation perfectly captures the sentiment. Never would I have expected for the teenager I once protected to become a colleague, or for us to check into a Canadian resort as husband and wife.

"Mr. and Mrs. Garcia, so wonderful to have you with us. You'll be staying in the Summit Suite. Jordan will take you to your room. Please enjoy your stay with us. If there is anything we can do to make your stay more enjoyable, please don't hesitate to let us know."

Sophia smiles cordially. Her full-length scarlet coat drapes over her arm, and she surveys the lobby with a commanding air. It's an aura I witnessed develop as she evolved from a skittish, skinny waif to a confident, driven college student.

This operation is surreal due to my partner, but it's a run-of-the-mill intelligence assignment. Sophia is clearly enthused and eager, but at this stage in my life, I'd prefer a more strategic role. Instead of being an operative gathering intelligence, I've reached that stage where I would prefer to be shaping strategy. With luck, I'll be promoted off this operational carousel soon. If this proves to

be my last stint as an operative, then I have to say, posing as a wealthy, upper-middle-class American living slightly beyond his means and staying at the Four Seasons is an unbeatable last assignment.

Sophia is silent as Jordan guides us through the luxurious mountain resort, to the elevator, and to our suite. She doesn't appear particularly impressed, but given the life she's led, why would she be? The suite features floor-to-ceiling views of the snow-covered mountains and includes two bathrooms, a kitchenette, a den, two fireplaces, and a master bedroom with a balcony. Golden flames with a base of blue flicker in both the den and the bedroom fireplaces. There's one king-size bed and a fold-out sofa in the den. Meets my needs and then some.

Our bags beat us to the suite, and both sit at the foot of the bed in the master bedroom. Jordan explains the Nespresso coffee machine and also shares that there's coffee downstairs each morning. In the kitchenette there's a selection of snacks, protein bars, wines, liquors, sodas, and waters. The room service dining menu is available twenty-four hours a day.

Sophia circles the room as he talks, listening politely enough but her slight frown tells me something doesn't meet her requirements. But we're here on the CIA's dime, so I'm at a loss as to what her issue could be. I tip Jordan, and after the suite door is locked, I join Sophia in the den.

Her vibrant auburn hair shimmers in the sunlight streaming through the glass. The new color offsets her light blue eyes in a way that had every man we passed in the airport doing double-takes. When I first saw her sporting her undercover look, red instead of blonde, I'd been floored. She's an attractive blonde, but as a blonde, she's the kid I watched over. As a redhead, she's a siren. There's nothing remaining of the kid. Her arms are folded, and her fingers lightly flutter, as if playing a piano on her upper arms.

"Is something wrong?" If she's upset about the beds, there's no reason to be. It's pretty obvious I'll take the sofa.

"The Toros aren't going to stay here. Surveillance got this wrong. They'll insist on a private residence."

"My last update said they have the suite two doors down."

"They'll change it when they get here. He'll insist." Her lips purse. Stubborn and defiant. Her dad had been damn lucky she'd been a pretty good kid because if she'd wanted to go wild, there's not a thing he could've done to stop her. If she'd shown any interest at all, those college boys would've been lined up at her door.

I stroll over to the kitchen, checking out the liquor selection. I need a drink. It's been a long, quiet trip to our destination. "If you're right, they'll still be around the property. And she'll definitely visit the spa. They have reservations at the restaurant tomorrow night. So do we, at the same time. We have a week. We'll bump into them. Want a drink?"

"Just water. I'm dehydrated."

I remove a bottle of overpriced water from the fridge and pour my bourbon from one of the airplane size bottles stacked in the concessions cabinet. "Don't stress."

She takes the water bottle from me and angles her eyes. I've seen that look. She's annoyed.

"Look, Bauer doesn't have high expectations. This isn't mission critical. Others have attempted this and struck out. If we do too, it'll be fine. Prior ops found it's hard to connect with them on their turf. Vacation may be an easier connection, or it may not."

"I don't want to fail." It's a quiet admission. And it's one I couldn't possibly comprehend more. Failure is a wound that quietly destroys if you let it.

"We'll do our best. They aren't getting in until late. Do you want to go down for dinner or do room service?"

"Let's order in. I feel grimy after traveling. Do you mind if I

snag a shower?"

"No problem. Pick out what you want for dinner, and I'll take care of it. You take the en suite bathroom, and I'll take the one right here." I gesture to the full bathroom off the hall.

She hesitates, chewing her lip. "You're the senior officer. Shouldn't you take the better bathroom?"

"Do I look like someone who cares which bathroom he takes?"

My question earns a small smile. She's been tense all day. I don't have a good read on why. I hope with food and a shower she'll settle down. Working together as equals is a new dynamic for us, and it's her first case. If she's got nerves or this is weird for her, we've got to work through it.

For me, this baby op is a holiday. Bauer wasn't wrong about that. The missions I've been covering will never make the news and will remain highly classified for the rest of my life. It's exhausting work, the kind of work that eventually ends in either death or a desk job promotion. I'll miss the thrill associated with a high-risk op, but at this stage in my life, studying the intel and developing strategic plans appeals more now than it did years ago. This baby op won't factor into my promotion, but if we score a win, it won't hurt. It's time for the promotion Bauer has been dangling like a carrot for the past two years to come to fruition.

By the time she emerges from the bedroom, hair wet, pale skin flushed pink from the heat of the shower, her room service soup is lukewarm. Loose sweater pants hug her narrow waist and flow out loosely from her hips. Judging from the tiny tank top and the shearling slippers on her feet, the shower helped her settle in. She lifts the metal cover over her soup and arranges the utensils. "You already ate?"

"Yes." I didn't wait for the bathing princess because I ordered a filet and had no intention of eating it cold.

I kick my legs up on the sofa, sitting back against it so I can see her at the small table. She looks so different now than she did at

fifteen, and it's not just the fact that her wet, dyed hair carries a sheen of black. The gawky teenager is gone. Beneath porcelain skin, the muscle tone in her arms and shoulders underscores her dedication to her cause. And just like when she was in college, she's seemingly oblivious to how clothes wrap around her tight body in a telltale... *Stop it.*

"We should review our backgrounds," she says as she stirs the soup.

"Already did that." We spent hours back at base drilling each other. "What I'm curious about is what's going on here."

She rips a piece of bread off and holds it over her soup, then drops it into the bowl.

"What do you mean?"

I cross one ankle over the other. There's no need for this to be confrontational, but we're a team. We need to be in sync. "You seem a little off. Tense. Is it nerves? 'Cause it's your first case? Or is it something else?" She was probably as surprised as I was to find us working together. "You okay working with me?"

"It's not you." She dips her spoon into the soup, as if that answer is sufficient.

"Well, I'm not wrong, am I?" Those eyelashes flutter, and she looks my way, but she continues eating. "Are you nervous?"

She dabs her pert, petulant lips with a napkin like the perfect little debutante, fastidiously avoiding my gaze.

I cross my arms behind my head and stare up at the ceiling. I'm probably reading into it. Highly developed observational skills can be a curse. She's also fresh in the field. Nerves are to be expected. Experience will settle them.

I drop my arms and regroup as she downs her bowl of pinkish tomato bisque.

"How'd you end up in the CIA?" That's something that's been bothering me. I watched her over the years singularly pursuing an FBI career. Prepping at the gun range and in the gym. Taking the

right classes and pursuing strategic connections. It was pretty clear to anyone paying attention she planned to undermine smuggling networks. Completely understandable, given her abduction.

"Recruited." She tears off another piece of bread and daintily spreads butter on it.

"Didn't like the FBI?"

She sets her spoon down, dabs her lips with her napkin, and sets her hands and the napkin in her lap.

"These days, there are some analysts in the field, but it became clear I wasn't on that path. The CIA offered me an alternate career path, and I took it."

"I've heard the bureau's mantra is it's where the bureau needs you, not what you want. It's not a personal thing." I'm being conversational, but her pointy chin juts out in classic defiance. Or maybe it's disagreement. "Disagree?"

She lets out a long, exhaustive sigh. Then she joins me on the sofa, squeezing onto the end of the sofa just beyond my feet.

"I suspect my dad had me assigned to desk duty. My guess is he probably pulled strings to have you assigned to this case. If I think about it too much... I have worked damn hard and—"

"Hey. To my knowledge, your dad had nothing to do with this. Bauer, our boss, knew our history and wanted to capitalize. I just came off another op. I can't speak to what happened in the FBI, but Bauer shared his logic in this assignment. Your dad didn't factor in." She stares at me, mistrust seeping out of those cerulean baby blues. The mistrust isn't deserved. I protected her for seven years. "You know, every person reaches a point in time where they realize the world doesn't revolve around them. This could very well be your time." I pause, studying her while she averts her gaze. She's difficult to read. I'm not sure she's listening, but I speak anyway, because that's how I am with teammates. "And I'm going to throw this out there too. Maybe your dad didn't influence your bosses at the FBI. When he agreed to end your detail after

graduation, he'd gotten his head around the fact that you were on your own. He was damn proud of you, too. It's possible your bosses simply had more openings on the AI side. Or they saw you have a strength they want to capitalize on. Or maybe they're overstaffed on the field side. Your dad calling HR and placing a request isn't one of the more likely scenarios. No matter how powerful you may think he is."

All those years watching over the Sullivan household, I never imagined Sophia was growing up with this kind of egocentric view of the world. She worked her tail off. At school, on the range, in the gym. Jack was proud that despite his wealth he didn't raise a kid who expected everything to be handed to her.

Over the years, Jack and I built a friendship. We didn't serve together, but the man's like a brother. Jack wouldn't interfere in her career. And she sure as hell can't blame him if she doesn't get the exact assignments she wants.

I get off the sofa and open the hall closet, searching for the linens for the sofa. There aren't any on the shelf, so I search for the phone.

"What're you looking for?"

"Phone to call the front desk. Want them to come up and get the sofa bed ready."

"You can't let them do that."

"There are no linens."

"It'll be too weird for a married couple. And word could get to the Toros."

"I don't think the Toros are going to be chatting it up with housekeeping."

"You never know. It's possible. It's an unnecessary risk."

"Fine." She's green. She's playing by the rules. I go back to the closet, pull down a blanket that's folded on the top shelf, stalk into the bedroom and grab two of the six pillows on the California king size bed, and return to the den. "Get up. I'm ready to call it a day."

My day starts early with a grueling workout and ends early whenever possible.

"Um, there is one more thing." She pushes off the sofa, and she runs her thumbnail over the pad of her index finger. I've seen her do that before. Nervousness? Was I right?

"Should we...um, you know, practice?" I stare at the scattering of freckles across her high cheekbones. Why didn't I notice them earlier? "You know, being together? So it comes across as natural tomorrow?"

"Being together?" I repeat the question. What the hell is she getting at? It's not like we're going to be fucking in front of the Toros.

"Um, like kissing or touching? I mean, it might be...unless you want to go with the unhappily married angle. That could work as a bonding point for me and Gemma. And since Rafael is on his fourth marriage, it could work for you to bond with him, too."

I pinch the bridge of my nose. "I don't think the state of our marriage is going to come up in casual conversation."

"Right, but if we look like we've never kissed before then they're going to pick up on it. Even if it's just subconsciously. I mean, I've been over the photos and videos we have of them, and Gemma and Rafael are affectionate. It's going to be awkward if we're around them and don't even touch each other."

"Sophia." I wait until her gaze rises from the floor and falls in the general vicinity of my face. "Kissing won't be awkward. Trust me." Her creamy, pale skin flushes, and another thought occurs to me. She didn't date much in college. None in high school. I would've known, because we would've conducted background checks. Is she inexperienced?

She's twenty-five. She can't be. But this is an awkward situation. Her first operation. I should do whatever I can to help her succeed.

"Sophia...would you feel better if we practiced?"

CHAPTER 4
SOPHIA

The silky sable crew neck sweater pulls tight across what I imagine is a rock-hard, sinewy chest. Every time I gaze into those steel-blue eyes, I hear Lauren's teen voice calling him god-like gorgeous. And the worst part is, with his longer hair that curls slightly on the ends, and that burly, dark chocolate beard, he's even hotter. It's distracting, yes, but not nearly as maddening as the smirk playing out on those all-too familiar stern lips.

Gah. This is weird. He's my dad's friend. He worked for us forever. And now I'm supposed to act like I'm his wife and it's natural for me to touch him. My suggestion is a good one, but he's making it strange.

And yes, I am nervous. My stomach hasn't been settled since LAX. It's my first operation. I want it to be a success. I need for this operation, which he and Bauer refer to as simple, to be a success.

"Sophia." His shadow crosses my feet before I feel his presence. His finger brushes my chin and gently presses, encouraging me to lift my chin. Sparks scatter from the point of contact across my torso. My breath catches.

The corners of his eyes crinkle with amusement, and the lines around his lips tell me he's struggling to hold back laughter.

I can't take it. I push back for some room. He's too close. "I don't need practice." I spit that last demeaning word out. Jesus. I'm not a virgin. "It's just weird for you and me." I wave a hand between us. He has to see it. It's not just in my head, and it's not just because I'm green. "I mean, you're, like, old enough to be my dad. It's gonna be weird."

He closes his eyes, and that's when it happens. He actually laughs. It's deep and barely there, so maybe more of a chuckle, but it's at me. The sound is as smooth as honey and as warming as hot tea.

"Way to catapult a man's ego. How old do you think I am?"

My gaze automatically flits to the laptop on the coffee table. It's in the project folder. I read it.

"I'm forty-two," he answers for me. "I realize that qualifies as old. To you." He raises his eyebrows for emphasis. The smirk comes back. "And yes, technically, I could have fathered you at the age of sixteen. But I think by most standards I'm not old enough to be your father."

"Well, you're friends with my dad."

"True." He turns his back on me, walking away to spread out the blanket on the sofa and set up his pillows. "Your dad is one of a small group of men I count as close friends. Our friendship is one reason I stayed on working for him while you were in college." He slowly turns around and crosses his arms again, stretching the thin sweater over the curves of his pecs.

Back home, he always wore a secured Glock on his belt, but tonight the sweater spills over the waistline of his jeans. He's not wearing a belt, and nothing is tucked in. The little details underscore the difference between then and now. His casual attire lends an air of not being on the clock, even though he is.

"If you want, we can practice tomorrow." He checks his wrist.

"After my workout, we can go down for breakfast. As a married couple." His fingers lightly brush my arm. It's skin on skin, and I'm mesmerized by the contrast of roughhewn skin and the gentle movement. He's attempting to comfort me, yet my lungs constrict, and his touch reverberates from that benign point of contact through my limbs and into my chest. "It's normal to overthink it all when you're first starting out. It'll get easier."

"It's not because I'm starting out." The condescending jerk is so damn amused with himself. "If it was any other man, it wouldn't." A huff escapes from the pit of my stomach, and I spin for the safety of my bedroom. I've got to get my head on straight. I'm coming across like an amateur. If I didn't know him, if it was any other man, I wouldn't have these issues.

"If it was any other man, it wouldn't what, Sophia?"

"It wouldn't be weird." My voice rises annoyingly high, and I reach for the door. I need to put an end to this. In the morning, I'll handle it better.

"Sophia," he says, stopping me right before I've closed the door. "When we kiss, it won't be weird." I can't breathe. "If our roles require it, I promise you, as the skilled officers we both are, we'll pull it off. It's acting. It's part of what we do."

He winks. He's never winked before. The action completely alters his serious persona. The teasing expression is... I don't know. Friendly. Younger. Real. I shove the door closed and pop in a meditation tape. We're both actors? Fine. Great analogy. Actors practice. But he thinks I'm green. Nervous. Silly. A colleague he doesn't need to take seriously.

I clamber onto the bed, cross my legs, lift my shoulders, touch my thumbs to my index fingers, and close my eyes. I need to clear my mind.

In the morning, bird chirps fill the room, enunciated with cracks of thunder. My eyes pop open and I fumble for my phone to silence the sounds of the Amazon. The bedroom door is closed, but I don't want to wake Fisher. Er, Damian.

Come on, Sophia. Get it straight. Today it's game on. His name is Damian. Think of him as Damian. Call him Damian. He's your husband. You've been married for eighteen months. You're his second wife. He doesn't have children. Do we want children? That's not in the brief. I'll say no. Keep it closer to the truth.

Shit. Are we in a happy marriage or not?

Our spending level exceeds his income. This is an important point. It makes him more approachable, and usable, to the Toro cartel. Maybe that's the angle we can play up. I'll push for him to spend more and more, and it will be a sore point between us. A rift in the relationship. And an explainable source of tension.

Yes, I like that. If we get to spend time with them, that's a good backstory. It exposes our weakness naturally.

Dressed in workout clothes and with our room card in hand, I carefully open the bedroom door. The drapes are pulled open, exposing the fading night sky and a scattering of stars. Two pillows sit neatly stacked on top of a blanket folded so tightly it possesses corners.

Fisher—er, Damian—is gone. And I thought I got started early.

Ninety minutes later, sweat drips down my brow as I pound through my timed intervals of weights, push-ups, pull-ups, and burpees. There are two others in the hotel gym with me. One middle-aged man on a bike, and an older woman with long gray strands pulled back in a low ponytail working out on the stair climber.

Damian enters the gym. He scans the room and steps to the back, where the weights are. I watch him through the wall of mirrors. Our eyes meet in the reflection. That frustrating tilt of the

lips returns. There's really no description for it other than "cocky smirk."

He strides straight up to me. "Good workout?" And cue the smirk. "After this, wanna meet back at the room, and we'll go down for breakfast together?"

He removes a thick sweatshirt, revealing a soaked workout shirt. It might be frigid outside, but it's not cold enough to prevent Damian's sweat from drenching his top. The fabric clings to his defined shoulders, his clavicle, and every curve and divot down a very taut abdomen.

"Sure."

I pop back down to the ground, push up through my arms and leap into the air. Damian reviews my form with keen observation.

Am I imagining he's studying me? Is that heat I'm feeling on my backside from his gaze? I drop to the ground, push up, and when I bend to push off into the air, he wiggles his eyebrows as if he's joking around with me. "Lookin' good, babe. See ya in the room."

It's the second time he's mentioned seeing me in the room. My timer stops, and I transition into stretching. Through the mirror, I scan the others in the gym. The man on the bike has black hair and an olive complexion. Could he be one of Rafael's entourage? The man's face isn't familiar, and I've spent years studying the intel we have on not just the Toro cartel, but all the organized crime rings. The biker is slightly out of shape, but only in the movies are they all ripped.

Damian just subtly schooled me. Always play the role.

CHAPTER 5
FISHER

After the gym session, I return to the suite. There's an update on the Toros' expected arrival time.

It's not until after my shower, when I'm drying off in the second bathroom off the hallway that I hear the door open. I freeze, listening. Light footsteps trail down the hallway.

"Sophia?"

"Yep. It's me."

From behind the door, I ask, "The Toros' flight's delayed. Not expected in until later in the day. I'm gonna hit the slopes this morning. You want to join me?"

"No, thanks. I'm going to stay in."

"Snow conditions are exceptional. You sure?"

"Yeah. I'm in the middle of some research."

Research. Right. I suppose when I first joined the company, I spent every second in work mode. With time, she'll settle down. Learn to enjoy life when she gets the opportunity. I'm not sure exactly what she's studying, but she spent the whole plane ride here pouring over reports and updates.

When I exit the bathroom, Sophia's locked away behind the bedroom door. I grab a protein bar and head outside.

The crisp, cool Canadian air, bright blue sky, and blinding yellow sun all scream holiday. The skis cut into my sore shoulder, but the endorphins mask the pain. It's hard to remember the last time I was set free on a mountain. With the blinding light of the sun reflecting off bright white snow and the crisp scent in the air, it feels like vacation. I could hug Bauer for assigning me to this op. He wasn't bullshitting me. This is a dream of an op.

If Sophia is correct and the Toros demand a different room, this whole effort could be dead in the water. If we're strategically hanging out with drinks near the check-in later today, we'll stand a chance of overhearing the Toros making a scene. Maybe we can offer a sympathetic ear to their plight of being stuck in one of the suites as opposed to a residence.

First world problems. Truly unbelievable one-percenter fucktards. Sophia included. But, to her credit, she could've taken her trust fund and never worked a day past college. She could've easily sat on a few charity boards and spent her days shopping, lunching, and spa-ing. But she works hard. Damn hard. She pushes herself. She's a spitfire. Always has been.

"Fisher?"

The male voice arrests my attention, and I scan the gondola line. Who knows me?

A black gloved hand waves from about twelve skiers back. Goggles are down, but I'd recognize that scruffy beard and wide, goofy smile anywhere.

"Trevor? What're you doing here?"

The line between us shuffles to the side, and he digs his poles into the snow, pushing forward to reach me.

"Stella and I came up. Normally, I take her out to Colorado, but she's never been here."

"Where is she?"

"She took a bad spill yesterday. She's back in the room taking it easy today. Pulled a muscle."

"It's just the two of you?"

"Yep. She prefers island vacations, but I'm slowly selling her on the merits of an annual ski trip." The gondola line moves, and we shuffle forward. "Who're you here with?"

I scan the line of families and friendlies, then let out a sigh. "Work."

His head jerks. He gets it. Of all the people I could run into, Trevor's a good one. He's one of the Arrow Tactical Security founders. We worked together for years. He mostly manages the training, keeping all the men up-to-date and fit. Arrow works covert ops for the CIA, FBI, and a few other government entities. He's fully aware I switched sides and joined the CIA about five years back. He'll play it cool.

"Where're you staying?" I ask.

"Fairmont."

"You?"

"Four Seasons." Small talk drivel. It's going on all around us.

Trevor and I shuffle onto the platform of the gondola and pile in with all the other eager skiers and boarders, five to a bench for the morning rush. A balding Australian asks if anyone will mind if he plays some music. We all shake our heads while his daughter whines, "Dad."

"I live to embarrass her," he says with a good-natured chuckle. He's directly across from me, so I'm in the line of conversational fire. "We're up from Brisbane. Love it here. What about you?"

Trevor answers first with a quick, "California." It's a damn good thing our cover story is similar to our real story.

"California too." And I add, "But I didn't realize this guy was also vacationing here. Haven't seen him in years." Lest he heard us in line, I offer up the explanation.

"What a small world, isn't it? We got a text from a friend that a colleague's sister from Sydney is here this week too. Haven't bumped into 'em yet, but that's bonkers."

A young twenty-something boarder decked out in bright orange and turquoise leans over. "Someone told me they call it Aussie season here. So many of you guys come up around now."

"Is that right?" the Australian man responds.

The conversation evolves into a discussion of the workforce on the mountain, and all the countries represented. Trevor pulls his phone out and texts Stella. He'll know to keep it low key, but I make a mental note to remind him to be sure to tell Stella to pretend she doesn't recognize us if we see her out and about. There's no reason to introduce Trevor and Stella to a man being groomed to lead a Colombian cartel.

I pull out my phone. It's my work phone, and I consider texting Sophia. If anyone were to see me texting, it would add to the construction of our cover. But I'm not sure what to text. I lean over to read Trevor's text to his wife, Stella. He's just coordinating the time and place to meet her for lunch.

That makes sense. A husband and wife on vacation would meet up for lunch if possible. Sophia and I need to be hanging around the lobby this afternoon.

DAMIAN TO SOPHIA:

Meet at 1 in Braidwood Tavern for lunch?

SOPHIA TO DAMIAN:

K. How's the snow?

DAMIAN TO SOPHIA:

> About to head out. Ran into an old
> friend. Will tell you later.

We approach the mountaintop, and everyone in the car begins fussing with gloves and goggles. I slip my phone into my jacket pocket and lumber in my ski boots onto the platform.

Skis on, Trevor and I head away from the others and pause near the trail map board.

"Who's Sophia? Colleague?" Trevor scans the crowd, wisely asking in a hushed tone. To a casual observer, we're two friends planning our track down the mountain.

"She's my wife." It feels odd using that term for Sophia, but you never know who is listening, even when it feels like no one can.

"What?" He whips around and bumps my arm.

"Shh." I hiss. "Work."

"Ah. Because I know I would've heard about a wedding."

"Yes. You would've." We have documentation, but there was definitely no service. Although, interestingly, in our back cover folder, and on our phones, there's a folder of wedding photos courtesy of CIA magic and a platinum band on my finger that fits but I'm still getting used to.

Trevor taps me and points. "Let's head that way. Go through Overbite then regroup."

I follow him down, nearly wiping out before fine-tuning the bend in my knees.

Ever the athlete, Trevor seeks out jumps. I focus on my path, given I can't afford to get injured before the Toros even arrive. Sure, the stated objective is for Sophia to bond with Gemma, but they've set me up to be of interest to Rafael.

My cover is that of an owner of a small brokerage in debt. The debt makes me attractive should he be in the market for an additional money launderer in the States.

Once we're back on a lift, a shorter lift with just the two of us on the bench, skis dangling below us, Trevor takes advantage of the privacy. "So, how're things going?"

I stare straight ahead, considering my answer. I'm pretend-married to our buddy's daughter. To my former boss's daughter. His business partner's daughter. Running into Trevor drives home the insanity of the situation.

"I don't mean with whatever you're out here for. I mean, with the new gig."

I study the friend beside me. He's always had it all. He made it through BUD/s. Served as a SEAL for several years and quit. I'm still not sure why he walked away from the dream. Yeah, he went through some crazy years, but now he's married to a fantastic woman. No matter what missteps Trevor makes, he lands on his feet, seemingly better off than before. We don't all have that luck.

"It's good."

"Bureaucracy doesn't get to you?"

Truth is, I've been on nonstop missions since joining an elite group within the CIA. One of the benefits of constant assignments is I'm less aware of the bureaucracy. Or at the very least, less encumbered by it. We gather intelligence. Eliminate a risk here and there. But out in the field, the bureaucracy isn't stifling. "It's not too bad."

"If it ever gets to be too much, I hope you know you've still got a home at Arrow."

"I appreciate that. I do." We can't see each other's eyes with our reflective goggles pulled down, but I shift in my seat and look straight at him. It's the universal sign for I see you, and I hear you.

Years ago, when I wasn't in a good place at all, Ryan, one of Trevor's partners, sought me out. He gave me a purpose when I

was dangerously close to hitting bottom. Trevor stepped in and helped me with PT and got my ass back in line. I owe the two of them. They helped me see failing didn't mean I was a failure or a worthless sack of shit. I'll forever be grateful for them.

"At the risk of stepping out of turn, life's short. You're due some good things. There's more to life than the next mission." Trevor's always gotta be the trainer, the coach.

The top of the lift comes into view. "Says the guy who has it all."

"Can't argue with you there. I do have it all. You can, too."

The full personal life Trevor's referencing isn't in the cards for me. Not when I'm never who I say I am. Not when I'm full of lies and disappear for months on end.

"Seriously. I wish the marriage thing were real."

I pull my face mask up from my neck and over my lips to hide them. He has no idea what he's saying. Or I guess he does, if you consider he's wishing for what Sophia represents, not who she actually is.

"I'm up for a shift change." It's all I'll give him. If I get that promotion, I'll spend time in one place. Then, who knows.

"Whatever happens, just remember, we're here." It's clear from his tone, he means it.

"I appreciate that." As we prepare to get off the lift, I hasten to add, "And, down at the base, this week...if you see me or..." Hell, I might as well tell him. "Sophia Sullivan, you and Stella need to act like you don't know us."

"Holy shit. Sophia's on your op?"

"No one." I say it with an edge, so he gets I'm deadly serious. "No one can know."

CHAPTER 6
SOPHIA

The restaurant's rough-hewn wood walls and ebony table tops evoke a cabin aesthetic. Low level nerves strum as I play with my phone, striving to blend into the scene. There's another woman sitting at a table alone, but she dragged an extra chair over, so she's definitely expecting a group. At the table closest to mine is a thirty-something woman with two young kids. The youngest sits in her lap, while the toddler sits on the floor playing with a game she took out of her bag. In the far corner, near the fireplace, two middle-aged couples in ski clothes gather around a table.

Given the Four Seasons resort isn't directly at the base, for the most part, only those who didn't go skiing would be here at lunchtime. The one table of couples looks like they skied earlier and are done for the day.

I purposefully got here before the lunch crowd and staked a claim to the best positioned high-top table with an indirect view of the lobby and, through the front entrance, the covered drive.

Two black Range Rovers pull up, and uniformed men scurry to assist the guests. I swirl my water and glance down at my phone. The last text from Fisher said he was on his way.

A woman with a veil of smooth, shiny black hair exits the first

Range Rover. A tall dark-haired man drapes a full-length fur around her shoulders. From my position, I count four men of similar age and build. The woman in fur is Gemma Toro.

One of the men steps up beside her, and they enter the lobby side by side. He's slightly shorter than she is, but she's wearing spiked high-heeled boots that have no place near snow and ice. The man wears a Canada Goose black coat, dark slim-fitting jeans, and snow boots. He pushes sunglasses up onto his close-cropped dark hair. It's Rafael.

I glance down at my phone and consider tapping out a quick text to Damian, but there's no point. Rafael and Gemma approach the lobby desk, hands linked. Four Hispanic men, ranging in height from approximately five-foot-seven to six-foot-two, enter behind them and gather around the water and hot chocolate table. One man wears sneakers, one has on loafers, and the other two wear snow boots. They all wear thick winter coats.

The woman behind the lobby desk taps furiously at her keyboard and frowns. From where I am perched, I can't hear what's being said, but as a frequent traveler, I can piece together what's happening. As I predicted, Rafael Toro is demanding a private residence.

Originally, the Toros reserved an enormous home on the mountainside, but the analysts determined it was too far away for us to ensure we would run into them. Thanks to clandestine efforts, the unit had an unexpected pipe burst less than twelve hours earlier. We had a good hunch the Toros would fall back on the Four Seasons, as Rafael and his father are both private residence owners, which gives them priority at all Four Seasons. But the Whistler location only has four private residences available as rentals.

The woman behind the desk fervently taps the keyboard, but she can't exactly kick out existing VIPs for another set of VIPs.

Gemma leans into her husband. She perches her head on his

shoulder, and from this distance it appears she's kissing the side of his neck.

Fisher enters from the back of the hotel. His helmet and goggles are shoved under one arm. His outer coat is unbuttoned. His ski boots are off, and in their place are snow boots. His ruffled hair and ruddy complexion tell the story of a day on the slopes.

As he trudges past the table of Rafael's friends, one of them asks, "How're the conditions out there?"

"Phenomenal." Fisher continues, eyes locked on me. His behavior tracks exactly like a guest heading to meet his wife for a late lunch.

One of the men holds up his hand and high-fives the guy standing closest to him. The other two stand off to the side checking their phones. These four men accompany Rafael everywhere. Our file includes photographs of their wives, but the wives have been conspicuously absent from public outings since Rafael married Gemma.

Damian arrives and loops an arm around my back. The wiry hair on his beard tickles my earlobe and my body reflexively leans into him, like this is normal and natural for the two of us, even though it's anything but.

His dark blue eyes assess the table, and as he takes his seat, he scans the area. He lifts his phone to access the menu. "You waited to order?"

"Of course."

A deep voice echoes through the lobby, and I take advantage to turn and observe, as does everyone else within hearing distance.

"Rafe." Gemma loudly states her husband's name, and it's a mix of reprimand and calming. "The suite *es fabuloso*."

It's clear she's calming him down. He points to his motley band of friends, and one man, I believe his name is Carlos, leaves the others to join at their sides. They've got a suite next door to Rafael and Gemma. In theory, they could all stay in one suite, but

based on what we could dig up, Rafael and Gemma never share their accommodations.

According to our file, Rafael is forty-three years old, but a casual observer wouldn't guess it. There are no grays in his thick, black hair. He's got a zestful energy that comes off as more kid-like than mob boss. In the surveillance photos, he's often moving, head down. Here, in person, he holds his head high, uninhibited, and his dark eyes are observant.

The employee checking them in somehow miraculously creates satisfied customers. Rafael smiles wide, revealing straight, bright white teeth. He bumps fists with Carlos and scoops up Gemma. Both her legs wrap around his waist, and she squeals.

She glances back in our direction, seemingly aware others are around. Rafael shuffles, carrying a giggling Gemma, back to the elevator bank. The Four Seasons employee leads the way, while Rafael's entourage remains at the lobby desk, presumably picking up copies of room keys.

As Gemma bounces, laughing, her gaze continues to flit in our direction at the bar. But it's like I'm invisible. She sees right past me, or maybe she's simply surveying the room to get a feel for how many eyes are tracking her, the most beautiful woman in the lobby.

I'm familiar with her type. Gemma Toro flaunts her wealth. Her six-carat diamond with a diamond band sparkles across the lobby. On the other hand, stacks of sparkly diamond rings glisten under the golden chandelier lighting. I'm almost positive those spiked leather boots are Louboutin.

If I'm going to make a connection with her, I'll need to up my wardrobe game. I visited my father's home in San Diego before departing on this assignment and packed a few pieces of jewelry. The CIA team offered up some pieces, but I didn't want to deal with logging them, and they also lacked a certain finesse. Pretty much everything in the CIA warehouse are items confiscated from criminals.

On my finger, my mother's engagement ring sparkles. It's not quite as obvious as Gemma's monstrosity, but it's elegant, as is the diamond band. The three-carat earrings in my ears are mine. A college graduation gift from my dad and stepmom. The diamond Rolex on my wrist is a gift from my uncle when I graduated from high school. My father cut off all contact with him after we discovered his role in fostering a gun smuggling operation, but he still sent gifts.

When the Toros round the bend out of our view, clinging to each other like a pair of over-the-top newlyweds, I ask Fisher, "Do you think we'll see them again?"

"Maybe in a few hours." He studies the menu on his phone.

"They didn't seem to notice us, but he seemed observant. Will it be weird if we're still here?"

"We're staying at the hotel. Shouldn't be odd. They open up wine tasting in a couple of hours. We'll commandeer the two chairs by the fire. Enjoy some wine. Those are the best seats. If they come down, we'll be here."

"After lunch, I'm going shopping." I shift my stool closer to Damian's. I want to be able to talk to him without having to speak loudly above the televisions and voices. "You know, they weren't exactly what I was expecting."

"What do you mean?"

A waitperson arrives and takes our orders. When she leaves, he leans closer and wraps his arm around the back of my chair.

"Were you expecting them to look like bad people? Like straight out of *The Sopranos*?" He freaking smirks.

"No." He must think I'm inept. "I studied organized crime for years. But..." I've seen reams of surveillance photos. This is my first real-life observation. "Maybe."

Fisher's smirk breaks into a full-out mocking grin, and I give him a playful glare.

"They seemed normal. Friendly. I mean, other than having a pack of friends following them around."

"Nice people can do horrible things. You took all the classes. There are many serial killers out there who are by all accounts charismatic and charming."

"Yeah." My virgin Bloody Mary arrives, and I pick up the toothpick with an olive perched on the end. "But you realize it's quite possible he isn't involved in the shadier side of the family business at all."

"In theory, he doesn't travel with security, so it's possible. We're just looking to make friends should he take over for dear old dad."

"I know that." I've spent more time studying this case than he has, yet of course, he needs to mansplain.

He dips closer. The tip of his nose rubs the side of my face. Electric tendrils swirl. He smells like cedar and man. He's closer now than he's ever been, and between his scent and his warmth, his proximity kicks off a flurry of intense physical responses that sends one leg crossing over the other and heat climbing up my neck.

The physical sensations throw me. We role played in training, but this didn't happen. Casually, I turn my head, stretching my neck muscles and breathing deeply to regain control. This is probably Lauren's fault. All those years of her drooling over Fisher, as if he was an actor or a model.

"Just remember." Fisher warns, his deep voice low and gravelly, "no matter how friendly they seem, three of his wives died untimely deaths. Many in his circle drop off the radar without explanation. Always be careful."

CHAPTER 7
FISHER

The fireplace roars and kids' laughter blends in with the melodic beat of the world music soundtrack. The bartender expertly weaves between customers, eliciting conversation and smiles.

An older man in a baseball cap and wool sweater approaches and gestures to the leather chair opposite mine. "Is this available?"

"No, sorry. My wife will be here momentarily." He glances to the side, at the two additional chairs set off to the side. "My friends," I volunteer.

It's total bullshit, but with luck, this place will fill up, and if Gemma and Rafael come down, our invisible friends will text us and bail on joining us.

I make a show of checking my watch, as if I'm annoyed to be waiting. It's nearly five, and the lifts are closed. Skiing is done for the day, and while a good many will après-ski closer to the base, many will find their way back here. A brunette at the bar glances over her shoulder. In a different tavern, the over-the-shoulder glance might mean something. In this one, she's checking out the remaining available seating. The diamonds lining her fourth left finger, plus the fact this is a pricey family vacation resort, say her husband is nearby.

Outside, small fires burn in circular stone pits, and kids wave sticks with marshmallows on the end into the flames. Hot chocolate loaded to the brim with whipped cream fill copper mugs.

A young woman, early twenties, blonde hair in a ponytail, of average height and build approaches. The crisp white button-down and black jeans match the bartender's outfit.

"Sir, can I interest you in a wine tasting?"

"Maybe." I check my watch again. Where is Sophia? She left to go shopping four hours ago. "My wife should be here soon."

She leaves a sheet outlining my options, and I review the choices, knowing I'll need to order the most expensive. If Gemma and Rafael arrive, wine could be a discussion entry point. Plus, I need to play the role of a jackass spending more money than he earns.

A table of rowdy men off to the side, mid-twenties to early thirties, one by one, look to their right. I follow their gaze. The largest entrance to the tavern opens into the lobby, but there's another entrance in the back which leads to a long hall of shops and services. Immediately, I see who caught their attention.

Sophia approaches, but it's not the Sophia from four hours ago. Eye-catching, glossy auburn tresses bounce with each step. She's wearing a tiny, form fitting top, cut so low the smooth, creamy skin above her breasts reflects light. The miniscule top is missing the bottom half of the shirt, revealing smooth, seductive contours. Her low-rise pants hug her hips and thighs then widen down the length of her legs, draping black leather boots with sky-high shiny silver heels that could double as a weapon.

She wiggles her fingers at me as she approaches, and I notice her once short, square nails are now talons. How the hell did she do that?

She perches on the edge of the seat across from me and sets an enormous black handbag on the ground beside her feet. She

reaches for me and clasps my knee. The movement lowers the neckline of her shirt, and I get a full view of her revealing lace bra. On instinct, I straighten her top, covering her, well, assets.

"Good afternoon?" My pants, the jeans Sophia set out earlier for me to wear, are uncomfortably tight, much more so since she arrived in this outfit. Her makeup is different. More present. Noticeable. She's the picture of a fucking vixen. Those blue eyes pop like never before, but then again, her whole body fucking pops. "What're you wearing?"

"Do you like it?" She twists and flips her glossy mane back over her shoulder. Her nails are a swirl of light pastel colors and shaped like, I'm not sure, maybe pointed tear drops. A vision of those long fingers wrapping around me flashes, and I blink it away.

"Sir? Here are the wines you ordered."

"Thank you." I shift again and lean forward in the armchair, resting my forearms on my thighs. Regardless of her provocative attire, she's still Sophia. My friend's daughter. As the sommelier drones on about the wine's merits, I focus on my breathing techniques and reining in my wayward body. She's undercover. That's why she looks completely different. And no matter how mature she appears, she's still the girl I protected for seven years.

After the waiter leaves, Sophia picks up the first glass and swirls. "I figured if I'm going for PLU status, I've got to fit in. Dropped about eighty K. Worth it?"

Uncertain I heard her correctly, I lean in to question. "Eighty thousand?"

The shirt's nice, mostly because of the absence of material, as are the soft leather pants that hug a shapely derrière, but come again?

She tilts her head back and laughs. "That expression. I wish they were sitting here beside us. That's the look of a husband who is in duress."

"There's no way that expenditure will be approved." But even

as I say it, I remember. She might be a working girl, but she's got a bank account that's larger than some island nations.

"I have no plans on submitting the receipts." She runs a thumb over the ends of the talons. "And this is so not me. Back in the room, I need to practice holding my handgun with these puppies. I doubt anyone could really punch with these." She splays out her hand, examining the new attachments on her nails.

"What's a PLU?"

"People like us. Haven't you heard that before? Anyway, I can't do this to my hair myself. Had to get it blown out. Took some work to get them to do my nails while doing my hair, but that's one thing I learned from dear Dad. With enough money, there's never a no. Also, new outfit." She waves a hand down her svelte, seductive, overpriced costume.

She's fucking stunning. Eye-catching. Sexy as hell. I catch one of the young guys at the end of the table stealing another glance our way. He may be close to her age, but unfortunately for that young man, she wouldn't give his baby soft face a second glance. Even if she wasn't my wife.

I reach across the space between us and clink my glass against hers.

"To makeovers."

"To shopping." She grins, and those light blue eyes sparkle. She's fucking mesmerizing.

"Ah, excuse me, are these chairs available?"

"Yes." Sophia dramatically flutters her talons as she gestures to the open chairs.

Gemma sits in the chair closest to Sophia. I stiffen and swirl my drink.

"Babe, the guys can't all fit here." The deep voice resonates from behind my high-back chair.

Gemma waves a hand. Her nails are shaped exactly like

Sophia's, only they're painted light blue. "They can pull up chairs. Otherwise, you heard the man...it's, like, an hour wait."

"I thought I made reservations." Rafael's annoyance is clear in his tone, but he's not throwing the fit one might expect from a spoiled international playboy.

The waiter arrives within seconds, and Rafael listens intently while Gemma reads the cocktail menu.

While swirling my wine, I stare appreciatively at my wife. She returns my gaze with a flirty smile, and the lightest of blushes coats her smooth cheeks. She crosses one leg over the other and snuggles into the armchair, angled conversationally to the pair seated near us. Her gaze and smile are for me, so much so that any onlooker would assume she's mine. Young Sophia may have missed her calling as an actress.

"Oh. My. God. I love those boots," Gemma says. "Where'd you get them? Are they Chanel?"

"They are." Sophie's eyes widen and she leans forward, uncrossing her legs and placing the boot in question down on the floor. "In the shop down the hall. Can't remember the name. Aren't they fantastic?" She scrunches her nose and smiles. Then she flutters those talons in my direction and grins. "See, honey? I told you they were worth it."

I simply stare at the chameleon. If she were actually mine, I'd take her across my knee. I can only hope that thought plays out in my facial expressions. The tiny, sexy smirk flirting across Sophia's glossed-up lips tells me she's reading my thoughts just fine.

"I love those," Gemma says. She leans back in her chair, effectively separating from us to converse with her husband. "I might go shopping tomorrow."

"You have a full spa day," Rafael says, sounding ambivalent.

"Pretty sure I can fit in some time to get a few new things." Gemma lurches forward onto Rafael's lap with a girlish giggle as the four friends join them. Ivan, the friend with a shaved head,

pulls up two chairs. We've been watching Ivan for years, but we're light on background details. Carlos waves down a waiter, communicates the order, and collects another chair.

Rafael jokes with his friends, while Gemma's hand continually roams his chest, smiling at the men and occasionally laughing. Carlos gives us a curious glance, and I lean forward and capture Sophia's hand in mine. I press my lips to her knuckle. There's too much distance between us, so I shift the armchair forward a few inches until our knees bump.

"What do you want to do for dinner?" I ask her as I gaze into her light baby blues that are now framed by seemingly darker eyebrows.

It's a legitimate question. We need to eat. I expect she'll wave a waiter down and order food right here, since we're seated beside our target.

"Let's order in." She gives me the sexiest fucking look and drags the tip of her nails across the edge of my jaw. With that simple touch, I'm hard as stone.

Guess we're not playing a married couple with problems.

I raise my hand and get a staff member's attention. I gesture to write in the air, and he gives a quick nod and heads off to get our receipt. Sophia's fingers return to my earlobe and venture down my neck. Her touch sends sparks down that side of my body that culminate in my groin. I lean back in the armchair, scanning the room for the arrival of the check.

I sign and stand, adjusting my jeans. Her gaze falls to my crotch, and there's that tiny little entertained, flirty smile. Does she know what she's doing to me? How my body responds to her?

She picks up her enormous bag and scoots by Gemma and Rafael. Her handbag bumps their armrest, and she says, in a tone that somewhat matches Gemma's, "Oh. Excuse me."

Gemma's eyes widen. "Is that from Gucci's spring collection?"

"No, actually. Fall. It's downstairs too. Same shop as the boots."

"Do they have Louis Vuitton here?"

"A few things." Sophia does this strange thing with her hands and eyes I've never seen her do before. "Small selection. But good stuff."

"Good to know."

I pointedly keep my gaze fixed to the lobby. Rafael's friends study us, their conversation halted by Sophia's traipse through their circle of chairs.

Sophia takes one step away from the circle, then pauses to add, "Maybe I'll see you tomorrow." Gemma squints in confusion. "Heard you say you have a spa day planned. I'm getting a facial and a massage."

"Oh," Gemma responds with girlish glee. "Yeah. I'm hoping they're good here."

"They are," Sophia says authoritatively. "We come every year." She wiggles those talons, and her ass sways as her long legs move with fluid grace. I give one quick nod to Rafael and Gemma, and dutifully follow my wife.

I catch up to her at the elevator. "You're good," I tell her in a hushed voice. A young family joins us in front of the elevators, and we remain silent until our suite door closes behind us.

"You know why I did that, right?" Sophia gushes the second I flip the lock on our suite.

"Yep."

Better to walk away and not seem too interested. Any connection can't be forced and must feel natural. I stride down the hall, checking each room as I go. Room service has been in and turned down the covers and pulled the drapes closed. After checking the rooms, I push against the drapes and scan the floor below them.

When I return to the den, Sophia is unzipping her second boot. The first lies haphazardly on the ground beside her.

"Not so comfortable?" I ask.

She gives me a look that says something along the lines of 'what do you think, smart ass?' "Can you pull up the room service menu? I'm starving."

"Certainly."

"Plus, that wine is going to my head."

After ordering for us, I reach into the refrigerator and grab a sparkling water for Sophia. My friend's daughter. A young woman. My colleague. "So not a bad day, huh? You made a connection."

"Not a bad day." She smiles in agreement. There's a lightness to her expression. A solid layer of make-up masks her pale skin, but there's a brightness to her eyes. She's happy. Probably relieved. "I think we'll nail this."

She pulls her feet up under her on the sofa, and I sit on the opposite end, far away from her plunging neckline and exposed midriff.

"You're a natural," I tell her. She smiles and dips her head in subtle acknowledgement. "But you know, I always thought you'd go after the Morales cartel." Her career trajectory puzzles me, because I assumed she went into law enforcement to dismantle the cartels. The cartel wasn't directly involved in her abduction, but the man responsible hired men from the group to carry it out.

Her gaze travels up the wall and her lower lip protrudes, like she's weighing my expectation. "In the bureau, they have a viral theory regarding criminal organizations. Be it Chinese, Mexican, Colombian...they all seem to learn from each other. You shut down one group, ten more spring up. And they've gained the learnings from the exposed group. They're all interconnected. An octopus with a gazillion tendrils." She swallows her water and wipes her lips with two fingers. "Do I believe in a mystical viral theory? No. I

think the key players know each other. They're sharing information. One operation, one battle, won't win the war, because invisible, powerful players are calling the shots. The mafia, cartel, even some of the powerful crime syndicates, they're more like pawns on a chessboard." She drops her gaze, and those blue eyes look straight into mine. "I like the CIA strategy. Gather intelligence. Learn. Assess. Covert, deniable strikes. It's a war. We're all on the same side, and all playing important roles."

Mahatma Gandhi once said that to lose patience is to lose the battle. This is the quote I repeat to myself over and over as I strain to keep my fidgeting digits still and my breaths even while the aesthetician smears creams around my face.

"You have a beautiful complexion. I see a couple of blackheads. Do you mind if I work on those?"

My eyes are closed, and I can't see the kind, gentle woman, but I've endured enough spa treatments to know that if I decline, she'll just find something else to do to my face to fill the fifty minutes. I respond with, "Sure," and an orange-red glow pierces through my eyelids.

Once I'm done with this treatment, I'll go sit in the relaxation room, drink tea, and flip through magazines for hours hoping I coincidentally run into Gemma. I would prefer to be there right now, and considered simply buying a spa pass, but they don't offer those here at this spa. A guest must endure a spa treatment in order to partake in the spa facilities.

Over the years, my stepmom and I have done the spa thing together over and over. Dad loves to pamper us, and somewhere along the way he decided spa treatments are a fantastic gift. I truly

do love that my dad found Ava and derives so much happiness from spoiling her. And, typically, I possess the ability to calm down and let someone dig into my pores and scrub the calluses on my feet.

But today the process is akin to torture. My body pulses with the energy of a live wire. I laid the groundwork yesterday. Gemma will recognize me. I'm almost certain. Thanks to my shopping venture, she saw me as someone like her. I'm going to nail this first assignment, even if it is an innocuous, boring mission.

Patience.

I'm going to prove myself and become such a valued, impressive CO they'll have no choice but to place me in roles where I can make a real difference.

Patience.

The bright light transitions to black, and latex covered fingers smear another layer of cream over my face. A crisp, herbal fragrance almost has me asking what products she's using, but instead I focus on the gurgling creek and high pitch chimes emitting from nearby speakers.

Fisher's probably correct. It's unlikely Dad has anything to do with my current situation. But if Dad did somehow pull strings to get my old bodyguard assigned to work with me, can I really hate him for it? He's a protective father because he loves me. When I pull this off, Fisher will see I'm capable, and he can reassure my dad that he doesn't need to worry.

A soft squeeze on my shoulder brings me back into the room. "How do you feel?"

"Fantastic. Thank you."

"I'll be right outside with some fresh water. Take your time."

I swing my legs off the table and lift the spa robe off the hook on the wall. The luxurious robe has plush, absorbent cotton on the inside and a satiny smooth exterior. A glimpse of deep red hair jolts me, and I do a double-take at my image in the small mirror. I

take a second to smooth a few strands and braid the ends so they fall neatly down my shoulder. But no, the reflection is too schoolgirl. It's not Gemma. So I toss my head down, fluff my hair, flip it, and let it cascade loosely over one shoulder. My cheeks flush against pale, dewy skin. The deep red hair overpowers my unnaturally dark eyebrows and pale skin.

Before visiting the relaxation room, I stop by my locker and apply eyeliner, mascara, and lip gloss. Not enough for it to register that I'm wearing makeup, but enough my face won't blend into the wall.

My locker key jangles in the oversized spa robe pocket. It's early in the day, but the spa is booked at capacity, and other guests have assumed several of the chairs in the relaxation room. A roaring gas fire lights one end of the room. The room overlooks a breathtaking view of the Coast mountains. Beyond the glass door, wafts of steam rise from a circular hot tub nestled into the concrete patio. And that's where I spot Gemma holding a champagne flute of what I suspect is a mimosa.

Cold air punctures my skin when I hang my robe, and I scurry in my heavy plastic spa sandals to the edge of the hot tub, drop my towel, step out of the slides, and submerge my body into the piping hot water. Gemma smiles and lifts her glass as if in a toast.

"It's gorgeous out here," she says.

"It's ten below zero." She's from Colombia. How on earth is she taking the freezing temps so easily?

She holds her glass in a haughty manner benefiting royalty, just above the water, with her hair wrapped up in a twisted towel. Artfully applied black eyeliner flatters her dark brown eyes, mascara lengthens her lashes, and there's a hint of rouge on her cheeks. Deep red lipstick mars the edge of her glass, although little evidence remains on her lips. She empties the glass and rises to place it on the patio behind her. A waitperson appears out of nowhere.

"Would you like another?"

Gemma eyes me. "Are you going to have something?"

"Was that good?" I point to her empty glass.

"*Sí.*" Gemma looks to the waitperson. "Two, please." As the woman walks away, she says, "Thanks. I don't really like to drink alone."

"Any time. I love a good mimosa."

"Well, they're a little stingy on the champagne and the oranges aren't freshly squeezed, but it'll do."

"Yeah." I wave a hand at our stunning surroundings. "This'll do."

Gemma laughs and dips down lower in the water until she's submerged up to her chin.

"I'd much rather be in here than out there." I gesture to the mountain.

We're light on intel on Gemma's background, but our guess is skiing wasn't a part of her Colombian childhood, and from what we know about Rafael, he likely wouldn't tone down his extreme sport tendencies for anyone.

"Ah, yeah." She breathes out her answer and slams her palm down on the water. Tiny droplets splatter. Her flawless face scrunches up as if she's smelled something rotten. "I have to go to ski school *mañana.*"

"Me too." It's a lie, but this is an opportunity. Possibly. Knowing Gemma, she's got a private. "Or, well, I have a private."

I swirl the water back and forth with my hand.

"Me too. I don't know why, though. I could be in ski school continuously for the rest of this month and I'd never be able to ski like Rafe."

"Oh, I'm in the same boat. Damian can ski anything. He likes to jump off helicopters. As if."

Gemma's eyes widen and her mouth gapes open. "Oh, my god. I thought Rafe was the only crazy. Well, and Rafe's

friends," She spits out the word friends, her dislike evident. Interesting.

Our mimosas arrive, and she taps my glass with hers and says, "*Salud.*"

"Cheers."

"You know, your husband is quite handsome. *Un papacito,* no? Sexy?" A coquettish grin spreads and she raises her eyebrows.

Sure, Fisher's a good-looking man. But is she interested in him? Is she another Lauren?

"Don't tell me I shock you." She laughs, and it's a lighthearted, innocent sound. "Surely you know you married a... how do you say... hot man."

"Hottie," I supply. "Oh, I know." And I do. Thanks to Lauren, I've been aware of his looks since I was fifteen years old. One day, I really am going to have to find a way to tell Lauren he played my husband, without, of course, spilling any CIA secrets. It might need to be when we're eighty, but I've got to tell her one day. She will flip out.

"My friends, they think I'm *loca* to marry a man so much... older. But I think they're cray cray. Young men, they're all about them. No give. Older men, they know how to work a woman's body. And look at this." She waves her arm around, much like I did earlier. "You think my friends' men bring them to places like this? No way." She wags her finger in the air. "*Nada.* This, what we have, brilliant."

"True. Damian loves for me to go shopping." I curl my lips conspiratorially. "Well, love might be a strong word. I think I give him heartburn sometimes."

She laughs and stretches an arm over the edge of the tub, relaxing. Her breasts rise above the waterline, but she's oblivious. "Men. How long you been married?"

"About a year and half. You?"

"Ten months. We're talking now about what we'll do on our first anniversary. I wouldn't mind a baby moon, you know?"

This is interesting. According to our sources, Rafael doesn't have any children. And Gemma is his fourth wife.

"What about you?" She glances down in the water, presumably at my body. "You going to have kids soon? Or is...what did you say his name is?"

"Damian."

"Does he want to wait?"

"Well..." A Langley instructor's voice materializes. Stick to the truth when possible. "I don't know about him, but I want to wait. I'm only twenty-two." Really, I'm twenty-five, nearly twenty-six, but age doesn't matter here. And that would sure as hell be my answer if I was twenty-two.

"I'm twenty! But my mama, she had me at eighteen. She keeps saying, 'Why wait? Give that man babies. Give me babies.'" She sips from her glass and sets it back down. Her dark brows lower thoughtfully. "Your mama say the same?"

As close to the truth. Bond. "My mom..." I give my head a shake. My mother passed away a long time ago, but emotions still stir when I think of her. "She died when I was young." I force a smile and lift my glass to partially shield my face. "My dad has a young son from his second marriage. I think he's fine waiting for me to produce offspring." A moment passes between us, a softening of her eyes and a dip in her shoulder. I halfway expect her to give me a hug because she's got that kind of oversized, warm personality.

"And Damian, not in a rush?"

"He's a man. Why should he be in a rush?"

"Isn't that the truth?" She sips from her glass thoughtfully. "Does Damian have any kids?"

"No."

"Same with Rafael. He's... He sees kids as... He doesn't want

them." She shakes her head dramatically then tosses back the rest of her drink. "I'm in a rush. I want a baby. You know, my Rafael, I'm his fourth wife. What about Damian?" I pause, tempted to change the background we've prepped, and she touches my shoulder. "You are not the first. He's too damn hot. Oh, the things I'd like to do to..."

My mouth drops open, and I bark out a laugh. I can't believe she's telling me this. But then she laughs, and it's all a big joke.

"Are you?" She's right back to asking me about his status.

"I'm number two." She nods with a smile. "*Dos*," I add for good measure and her smile widens.

The glass door opens, and a woman in pale blue scrubs calls out, "Gemma Toro?"

"Oh, that's me."

"What treatment do you have?"

"Ah, I went big. Three-hour massage and body wrap. When Rafael gets back, my skin is going to be like butter, and I plan on spending the entire afternoon," she rises from the water and leans closer to my ear, "fucking his brains out."

"Good plan," I tell her, holding a thumb up. She runs from the edge of the tub inside to her robe, wraps herself up, and the door closes.

Shit. I don't have a plan to meet up with her. I toss back the rest of my mimosa, set it down, and spot my towel and robe. Ugh. Getting out of the tub is the worst part of hot tubbing. Thanks to the combination of alcohol and heat, a lightheadedness overtakes me.

The door cracks open and Gemma says, "Let's do our privates together, *si?*"

"I'd love to," I shout and the door closes.

By the time I return to the suite, I'm nearly floating. We'll spend the day together tomorrow. It's perfect. And the funny thing is, I didn't really need to make all these adjustments with nails and

hair. Gemma and I really could be friends. I doubt she has any idea what kind of family she married into. After all, his father is an esteemed politician.

The hallway bathroom door opens, and steam wafts into the corridor. My gaze falls first to the white towel wrapped tightly below a chiseled abdomen and over a sculpted chest and shoulders. A smattering of dark hair sprinkled with a couple of gray hairs cover the well-muscled terrain, and I sort of want to run the tips of my fingers through the curls.

"You're back early."

I force my gaze up to his face because he's a colleague, and that's where my gaze should go. Damn. Gemma was right. My husband is fine. Maybe I should've complimented hers?

"Everything go okay?"

"Yeah." His question reminds me of my victory. "I scored huge. Chatted in the hot tub with Gemma, and we're going to meet up tomorrow." I snap my fingers. "Which reminds me, I've got to get a private scheduled." I pause, waiting for him to move farther down the hall so I don't need to squeeze past him. "What're you doing? Shower in the middle of the day?"

"Ah, went out for a few runs on the off chance I might run into Rafael or any of his friends."

"Anything?"

"Nope. Didn't run into anyone. Not even Trevor and Stella." He turns, and my gaze falls to his sculpted ass, covered only by the towel.

That's something I've got to nip, meaning I need to stop looking him over like he's a tasty treat. Gemma is getting to me. And then there's Lauren. *Gah.*

"What's your plan for the afternoon?" Fisher asks. "You going to head back out to try to cross paths again today or—"

"There's no point. We're free to do whatever. Gemma plans on fucking Rafael's brains out all afternoon." Fisher's pupils enlarge,

and the darkening of his eyes somehow eviscerates the oxygen from my lungs. "Her words, not mine."

I sidestep him and inhale wintergreen. My throat tightens as I reach my bedroom. Sure, he's a good-looking man. Gemma's correct. So is Lauren. I'm not blind. But he's Fisher. And I am not a woman who gets tongue-tied or goes girly. Ever. And, with the rest of the day open, I have work to do.

CHAPTER 9

FISHER

A few flurries descend from the milky white sky, thick enough to obscure the mountain peaks. When I left the suite, Sophia was camped out on the bed, engrossed in her laptop, working on what she called a personal project. I thought about asking her exactly what she's working on but refrained. It's not my business.

Playing the role of businessman, I continue down to the resort's ground floor and along the hallway to the business center booths allocated for private meetings and internet access.

A glass pane covers the top half of the door, but the booths are soundproof. Few guests wander through this part of the resort. At this time of year, guests visiting the Whistler region are here for the winter wonderland, not for business conferences. I pull down the booth's light shade and out of habit check below the desk and under the chair. All clear.

Using my government issued cell, I dial my handler. Rita and I have worked together for several years.

"How's my favorite wasp?" Rita's greeting has me smiling. She's a sixty-something Black woman based in Langley. She's a top-notch handler because to look at her, you'd think kind, cane-carrying grandmother. But she can beat the living shit out of

someone if she so chooses. Legend has it she spent a couple of decades as a case officer before transitioning to become a handler. I suspect she lives outside of DC, but I don't really know. Rita gave me my CIA code name, Wasp. She looked up the deadliest ocean animal, the box jellyfish. A nickname for it is the sea wasp. A run-in with the tiny animal means death in under five minutes. I like Rita. She's creative.

"Living my best life."

If we were on a high security operation in a hostile territory, I wouldn't be contacting her this way. But I'm in Canada on a low-risk op, so a simple phone call works. I could call her from our suite, but I wanted out of the suite.

"I see the princess has been making use of the spa. Must be nice." Rita's a good soul, but I'm not a fan of the attitude she's been throwing Sophia. One, she picked her code name, Princess. It's not like Sophia needs her wealth thrown in her face within the CIA ranks.

"She scored. Meet planned for tomorrow."

"Good for her. Get the digits and you can come on home."

"Yep. How're things back there?"

"Oh, you know, typical. Jerry got the Latin America post."

My skin goes numb. Bauer fucking promised me. That was my post. That fucker sent me to Canada on a joke of an assignment to keep me out of the office for the announcement. Rita's chatter continues. The words blend into incongruous background noise.

"Wasp? You there?"

"Here."

"Did you hear what I said?"

"Yep."

I can practically see Rita's speckled gray eyebrows knitting together. "You didn't say anything?"

"Had to go quiet. Footsteps outside the booth."

"All right. Well, touch base Thursday? Eight a.m. PST?"

"Copy that."

"I shouldn't have said anything. There's a lot of movement right now. You've impressed—"

"Speak later." I end the call.

There's no point in contacting Bauer. One, that would be an extreme violation of policy. Two, Rita shouldn't have said shit to me, and there's no reason to burn her.

I step out of the booth and make eye contact with an Asian woman bent before a hallway bench. She's tugging on her kid's ski boot. I give a quick nod, scan the hall, and head to the elevator.

If ever there was a sign I should think twice about what Trevor's offering, this is it. He's right. Bureaucracy sucks. I barely know Jerry. Met him once or twice in the halls of Langley. There could be ten other Jerrys in line above me for territory spots.

When I push open the suite door, I hear movement. The only exit is through the door at my back. "Sophia?" I call.

"Hey?" Her red head peeks out of the bedroom doorway. I must be getting used to the red. The first glance is no longer jarring.

I step out of my snow boots. I never went outside but put them on anyway as they blend in with everyone else here.

"What's wrong?"

I pause, wondering exactly what I did to tip her off. I scrub my fingers against my scalp and pass through to the sofa.

"Checked in. Communicated you made contact."

"Is there a problem?"

She claims the leather armchair closest to me. My gaze drops to her bare, milky white legs and travels past her knee, to toned thighs and the shade between her creamy thighs below the hem of her short sweater dress.

"Why're you wearing a dress?"

"Figured we might as well go out to eat. Besides, I'll need to

tell Gemma what we did last night. Saying we stayed in will sound boring."

We're here to get a phone number. This operation is the definition of snooze fest.

"What's wrong with you?" I drag my gaze up her body and look into those questioning baby blues. "Don't say nothing."

I let out a loud sigh and collapse against the back of the sofa. "It's nothing."

The concerned expression morphs into a don't-mess-with-me scowl that completely contradicts her youth. I close my eyelids and pinch the bridge of my nose.

"A post I wanted was assigned to someone else. Not a big deal."

"But you're pissed?"

My palms slap against my thighs, and I fix my gaze on a corner of the room. "Par for the course." I push off the sofa. "Should I get ready for dinner? What should I wear?"

She's got everything planned. Might as well let the fashionista direct this one.

"You're thinking about leaving the CIA, aren't you?"

"Where'd you get that?" Sophia is perceptive. I picked up that personality trait when observing her interactions with friends in high school.

"It's in your vibe. Plus, you said Trevor is here. Did he come here to lure you back to Arrow?"

"He's on vacation with his wife." I step away from the wise one. "I'm going to get a shower."

"You already showered."

"Yeah, well, I want another one."

"We have reservations in thirty. It's a twenty-minute walk."

"Fine."

"Fine."

Jesus. What a fucking op. I'm fighting with my fake wife like

she's a real one.

We sit through dinner at a restaurant in Whistler Village without saying much. It's a decent restaurant. They have a television over the bar set to an adventure channel, and I zone out watching skiers jump out of a helicopter and sweep the powder.

After dinner, I'm ready to call it a day, but Sophia's warm fingers tug on mine.

"Let's get a drink before going up."

She's thinking we might see Gemma and Rafael pass by, and she's eager to do a good job.

"Sure." I gesture for her to lead the way.

There are a couple of bar seats open, and she weaves her way through guests. Her thick winter coat drapes over her arm. That tight-fitting silver sweater dress glitters under the lights. Her black furry snow boots rise mid-calf and accentuate toned, svelte legs. I normally don't pay attention to women in tights, but her dress is so damn short it's a good thing she's wearing tights to ensure her bum stays covered.

As we approach the bar, I scan the crowd and count four different men sneaking glances. And those men are sitting with their wives. Unreal.

"What do you want?" Sophia asks.

"I'll order for us. What're you getting?"

She points the tip of her talon at a Cabernet Sauvignon only available by a bottle. I order her blasted bottle, because hey, we're on the CIA's dime, and I order a bourbon neat.

The bartender is a thirty-something Australian who keeps his eyes locked on Sophia as he slides me my drink. She's talking to him about how long he's lived in Canada and how much he enjoys working for the Four Seasons. I slam my drink back in two swallows and push it to him.

"More," I say.

"Sophia!" a high-pitched woman squeals from behind me. I

twist on the stool as Gemma stumbles toward us. Rafael appears to be partially holding her up.

"Gemma!" Sophia transforms into a squealing girly woman and pushes off her stool to give Gemma a big hug. Any observer would think they were besties.

"What're you doing?" Gemma asks.

"Just getting drinks."

"Oh, I want a drink," Gemma says as Rafael says, "We're going back to our room."

"Come with us!" Gemma claps her palms together. "Bring your drinks. We have a huge den and a gigantic fireplace."

I scope Rafael, searching to see how pissed he'll be if we join them. He shrugs and says, "Come on."

I pick up Sophia's coat and drape it over my arm along with mine. She grabs the wine bottle and heads off with Raphael and Gemma. I lag behind to sign our check, give the overly friendly bartender a mediocre tip, then catch up with the others at the elevator.

The four of us say little in the elevator. Gemma rubs her body against Rafael. Two teenage girls fill the space between Sophia and me and get off one floor below our destination.

The elevator reaches our floor, and Gemma takes Sophia's hand and leads her down the hall. Rafael and I follow.

"Girl can't hold her liquor," he says, but he looks amused rather than annoyed. "Not sure how long we'll be up."

"Just tell us to go when you're ready."

He bypasses the girls and opens the suite door.

Once inside, Rafael clasps a hand on my shoulder and asks, "What're you drinking?"

"Bourbon." I left the fresh pour back at the bar, sensing it might be in poor taste to carry my drink through the hotel.

Rafael steps into the small kitchen and pours us all drinks, emptying the rest of the wine bottle into two glasses.

Gemma grins up at her husband, rapidly blinks her thick, dark lashes, and says, "I love my husband." She giggles and holds up her generous pour as the implied reason.

Rafael takes a seat on the corner of the sofa and pats his thigh. "Sit."

Gemma complies, positioning herself on his lap. She dips her head and administers kisses up his neck.

Their den is like ours, only slightly larger. There are more doors leading off of their den, and they have more leather armchairs. I hesitate, waffling between an armchair or the sofa, and Sophia sidles up to me.

"Sit," she breathes into my ear and giggles.

Yes, she is quite the actress. Her palm caresses my chest. Gentle pressure directs me to the leather armchair. The cushion sinks beneath my weight and Sophia plops down on my thigh. She squirms on my lap, and my dick quivers.

I grip Sophia's hip to still her. If she keeps moving like that, I'm going to become uncomfortable real fast.

Gemma and Sophia chat back and forth comparing notes about the day. Gemma spouts off about a dress and shoes she saw somewhere. Rafael appears about as entertained by the conversation as I am. His hand ventures up his wife's thigh, and she finally stops chattering.

Sophia's long fingers venture along the edge of my jaw. The tip of a nail dips inside my earlobe, and I twitch.

Rafael and Gemma lip lock on the sofa.

A warm, wet mouth nips my earlobe as talons comb through my hair. Soft lips trail down my neck, and I stretch, giving her more room. Pinpricks trickle down the back of my neck, and my dick becomes an aching bulge.

She's mirroring Rafael and Gemma. I am aware of this. Both glasses of wine rest on the coffee table, nearly empty. Christ.

My hand slips from Sophia's hip to her ass. My palm flattens

against her rounded bottom, attempting to keep her from rubbing her thighs against my dick, because as good as it feels, this is an act.

Gemma shifts and straddles Rafael. Both his hands cup her ass, and she rocks her pelvis against him. Gemma's dress is longer than Sophia's. If Sophia attempts that maneuver, she'll be flashing her ass.

Sophia cups my jaw and turns my head away from our supposed hosts. Those baby blue eyes cloud over, and my lungs contract as her thumb brushes over my bottom lip. Her tongue slips out and curves over her luscious, full lip. My heart rate climbs.

She dips her head as her eyelashes flutter closed. Those warm, soft lips meet mine. A current jolts through my body, electrifying my skin. The electrical charge quickens my pulse and neutralizes thoughts. The perimeter of the room darkens.

Sophia lifts her head, and those sex kitten eyes blink. The pads of her fingers dig into the back of my head, and then she presses my head back down to her. Her lips open, inviting me in, and god help me, I accept.

Our tongues collide in a sensuous, sinful dance. One that leaves me wanting to shift her in my lap, to rub her against my aching crotch. Desires that have no rightful place spring up, and my breaths come short and quick. One hand clutches the cushion and the other clasps her thigh, torn between holding her in place or shifting her over me.

A moan infiltrates my senses, and I'm not sure if it's Sophia's or Gemma's, but I stifle a responsive groan. Then Sophia lifts my hand from her thigh and moves it up to her breast. *Jesus fuck.*

She's telling me she wants me to paw her breast. She wants me to play along. To mirror the lurid show on the other end of the sofa. I brush my thumb back and forth across the rough yarn. Judging from her squirms, I'm rubbing a sensitive peak. And Jesus, if she keeps twisting in my lap...

The suite door clicks open and deep, boisterous laughter fills the suite.

"*Hola*," one man shouts.

I jump up, lifting Sophia with me, pressing her body against mine as I palm her ass. "We're going."

Rafael's friends crowd around us, taking in the scene. I give them the briefest of nods, scoop up our jackets, and lead Sophia down the hall.

At the suite door, I glimpse Rafael pulling Gemma into the bedroom. Howls of laughter from his friends travel down the hall. The door clicks shut.

Sophia's gaze travels down my chest to my crotch, and the vixen gives a knowing grin. I raise my eyes to the ceiling.

"What?" Her voice is light and breathy and full of play.

"Oh, you know what."

Our suite door closes behind me, and I press my back to the door, willing my body to calm the fuck down.

What happened back there was all part of the operation. My body just... Jesus. In the past, I've slept with assets, even though you aren't supposed to. But people do it. I've never had an undercover op like this, though...with my friend's daughter. And he's not just a friend. I might end up working for him again. Technically, he would be my boss.

"Do you think they're swingers?" Sophia is all the way down the hall. She bends, sticking that delectable ass out in my direction, and unfastens those sky-high fur boots.

I consider her question. It got hot and heavy fast.

"Maybe."

"Interesting." She pops back up, picks up her boots, and offers a quick, "Goodnight," before closing the door.

She's good at this. The consummate professional. Intelligent. Instinctually savvy. Daring. Sexy as hell. She's going to have one remarkable career in the CIA.

CHAPTER 10

FISHER

Steam billows through the small bathroom and coats the rectangular tiles in a film of moisture. I rest my forearm against the back wall and let the overhead rain shower pummel my shoulders and coax my tight muscles. My free hand wraps around my dick, and I close my eyes.

The taste of Sophia's wine, rich and sweet, comes to mind. Her teasing tongue, and the way her teeth scraped my bottom lip. Her nails scratching my scalp, tugging on my hair. Did she have any idea what she did to me, rubbing that delectable bottom over my iron-hard erection, grinding my sensitive tip?

My grip on my shaft tightens. Up and down. I need to visualize a woman's mouth. Sophia's lips and those sky-blue eyes crystallize. I close my eyes, shutting that down. Not her. Anyone but her. I comb through memories. The last woman I fucked. A brunette. Yes. An olive complexion. Dark, sultry eyes.

My hand over her breast, palming her. But there's a coarse fabric. Sophia's breast. She's placed my hand over her breast, and my thumb flips over her tender crest. Sweetly curved mounds I've never actually seen, but damn if I can't visualize them.

I grit my teeth as I pump my release, knowing damn well this is

wrong. Sophia is the last person I should think about while jacking off.

I need to go into the village and find someone to fuck. To clear my mind. But I can't risk it. Someone might see me. It wouldn't fit with our cover.

Of course, maybe Sophia's hunch is correct. Maybe they are swingers. But what would that mean? I'd be with Gemma while Sophia was with Rafael? Would she do that for a nothing case? It's clear in training sex is not a requirement of the job. It's not expected. But there's an unstated understanding that sometimes it works. Hell, there are infamous instances of men and women being trained in other government's intelligence operations to seduce and use all means necessary.

It's just sex. And I wouldn't have a problem with it, but as I flip the lever to end the shower, I envision Sophia crawling on Rafael's lap. My muscles tense and my jaw tightens. No. Absolutely not. Getting a phone number, maybe securing a Colombian source, it's not worth that.

I swipe a large section of mirror with a towel and study my beard, judging if it needs a trim. What the hell am I doing? Since when do I do anything but brush and floss at night?

The lights outside the bathroom are off. I drop my towel, slip on a pair of flannel pajama pants, and head to the kitchen. I want more bourbon, but search for water. My muscles are too damn sore and tight to get loaded up on alcohol.

A movement on the sofa sends me into a crouch. My eyesight adjusts in the darkened room. A woman sits on the sofa, knees pulled up to her chest, arms wrapped around her legs, face down. Dark hair veils her legs.

I flip on the kitchen light. Sophia's pale skin nearly glows beneath a crimson halo.

"What's wrong?"

She sniffs, and I search her face. Sophia's been through a lot,

but in those seven years of watching over her, I only observed tears once. Splotches marred her perfect complexion back then. Here, there's no redness. No, if anything, her color is ashen, blanched.

In two seconds, I'm before her, kneeling on the floor, searching for injury. She's in a silky cream tank top with thin straps and matching long silk pants. Conservative yet alluring.

"Sophia?"

Those blue eyes lift, lost in a blank, unreadable expression. My gut twists. Something is wrong. Very wrong.

My mind skims over the operation details. There's nothing that could've gone awry in the twenty minutes I spent in the shower. Is her family—

"The parole board met today. They released Wayne Killington from prison on good behavior. My dad just found out."

Oh. That explains it. I rise and sit back on the sofa. Wayne Killington orchestrated her abduction. If memory serves, he got fifteen years. Being released now would mean he served about two-thirds of that time. But, given his connections and the state of overcrowded prisons, it's not surprising he got an early release.

"What's the point of doing all of this?" She speaks over her knees, as if she's asking the room. "I mean, they caught a gun smuggler. He smuggled guns into other countries for years." She blinks and her brow wrinkles. "Maybe decades. We don't really know. He fed guns to the cartels. We couldn't prove it, but I expect his clients included the mafia, the Middle East, anyone with assets. Why work to end the gun trade, the drug trade, any illegal trade, if the bad guys are only going to serve partial sentences?"

"His life is ruined. His marriage dissolved."

"His marriage was a joke to begin with." Wayne Killington had been her mother's lover. I don't know the details, never wanted to know them. But I understand what she means.

I let out a deep exhale. The man did pay. "He's going to be

lonely. He might have to sell his house. Getting a job is going to be—"

"Don't." Those blue eyes narrow into hostile storm clouds. "It's not going to be difficult. Did you miss the part about him having connections? Sure, he won't get his old job back. But the gun industry is small. Someone will hire him. If he needs to work. He's still got all that money he earned. Probably some we don't know about in offshore accounts." Her chin returns to her knee and the hostility blows past as quickly as it appeared. Curled around herself on the sofa, she's soft and small. Fragile. "I just can't believe they think ten years is sufficient for all he did."

"If it makes you feel better, from what I understand, the Morales cartel is a fraction of what it used to be." Killington hired members of the Morales cartel to carry out her abduction. They were more or less freelancing the job, but the connection exposed a larger gun and drug smuggling endeavor between the Morales cartel and Sullivan arms, and Killington played an instrumental role. She's right. He didn't get prosecuted for any of that.

"They've suffered from in-fighting and competition. Victor Morales going down damaged their network." She says it matter-of-factly.

"You've been monitoring them?"

"It's what I did in the bureau. An analyst studying organized crime in Latin and South America. Studied criminal organizations around the world. The bureau isn't only law enforcement these days. It's also an intelligence agency. Being aware is a big part of protecting US citizens. Of all the organizations I studied, most are spurred by greed, some by survival. Drugs, guns, diamonds, humans... It's all interconnected. I thought I could make a difference but..."

I'd love to tell her she is making a difference. But, when you're fighting in the trenches, it's impossible to grasp who's winning the war. I just spent years in Mexico, nursing informants, and what do

I have to show for it? Charges brought against a high-ranking diplomat. And passed over for a promotion.

Sophia curls onto her side, and her head rests on the sofa's armrest as if it's a pillow. With her legs pulled up to her chest, her position stirs a memory. So many years ago, when she found out Killington had been granted bail before his hearing, she'd curled up into the fetal position on her bed. I glimpsed her broken form when walking through the house doing rounds. I vowed I'd never let that bastard near her. Worked around the clock with a full staff until he was prosecuted. Then kept working, keeping Sophia and her family safe for years after.

There were quite a few men involved in her abduction. More involved in illegal gun smuggling with her father's company. But for her, while all those other men were breaking the law, Killington is personal. I shift onto the sofa and tuck her hair behind her ear so I can see her face. "Do you still think about it? The abduction?"

I've known men who years later can't forget what happened during battle. Trauma. People carry it differently. Killington abducted her, and that alone, holding her hostage, is traumatic. I've never been clear on what happened to her during the week or so he had her. The DA didn't pursue rape charges, but that means nothing. A girl as young as Sophia might not have wanted to endure a rape trial. Her dad's protective. He might have refused to put her through that.

"Yes. And no." She releases a pained, defeated sigh. "I remember fragments. They had me pumped so high my memory is...unreliable." My fingers skim her silky calf. I want to comfort her, but this isn't my area of expertise. Jack and Ava, her dad and stepmom, are far better equipped than me, and they struggled for years to help her.

"I'm sorry." Even as the words fall out, the inadequacy of the sentiment weighs down.

"To answer your question, yes, I think about it. But not every day. Not like I used to."

With a loud, exaggerated sigh, she places her bare feet on the floor, stands, and stretches, hands high in the air, leaning from side to side.

"What're you going to do?"

"What I've always done. I let my emotions infiltrate. I put words to them." Her hands fall to her side, then she drops her gaze to meet mine. "Now I'm going to proceed. Plan. Move forward. What's the other option?"

She pads softly to her bedroom but stops in the doorway. "Thanks for listening. I needed to just...verbalize." She purses her lips, and I can't help but think she's holding something in. "See you in the morning."

She closes the door, and the click reverberates through the room.

God, I am such a pathetic, fucked-up monster. I should've never thought about Sophia in a sexual manner. That was out of line, inappropriate, and wrong.

CHAPTER 11
SOPHIA

In the privacy of the suite's bedroom, I flip open my laptop. Not my CIA issued laptop, but my personal one, and I open Google Earth and enter an address I will never forget. I zoom in on the house and yards. He's maintained it over the years. He had no choice but to maintain the grounds, as the HOA would've taken legal action if he didn't.

There was a time when Arrow Security, one of my dad's investments, had full surveillance on the property. But that was ten years ago. I doubt any of those devices remain active.

Has he paid enough? Is ten years sufficient penalty for his crimes? For upending my world view?

Will he go back to his old ways? Will he be a source of leads and information? He could be. It would be fascinating to learn who he reaches out to. Who visits his house. Who he calls.

There's one man in particular I've been watching for years. A Texan senator who has eluded indictments for years. But Talbot's too smart. He's careful with what he says. Who he's seen with. Who his political contributions trace back to. Over the years, we've had eight different informants who could tie Talbot to the cartels.

All died quickly. I'll get Talbot one day. But it probably won't be through Killington.

In theory, ol' Wayne found religion in prison. But that's par for the course for a convict pleading for early release. *Dear God, please forgive me for I have sinned.* Parole boards are notorious for loving the converted.

I watch the video of his parole hearing without the sound on, paying close attention to Killington's facial expressions and to his hands. His head is angled down, a sign of contrition. He doesn't touch his face. The descriptive word that comes to mind is somber.

Does he truly feel guilty? If so, can I leverage that guilt?

Interrogation is an art. We studied it at Quantico. Langley too. Television shows might lead one to believe abuse leads to results. But one of my Quantico instructors taught a different approach. Get inside their head. Show empathy. Make them think you get them, even if it's inconceivable you could ever be on their side.

It would be helpful if I could read Killington's personal correspondence. If he had any personal contacts. But the guard I spoke to when I visited him years ago said he's a loner.

A vibrating hum sounds on the bedside table. The screen lights up with a photo of Zane, Lauren, and me taking a selfie in caps and gowns.

I swipe to answer and lean back against a tall stack of pillows. "Do you have any idea what time it is?"

"Oh, shit. You're back on the East Coast? Then why're you answering?" Zane's puzzled, and he should be. If it was really two a.m., there's no way in hell I'd answer.

"Because it's you." It's a corny response, but it's the best I can come up with on short notice. I'm known for not answering my personal phone. I'm not sure why I felt compelled to answer tonight.

"Aw, now you've got me blushing." Zane doesn't miss a beat. "When's your next trip home?"

"Nothing on the calendar." My screensaver flashes on my laptop, and blue jays fly into the edge of a Norwegian forest.

"Did you check out the event I sent you? The governor's ball? I really need a date. I'll owe you forever."

"Pretty sure I've heard that before." Zane's one of my oldest friends. A classmate and a neighbor. He and Lauren are the only two I spoke to that first summer after the abduction.

"I'll owe you in your next life too. And the one after that."

"Fascinating."

"And you know, you need to come back, anyway. Lauren's getting pissed at you."

"Seriously? Did I miss something?" Yes, I'm a bridesmaid in her upcoming wedding, but I live on the opposite side of the country from her. How much can she expect?

"Well, when did you last speak to her?"

Hmmm. I probably do owe her a call.

"Yeah, that's what I thought."

Zane's smug response irks me. I rub my hand over my face and make a mental note to call Lauren in the morning. "When is your event?"

"Two and a half weeks."

Night falls on my screensaver and stars shine bright through the opening in the trees. *My parents live in Killington's neighborhood. It could be an opportunity, if I'm not assigned to a different op by then.* "And I'll have some free time? To spend with Lauren?"

"Absolutely. I'll book you both a spa day. Maybe the three of us can go to brunch."

There's a tap on the door, and Fisher's head peeks through. I hold up my finger to my lips. "Sounds like a plan. Now, let me go to sleep so I'm not a total zombie at work tomorrow."

"You know, there are plenty of financial institutions here in San Diego."

"But New York is New York." He groans, and I laugh. "Goodnight, Zane."

I end the call, and Fisher steps through the doorway. His dark, thick hair is mangled, as if he's run his fingers through it endlessly. In only his black briefs, my gaze travels down his chiseled chest, sculpted abdomen, and muscular thighs. He's barely clothed, it's late, and I'm dazed. Gemma was right. And so was Lauren. Fisher's a gorgeous specimen.

"Thought I heard voices. Everything okay?"

My gaze snaps up from the noticeable bulge in his briefs.

"Yeah, just Zane."

"He know you're here?"

"No." I'd have to get clearance. Fisher knows that. "Absolutely not."

"You wouldn't be the first officer to tell a significant other the truth."

"What?" My lips stretch into a grin. Me and Zane? No way. "He's a friend. That's it."

"You sure about that?" The corners of his lips turn up into a disarming smile. "I remember he came around quite a lot back in the day."

This is Fisher. He probably got reports on my activities during the duration of my undergraduate career. "We dated," I admit. "But briefly. Didn't take long for us to figure out we're better as friends."

Fisher folds his arms, leans back against the wall, and crosses one ankle over the other. The stance flexes his strong, hair-roughened legs, his sculpted biceps, and his pecs. My throat tightens, but I refuse to look away because he's the one who entered my room in only briefs. And Gemma isn't wrong. My fake husband is hot as fuck.

"I'm glad to see you still keep in touch with your friends."

"You are?" Does he keep in touch with friends? Does he have a personal life?

"Yes, I am." His lips flatline. "In this line of work, what we do, it's easy to let the job absorb you. To lose all contact with real friends, with people who know the real you. Your whole life can, in the blink of an eye, become the job. It can be lonely."

"Are you lonely?" A warning sounds deep within. This conversation ventures into deeper waters than Fisher and I swim together.

His guarded expression speaks volumes. "It's not about me. You're new. Eager. You're going to have a distinguished career. Just don't lose sight of what's important. There's more to life than a job, and the CIA is an employer. Don't give them everything. You're worth more than that. Your life is worth more than that."

Thanks, Dad is on the tip of my tongue. But I bite back the sarcasm. Fisher is being real, and there's no need to put up defenses.

"Do you have friends? Outside of the CIA?"

"A few. Mostly through work." He runs his hand through his disheveled hair and gives me a half-smile that is toe-curling sexy. "Trevor, Ryan."

I nod. Ryan might as well be my uncle, given he married Aunt Alex. Sure, she was my mom's close friend and is technically an adopted aunt, but I see them both regularly. Trevor has a stepson I enjoyed hanging out with. Last I heard, he made it through BUD/s, which means he's on a SEAL team kicking ass somewhere. I never hear from him.

"Your dad. I count him as a friend."

The tilt of Fisher's head and his bowed shoulders convey guilt. And I remember how I practically pawed him earlier this evening. Is he feeling guilty about that? I totally enjoyed it, which was highly unusual for me, but it had been for the job. We played our roles.

But another thought crosses my mind. "Does he know we're here?" He doesn't respond.

Were my suspicions correct? Is Fisher here on behalf of my father, once again playing bodyguard, and he just lied to me earlier?

"Not unless Trevor told him. But I doubt Trev would mention it. He knows I'm here for work." I examine Fisher, searching for any of the signs of deception. "I swear, Sophia. This assignment isn't one your dad pulled out of his bag of tricks. He's not keeping tabs."

"If you say so." Fisher's countenance is stern. He doesn't seem to like me questioning his veracity, and that's fair. "Nah, you're probably telling the truth." My gaze falls over the rumpled comforter. "If Dad arranged this, there's no way he'd set us up in a suite with one bed."

Fisher grins and holds an index finger up in the air. He shakes it at me a couple of times, like I'm a naughty girl, then closes the door behind him.

I flip off my bedside light and lean back against the pillows with an inexplicable grin plastered on my face.

CHAPTER 12

FISHER

A haze of gray covers the sky with shades of steel over the mountains. The forecast calls for snow showers beginning sometime this afternoon. The frigid temperature forced my morning workout indoors, but the Four Seasons gym proved an adequate substitute.

I have the day to catch up on reports from my last case and to read through updates. My work cell rings, and I answer it without much thought. I'm in our suite, alone.

"Can you talk?" Bauer isn't the CIA officer I expected to be calling when I saw the area code. Technically, he should go through Rita while I'm on an op. I assume he's calling to clear the air about the assignment I didn't receive. The promotion he hung over my head like a carrot these last few years.

"Yep." I slide back on the sofa and stare out across the blanketed peaks.

"Your wife with you?"

"She's out skiing."

"With the target?"

"Yep."

"Good. This op is evolving."

"What do you mean?"

"A source claims Toro's father is going to declare his presidential candidacy."

"Okay." The information doesn't surprise me. We're here because Rafael Toro's father is an influential Colombian as much as because his uncle leads a cartel responsible for a significant percentage of Colombian cocaine and heroin production.

"FBI source. We're still fleshing out details, but it could have some implications for this op."

"Like?"

"How we're going to work with our fellow partners." He means other intelligence operations, primarily the FBI.

"Where's Rita?"

"She asked that I run point on this one with you."

"Oh?"

"Well, there's a chance this is going to extend longer than planned. You didn't have a break between UC roles..."

"She asked you to give me this update because she knows I'm pissed about the Mexican desk."

"True. And we're friends. Look, I don't know where this is going. All I know is that right now we want more than a phone number. If you guys make contact, we'll want you to keep it. Could be absorbed into a cross-agency endeavor."

"Our cover is based in California." The CIA doesn't run ops on domestic soil.

"Nothing is final. Miami feds brought in a fugitive's wife. The guy had been stealing printers, of all things. Or so we thought. In interrogation, she opened their eyes to an entire Colombian smuggling enterprise. They're still assessing the validity of the claims, but so far, it's proving accurate."

"And you offered this op as a potential source of intelligence."

"We're all one team."

Jesus. If our role is to be friends with Gemma and Rafael, it's

the kind of role that could go on for years and deliver next to nothing. "Well, nothing changes on our end this week."

"True. And, I wanted to tell you, personally, to not be discouraged by the Mexican desk. There are bigger things coming for you. Be patient."

Right. I've heard that one before.

My personal phone vibrates on the side table. Jack Sullivan's name appears on the screen.

"Gotta go."

"Check in with Rita within twenty-four hours."

"Copy that." I end the call and reach for my personal phone, reading the screen. *Bauer's such a fucking an ass.* I stare at the screen for a beat before answering.

"Jack."

"Fisher. Hope you don't mind me calling you. Do you have a minute?" Jack is aware I work for the CIA, but there are a lot of roles within the CIA that don't involve field work. To my knowledge, Jack isn't familiar with my role within the agency. It's definitely something I'm not authorized to share.

"Sure. What's up?"

"I've been running through scenarios with a team, and Ryan suggested I touch base with you."

"Okay."

"They released Killington on parole yesterday. You studied him as much as anyone. What kind of threat do you think he poses?"

"Jack, I studied him ten years ago. I haven't kept up with him. Ambition and greed motivated the guy ten years ago. Without a motive, he wouldn't come after your family. But..."

Prison can change a man. Is revenge a motivator now? He wouldn't be the first man to go through prison and come out with new motivations.

"I hear you." Jack sounds tired, maybe resigned.

"I'm sure you've still got a full security detail. I can't imagine he'd risk a parole violation by coming after you. Staying out of jail is bound to be a big motivator for a guy like Killington." The guy's house isn't oceanfront, but it's technically a mansion, and he's got a stunning lap pool in a back yard that borders a golf course. Far better accommodations than the Texas penitentiary.

"That's what I hoped you'd say. How're things going with you?"

"Good."

"Heard a rumor we might persuade you to come back and work for Arrow."

"What exactly did Trevor tell you?"

"Not much. Intelligence gathering can be mind-numbingly boring. Bureaucracy, ten times worse. Next time you're on the west coast, you should at least meet with Ryan. You'd be an asset for us. And we might be able to offer you a better life. At least, if the CIA is like I remember it."

"Doubt it's changed."

"Next time you're in town, let me know. Ava and I would love to have you over."

"Sure thing." The door to the suite clicks open, and I jump up. Movement sounds from the end of the hall.

"Gotta go." I end the call and pad to the side of the wall. Room service would announce themselves.

Footfalls grow louder and I crouch, hands up, ready. Around the corner, I glimpse auburn hair.

"Sophia." I let out a loud huff and straighten. Bright blue eyes sparkle with amusement. "What're you doing back?"

"Did you think I was a burglar?" She steps into the small kitchen and reaches into the fridge.

She can mock me all she wants. She's cautious, too.

"Who were you speaking to?"

"Your father."

Her water bottle hits the counter with a dull thud. "Did he want an update?"

"Sounded like he simply wanted me to confirm the risk assessment Arrow provided him."

She twists off the plastic cap and narrows her eyes, scanning me up and down. "Killington?"

"Yep." I return to the sofa and tap my laptop to bring it back to life. "What're you doing back?"

"Winds were too strong. Rafael's heli-skiing adventure got postponed. We're supposed to meet them at their place to go hot tubbing."

"When?"

"In thirty." I give a quick nod while I try to recall if I packed swim trunks. But I did. I thought I might find a pool for laps. "You realize Dad knows I'm here with you."

"Didn't give any indication that's the case."

"You're naïve."

"You're paranoid."

I'm unsure if her contemplative frown means she's certain in her declaration or if she's doubting herself, but it doesn't particularly matter.

Since I apparently won't be finishing that report, I close the laptop and stand, then judge my hunger level. We don't have time to eat before our scheduled hot tub excursion.

"Why did Dad say he called you?"

"I told you." Those baby blues cloud over with clear warning. I release a gruff huff, warning her right back. "We're friends. He got some intel and because it was about one of the most important people in his life—you—he wanted a second opinion. He just wanted someone to verify his conclusion. End of story. No need to read into it."

"And you still think it's a coincidence that they assigned me on this case? That the officer they place as my fake husband is my old

security guard? You really don't think my dad pulled strings to make that happen?"

"Jesus fucking Christ, Soph!" The world does not fucking revolve around the princess.

"Just hear me out. Think about it. Dad wouldn't want me in a position where I'd be with someone who might take advantage of…"

I dramatically lean my head forward. "Of what? You realize you're twenty-five years old, right? I don't think your dad is staying up late at night worrying about whether you've had sex. To the contrary, I imagine if pressed he'd say he hopes you have a healthy sex life. He's not the Puritan you seem to think he is. And trust me…if I thought for one minute I was on this bullshit assignment to babysit, I'd be the first to let your old man have it." I sling open the closet door that holds my suitcase, and the door ricochets back from the wall. "And another thing, if you must know, not that it's any of your goddamn business, but I'm considering returning to Arrow. In a different role. Not in personal protection. If dear old doting dad wanted me to be your personal protection while you did your grown-up fucking job, I don't think he'd be calling me about a job offer that would take me out of the CIA, now, would he?"

In the blink of an eye, those storm clouds shoot bolts of lightning. I grit my teeth and growl into the storm's fury. "Daddy Warbucks might be a billionaire, but he's not pulling strings at the CIA. It's time for you to see that and grow the fuck up."

Her thunderous glower might scare a weaker man, but not me. I head to the bathroom with a change of clothes in hand and slam the door. Just a few more days of this shit.

But then I remember Bauer's call. This has the potential to morph into a longer assignment. *Fuck me.*

Once I change, I exit the room and enter the kitchen to dig out

a protein bar. I sense her approach but pointedly avoid looking her way.

"Did you see the latest backgrounds on Rafael's friends?"

"No." The remaining flavors of protein bars are decidedly too sweet. Birthday cake and lemon chiffon.

"They all spent time in the Colombian military."

"They're from Colombia. Not unusual."

"Maybe. It's also possible they pose as his buddies but are actually bodyguards."

I rip open the lemon chiffon bar, take a bite, and consider her theory. It's not out of the realm of reasonable. Rafael travels everywhere with those four men, Carlos, Enrique, Alros, and Ivan. And they don't bring their wives. We assumed it was because Gemma didn't get along with the wives. When Rafael was younger, the CIA didn't watch him as closely because he was a professional extreme sports athlete. The CIA's interest has increased in him recently since rumors surfaced he's being groomed for the family business. And he's older now. He's not the competitive athlete he used to be.

"By the way, Gemma told me the other guys won't be joining us in the hot tub."

I bite about a third of the remaining bar. It is interesting how they appear and disappear around Rafael. Friends along for a vacation would probably expect to après-ski and hot tub together.

"And by the way, she warned me Rafael prefers *au natural*."

"What?"

"No swim trunks."

"Seriously?" Now she has my attention. I don't give a damn about going hot tubbing nude, but this could be a swinging invitation.

With a smug, coquettish grin she wiggles her eyebrows and asks, "Ready to go hot tubbing?"

My gaze falls over her teeny, tiny, barely there red bathing suit.

Milky white breasts spill out of miniscule red triangles. I blink. Fuck. And she's planning on taking that off? If Rafael isn't a swinger, he's going to want to be one.

"We should beg off this. Say I have a migraine. This isn't—"

"Don't you fucking dare. You just yelled at me that I need to grow up. I think your exact words might have been 'grow the fuck up.' This is my first operation. And according to Rita, because of an ongoing intra-agency op, this one just got escalated. We're all in. Don't you dare bow out because you're trying to protect me."

She turns and saunters down the hallway, her two perfectly rounded ass cheeks on display because that damn red thong barely covers her ass crack. Those sparkly, bright blue eyes and crimson mane lend her a wild beauty. But that body combined with a daredevil arrogance... Jesus.

"You're wearing that through the hotel?"

"No. I'm going to put on a spa robe. That's what people do." The look she gives me is a mix of unfiltered annoyance and disbelief at my ignorance. "Come on, growly fish. Time to go skinny dipping."

CHAPTER 13

SOPHIA

There's a little extra in my hip sway as I pad down the hall to the closet with the hanging robes. Because, yes, I am fairly certain Fisher's eyes are on my bum.

Grow up. Yes, that's what he said to me. I'll show him I have grown up. Fucker. The Fisher Fucker.

That's a kind of funny phrase. I take the robe off the hanger, halfway expecting Fisher to step up behind me and assist like a gentleman, but he does no such thing. After donning my robe, I remove the second one and turn to give it to him, but he's not behind me.

"Fisher?"

"Where's your CIA phone?" he calls from the bedroom.

The poorly sized spa slippers clomp on the hard floor as I head his way.

"Over here." I go to my trim backpack that I use for all my electronics and unzip the outer pocket. "Why?"

"Give it to me. Also, anything CIA sourced. Did they give you a tracker?"

"Yeah." I dig it out of my suitcase. "What's up?"

"Just being safe. We're going to be otherwise occupied and out of our room with Gemma and Rafael. If his friends are working for the Toros, that would be an opportune time for them to check out our room. No need for them to find CIA issued equipment."

"You think they'd know what to look for?"

"Absolutely."

"Where are you putting it? The safe?"

"Too obvious."

He opens his toiletry bag, takes out a Swiss Army knife, unfolds a screwdriver, goes to a wall vent, and, using the screwdriver, opens it up and places all of our equipment inside. He pauses and narrows his eyes thoughtfully. "Did you pack any guns? Any weapons?"

I shake my head. I didn't bother carrying on the plane. Also, this isn't considered a high-risk operation. Contrary to common beliefs, it's much more common for CIA officers to be unarmed as opposed to armed. "You?"

"No." He takes to screwing the screws tight. Then pauses. "Do you have a small ribbon? String?"

I go back to my shopping bags and find a clear plastic piece that held a price tag and bring it back to him. He has me place it so it's captured against the grid and the wall. If someone breaks in and thinks to check this spot, the plastic should fall unnoticed. But we'll know someone has been here and our stash was discovered.

"You don't have any weapons?" In my memories of him, he always had a gun concealed on his person. I used to make a game of figuring out where he had his piece tucked away.

"Knives. But if they find them, they won't think anything of it." He stands then cocks his head, examining his handiwork. Also possibly memorizing the wall and the grid for any identifiable markings. "The Americans we're playing wouldn't carry guns internationally."

He returns his screwdriver to the brown leather bag. Since it's a part of a Swiss Army knife, if someone finds it, they wouldn't think twice about it.

"What other knives do you have?"

"This one. And one other like this in my ski bag. The kitchen knives are more lethal."

"You really think they'll come in here?"

"It's conceivable. You and Gemma are getting closer. Would make sense to check you out and clear you." He lets out a sigh and glances down my body.

The robe hangs open. My skin prickles under his scrutiny. He scratches his hair and mutters as he steps by me. "Let's do this. Just remember... I'm human. Play carefully. And," he pauses, wincing as he pulls on his robe, "what's our plan if they're swingers?"

"We play along."

"I was afraid you'd say that." He rubs his fingers through his hair, head bowed down. He takes a step, then stops. His jaw flexes, and he directs those steel-blue eyes at me. "Sophia, this isn't an operation that's worth having sex with these people."

"Really? You'd sacrifice an op over sex?"

The flex in his cheeks and the hard glare warn me I'm picking at his last nerve. *Tough.*

"It's totally believable as a married couple we'd turn them down. And, if you play it right, it could endear her to you. Make you closer friends."

"We'll see how it goes. If something more happens, it's just sex, Fisher. We're role-playing, and it's a job. Don't make it into more than it is."

My shoulder smacks into his as I stomp down the hall. Yes, any playful sashay is long gone. But, when my hand falls on the doorknob, I breathe deeply and consider what he's saying. He's been in the field longer. He's right. There are unspoken expectations, but if it came out we were both sleeping with our

targets for a mission like this, where we're simply supposed to flesh out contacts, maybe lure an informant, it wouldn't reflect well. Not to mention, it would be an unnecessarily dangerous play.

If we swapped partners, they could choose to end contact and never see us again. The only information I have on Gemma is she wants a child. She's still in the honeymoon phase of their relationship. If he's into swapping partners, she might not be at all. It might be a side of him she abhors, and playing into it wouldn't be a good long-term strategy. Of course, she did say my husband is hot.

I rest my forehead against the cool, painted wood. I'm not sure how to play it. When I turn, Fisher stands, robe tied, patiently waiting.

"We'll have to play it by ear. But I agree, the goal is to avoid swapping partners."

He leans down close enough his breath warms my ear and his musky cologne surrounds me. "And when we return to our suite, until we sweep it, we stay in character."

Side by side, we travel down the hotel hallway. Fisher's fingers link with mine, a smart touch. Anyone watching would assume we're happily married. My nerves kick up a notch, and my stomach flips.

I've spent time with Gemma. That's not the part that's got me on edge. No, it's the fact that there's a good chance there's about to be a replay of the PDA from earlier. Anticipation for kissing the grumpy guy who still treats me like a kid is irrational. Yet there's unmistakable adrenaline pumping at unusually high levels. My heart beats stronger and faster. The tips of my fingers are chilled. My lips tingle.

Fisher—no, Damian—raps his knuckles against the door. Carlos swings it open. The rope chain necklace around his neck glitters under the hallway lights.

"Gemma, your friend is here." He glances down my body,

covered in the tightly bound spa robe, then his scan travels over Damian.

Rafael and Gemma's larger suite is more like a townhome. Stairs lead to an upstairs area. Sliding doors open onto a snowy deck. Steam rises from a circular sunken hot tub.

Gemma rounds the corner. She's in a two-piece bathing suit and Gucci sandals. A solid gold collar-length necklace gleams, and her thick, black hair is swept up on top of her head.

"Come on in. What can I get you to drink?" Gemma asks.

Carlos, still standing by the door, asks, "Can I take your robes? Ivan will get your drinks."

"Aren't you guys leaving?" Gemma asks Carlos. There's an attitude to her tone. It's not hostile, but it's clear she expects him to leave.

"Yes, ma'am. We've got reservations at a place in the village. Gotta have reservations in this place." His cocky grin comes across as relaxed and harmless. He lifts a hanger out of the side closet in the hallway and holds an arm out, waiting for me to de-robe.

I don't really care to pass mine over to him, but I suspect he's not leaving until he knows what I've got beneath the plush robe, and I also suspect his reasoning isn't at all sexual.

I shrug out of the robe but make a show of holding my arms like I'm cold. The reaction isn't complete show. It is chilly in their unit. The high ceilings probably make it harder to heat, and the snow outside the windows underscores this.

Gemma tugs at my wrist. "Come on. Let's head out. The guys will bring us our drinks. What do you want?"

"Whatever you're having."

"Carlos...make us that champagne cocktail you fixed the other night?"

I follow Gemma. Like me, she's wearing a thong bikini. Her curves are voluptuous, her bronzed skin smooth. Compared to her, I'm a rail-thin waif with skin as blinding as the snow.

On the deck, the frigid air burns and sucks the oxygen out of my lungs. I rush to the water's edge, kicking off my hotel-provided slippers, and drop into the hot tub.

Gemma takes a little more time, setting her Gucci thongs off to the side, far enough away from the hot tub they won't get splashed, then dashes to the steaming water, grinning as she slides in.

"Where's Rafael?"

"Oh, he's wrapping up a meeting. He'll be back shortly. My muscles are so sore from today."

"We were only out for a couple of hours."

"Are you not sore?"

"A little." My thighs are slightly sore. I work out religiously, but skiing uses a slightly different set of muscles.

She waves her hand and makes a dramatic noise of exasperation. "If you're not sore, then you exercise too much. That's why you're skin and bones."

She dips down in the water, letting it rise to her chin, and I mimic her. The heat over my shoulders feels divine.

Gemma glances to the den, and I follow her gaze. Rafael is back, and he's with his buddies, standing in a circle talking. "Now, don't you let Rafe push you. If you want to keep that top on, girl, you do it."

I swirl the water with my arm. "I thought you said he had a strict rule. European style bathing. No tops."

She raises eyebrows and grins. "That man loves swimming naked. But no pressure. Seriously. We just met you guys, and he understands you're American."

"What does that mean?"

She tilts her head back and laughs. "You do things differently." She waves her hand around and looks to the ceiling, like she's searching for the right word. "Uptight."

"You were born in the US. You're American, right?"

"Sí." Then she waffles her hand. "Sort of. It's like my English. I

moved at a young age. It's still there," she points at her head, "but here, I'm Colombian."

"What language do you dream in?" Languages have always fascinated me. An instructor once told us that once we dream in a language, we've mastered it.

"Spanish. Always Spanish. Do you know *Español*?"

"Sort of. *Asi asi*." I waffle my hand back and forth, lying through my teeth. I studied Spanish in high school and college, but I mastered it when I was in the FBI.

The sliding door glides open and Rafael and Damian exit, each holding two drinks. The other men are gone.

"Ladies. What's going on out here?" Rafael's loud voice carries. He's so boisterous it has me wondering if he's been drinking, and if yes, how much he's had.

Damian steps down onto the bench, hands me a champagne flute with raspberries floating on the top with a sprig of mint, then he slowly sinks into the water beside me. Our thighs touch on the bench, and an air bubble pushes his swim trunks higher.

Rafael jumps into the middle, feet first, sending hot splashes of water every which away. Gemma squeals.

"Tops off, girls! What the hell?" He sits down beside his wife then reaches behind him to set his beer down. She squirms, and with a dramatic flair, he raises her top and tosses it behind him.

Gemma's breasts are enormous compared to mine. They're so full they spill over on her sides, wider than her rib cage. They are perfectly shaped, and her nipples are round, the darker skin tantalizing.

She glances up at me with a timidity in her expression, and it hits me that I'm staring. Total social faux pas. So I lean into Damian, snuggling against him, and press a kiss below his ear. He wraps an arm possessively around me.

"Did you make it out skiing today?"

Rafael's face twists. "No."

His disappointment is evident, and Gemma shifts, awash in sympathy.

"But we're going to have a great afternoon. And you've got the rest of the week."

He grumbles. She proceeds to chatter away, telling him about our morning out in ski school. She wraps up a rather long, convoluted summary of us practicing snowplows with a cheerful summation. "It's gonna be a few years before we're ready to go skiing with the boys."

Rafael pulls Gemma up onto his lap, lifting her up so her breasts are no longer partially submerged. He then motorboats his wife, slapping his face against her breasts, shaking his head back and forth, and she howls with laughter. The man has most definitely been drinking.

Gemma warned me. This scenario isn't unexpected. But suddenly I'm awash in nerves. I should play into that. What I'm feeling is exactly what my American character would feel. And my American character would follow her husband's lead. I'm much younger than he is, and he's the breadwinner.

But I also feel awkward tucked against Fisher's side, watching Gemma and Rafael. I should do something other than stare. So, I move onto Fisher's lap, placing a knee on each side of his thighs and rest one hand on his shoulder. My thong rides up my center, and the steaming hot water coats my newly exposed walls. In this position, I'm slightly higher than Fisher, and I bend to press my lips softly to his, then teasingly bite his lower lip.

When I pull back, Fisher's chest lies still, as if he's ceased breathing, and those dark blue eyes narrow speculatively. His features remain unreadable, but those deep pools of blue smolder and light a tingling in the pit of my stomach. I breathe through the unruly, inexplicable nerves. This is role-play.

Climbing on his lap isn't particularly considerate of his only human warning, but his 'grow up' words are fresh in my mind. Behind me, Gemma's giggles continue.

"What do you say? Top off?" I raise one questioning eyebrow and wait.

CHAPTER 14
FISHER

Decision is a sharp knife that cuts clean and straight. Indecision is an unwieldy blade that leaves jagged edges. I train for decisiveness. It's the difference between life and death. Yet here I sit, struck with indecisiveness.

I've got a hot, sexy, twenty-something on my lap in a string bikini, and she's asking about untying those strings. But the light blue, questioning eyes tempting me belong to Sophia Sullivan.

Rafael's wife removed her top. There's no way to walk out of this without offending Rafael. Plus, refusing to have my wife go topless isn't exactly an approachable quality. Rafael gravitates to rough and tumble, live-out-loud guys.

A buddy of mine once worked a UC gig in Colombia. He shared that Colombians were notorious for wanting to work with fellow Colombians in the US, because they'd likely have family members back in Colombia, and that gave them leverage.

A sex tape, or even nude photos, are hardly leverage on a married couple. This could be Rafael's personality. How he likes to play. Or he could be sizing us up. We've already had two CIA officers fail at attempting to get close to him. Maybe he's wising up

to intelligence agencies around the world wanting to infiltrate his circle.

Sophia inches forward, her thighs pressing down on mine. Her movement sends a rush of water brushing over my dick, which is getting harder by the nanosecond. Her thumb caresses the side of my cheek, but her speculative gaze tells me she's following my lead.

My head is all over the place, and my swollen cock is proof my body is in quite another. Giggling from the other end of the tub invades the space between us, reminding me I need to act.

She rises. Her inner thighs strain against mine. Streams of water flow from the bottom of her breasts down the inches of skin over her ribcage, returning to the hot tub. Her baby blues probe. What am I going to do? How am I going to play this?

What do I want to do? Nothing good or right.

My fingers tangle with her auburn hair, and I press her back down until her ruby lips press against mine. My tongue asks for entry, and she opens. The pull to her intensifies, and as if she's affected too, her hips undulate, but she's inches from me and the movement sends a current around my erection. My hips shift of their own accord closer to hers.

My lips trace the damp lines of her neck to the pulsing hollow at the base of throat as her hips grind forward over me. The muscles along her back contract with each thrust of her hips. I follow along the thin string to her ribs, below her arm and then to the soft underside of her breast. My thumb flicks over her aroused, perky nipple.

I flick my eyes up to hers. Those eyes are ablaze with desire, so much so it knocks me back and I grow dizzy from the heat. Her back straightens, putting distance between us. Cool air wafts over my face and shoulders, letting reason flicker through my lust-addled brain.

She reaches behind her, and the fabric beneath my thumb

collapses. I suck in air as the red strings tied to triangles float in the bubbling water. Instinct reigns supreme and my mouth covers her peach-colored peak, and I lash the tip of her nipple with my tongue. Her head tips back and her hips grind forward. Slender fingers reach between us, over my bathing suit, caressing my tip.

"You two are like a porn movie." Rafael's statement has the effect of a splash of cold water. The side of the deck comes back into view, the lightly falling snowflakes dotting Sophia's auburn crown. Auburn, so different from her natural blonde. Dyed with purpose.

I grip her ass and rise, stumbling, reach for the metal railing, and pull us both out of the tub. Sophia's arms wrap around my back and her thighs squeeze my hips.

There's one thing a man like Rafael will understand.

"It's time for us to go."

His laughter follows through the sliding door, followed by, "I like hanging out with them."

"Grab my robe," I say to Sophia, unwilling to put her down.

A pulsing need to have her close keeps her pressed against my chest as I forge a speedy path to our suite. I fumble with the room key, push the door open, and the second I'm in, have her back up against the wall.

My forehead presses against hers and my lungs contract. My breaths are rapid, like I've run a marathon, and my dick throbs. Fuck, I want her. So fucking badly.

"Do you see what you do to me?"

There's just a strip of fabric covering her. I could easily move it to the side.

Her probing gaze asks questions my brain can't process. My gaze drops to the floor, then down the hall, and I freeze.

Someone's been in here.

Sophia's palm presses against my chest, asking for space. She's figured it out, too. Her feet slowly drop to the floor. I hold on to her

until she's stable. Once she's standing on her own, topless, I hold an index finger up to my lips.

My gaze falls to her perfect, delicious breasts. And the fact this is an operation hammers home, because if this were anything else, anyone else, we would not have stopped here. I'd be balls deep by now.

She bends and picks up the scrap of material from the floor. But if someone's in here, I'm not waiting for her to tie that on.

I take the lead down the hall, crouched, on the ready. The bed is made, the downy white comforter pulled tight with the decorative pillows in place. The cleaning service came through.

My muscles relax, but I still clear the place, checking the bathroom, closets and behind the floor to ceiling drapes. After securing her top, Sophia checks all lightbulbs, outlets, and ceiling vents. I bend down in front of the hallway wall vent and carefully unscrew the fastenings. The thin plastic flutters to the ground.

The shower turns on in the bathroom. Soft footsteps grow louder. Two feet with bright pink polished nails come into view. Sophia gathers our stuff out of the shaft, and I screw the vent back on, careful to avoid scratching any paint.

Fingers lightly tap my shoulder, and she motions for me to follow her. The light reflects along her skin. Visible goosebumps cover her arms.

"Are you cold?"

She pulls me into the bathroom and closes the door. Steam gathers behind the glass door of the oversized shower.

"Is it safe to talk?" She's whispering, and for whatever reason, the action amuses me.

"Yeah. They weren't in here." We have a device that I can use to confirm there are no bugs in place. I'll use that, but we weren't gone that long. Chances are if Rafael wanted his guys to come in here and check things out, the cleaning service sidelined them.

The CIA breeds paranoia. Just ask any officer who takes a gazillion left turns before arriving at a destination.

Electricity buzzes between us. The adrenaline coursing through my veins insists a rousing need has yet to be sated. But this is Sophia. Sullivan. My friend's daughter. This is work. She's taking a hot shower, but I need a cold one. I turn to leave.

"What you did back there was smart."

I pause, my hand on the bathroom doorknob. "What do you mean?" I glance over my shoulder.

She fidgets and her cheeks blossom. Nerves? But then again, we've gone from hot to cold to steamy. The temperature changes alone could be responsible.

"It's..." The tips of her auburn hair are soaked and cling to bare, tempting skin. "If he was doubting whether we were really a couple, he won't be after that. You played it right."

I played it right. I let those words filter through, open the door to let some of the steam out and press my back against the doorjamb, forcing my gaze to remain on her face, while I weigh her statement. The truth is, I essentially forgot where we were. If we'd stayed there, I can only hope I wouldn't have actually slipped her suit to the side and finger fucked her, or worse, lifted her up and fucked her over the edge of the tub.

"It's something about being with the two of them." Her lips press together and her shoulders shrug. She's blowing off what happened between us. That's smart. I should follow her lead.

"He invited me to go heli-skiing with them. Tomorrow."

She beams up at me, excitement clear. The girl wants to nail this assignment. If we each form contacts, that equals unequivocal success.

"That's great. All day tomorrow?"

"It'll take most of the day." The doorjamb digs into my spine, and I shift, massaging the wound-up muscles. "We'll fly up to a

remote peak, ski down through untracked powder, and depending on how we're feeling, hike back up said peak and drop again."

She slips past me, shower still pouring, and I follow her into the den. "What're you doing?"

She picks up the hotel phone and dials. "Yes, can you connect me to suite 914?"

She bounces on her toes. The movement flexes her ass cheeks. Goosebumps reappear. She's in a wet suit and the temperature in the room is brisk.

"May I please speak to Gemma?" There's a pause. "Sophia. From next door." There's another pause. Sophia glances back at me and giggles. She's not a giggler, so I can only assume she's playing along. "Sorry. Didn't mean to interrupt. But Damian just said he's spending tomorrow with Rafael and the guys. Do you want to meet up again?" There's another pause. "Great. Yeah. Here's my cell. Text me and we'll coordinate." She rattles off her number, the number our team set her up with for her assumed identity.

She hangs up the phone and squeals as she turns around. "She's going to text me tomorrow!"

"And you'll have her number." Her enthusiasm is contagious and despite this brewing mix of consternation and frustration, I grin. "Good work. Impressive."

"Do you think so?"

I counter her skepticism with a firm, "Absolutely. Good work." Before I do something stupid, like pull her barely clothed body back up against me, I escape to a cold shower.

CHAPTER 15
SOPHIA

The patio offers a sweeping view of skiers and boarders making their way down Blackcomb. The lifts close at four, and the base area becomes more crowded by the minute as folks finish their last run of the day.

Gemma taps away on her phone, then slams it down.

"Something wrong?" She's replaced her goggles with enormous sunglasses that cover so much of her face it's difficult to get a read, but based on her clenched lips, she's not happy.

"No word back. Rafe knows I worry when he goes out. You know what they're doing, right?"

Slowly, I nod. I'm familiar with the idea of heli-skiing, but it's something I haven't actually done. My father took us on plenty of ski trips growing up, but a double diamond is about as savage as I've ever managed. But pretty much every ski resort bar in America plays heli-skiers on loop on at least one of the hanging television screens. It's disconcerting the guys haven't checked in, but I trust Fisher wouldn't hurl himself out of the helicopter if he couldn't get down in one piece. The guy stretches every single day, which strikes me as the action of a conscientious athlete, one who fervently wishes to avoid injury. He's former Navy. From what

I've seen, he can hang with my dad, Ryan, Trevor, or any of the former SEALs, Rangers, or other military elite hired by Arrow. He's a badass.

"Rafael acts like if he has his buddies with him, he's immortal. Damn fool is what he is."

A woman with a toddler bundled in a light pink snowsuit veers near our table, apologizing profusely when her child's boot flails out and kicks me in the shoulder.

"No worries," I say as Gemma says, "Aren't you just adorable?"

The toddler chews on her glove. She's a cute one, with her blonde hair tied into twin pigtails and bright pink chapped cheeks. But the runny, crusty nose negates the cuteness factor by a few degrees. The mom is on a mission to meet up with another table, and she passes us quickly.

Gemma shifts in her seat to continue waving to the toddler, a maniacal grin plastered on her face. It's a clear case of baby fever. Which is odd to me, because she's twenty, but she's also crazy in love with her husband.

Based on the selection of photos in her file, it was difficult to tell. But every break she checks her phone, and the moment he's down the mountain, she rushes to be with him. My friend Lauren is like that with her fiancé. My stepmom, Ava, calls it the starry-eyed phase, but I'm not sure why she of all people calls it a phase. She and my dad are still like that, and they've been together for over ten years now.

It's not until the toddler disappears inside that Gemma lets out a sigh and shifts to face me once again. "What?" she asks.

"You've got it bad." I say it with a teasing grin.

"Yeah, I do." She settles back in her chair and gazes over the mountain, the smile erased.

"It's only a matter of time," I reassure her.

She shakes her head, disagreeing with my assessment. "No.

We talked about it last night. He's committed to the no kids thing. He refuses to reverse the surgery."

Ugh. I can feel the disappointment and sadness rolling off her in waves, and I reach out to cover her hand and give it a supportive squeeze. "He could change his mind. You're young. You've got so much time."

"No. He's not going to change his mind."

"What's his reasoning?" I don't want children. It's so rare to come across someone else who doesn't want children, that I am genuinely curious to hear his rationale. Children don't define us. They're not a requirement for a fulfilled life.

"It's..." She inhales deeply and unzips her winter coat a few inches. "Back home, it's... I don't know how much you know about Colombia." She shifts her gaze from the mountain to me, and I can't see her eyes, but I feel the heavy weight of her inquisitive examination.

"Never been there."

"Rafael's father is a politician. In the public eye. When people want to threaten his father, they do so by threatening those he loves. His mother was killed in a car bomb ages ago. His first wife, shot in a drive by shooting."

"Oh, my god." This information somehow isn't in the CIA files. But, depending on when his mother died, Rafael's father might not have been on our watch list. Our records show his first three wives disappeared, but now I wonder...

"He's insistent. Says any children will be targets."

"But he's not in politics, right?"

"I thought he would change his mind. He told me before we got married. I am to blame." She lifts her sunglasses and pinches the bridge of her nose, securing tears that welled up and leaked out. She holds the glasses up on her brow and shows me her face, "Did I smear my mascara?"

"No." My heart hurts for her.

"Eyeliner okay?"

"It's a little lighter near the corners but it's not smeared."

She sniffs. "Rafael can tell if I've been crying."

"The make-up's good. Really."

Her phone rings. She picks it up. A second passes. Her posture stiffens and one hand clutches her coat's zipper. I lean forward in my seat as uneasy nerves fire off.

"Which infirmary?" she asks in rapid-fire Spanish. "Imbecile. Sí. We'll be there."

She disconnects, and I dig out my wallet to throw cash on the table. She reaches for my wrist and squeezes. It's the same comforting squeeze I gave her minutes ago. I search her face as my pulse quickens and the pit of my stomach free falls.

"He's okay. But injured. He's refusing to go to a doctor." She shakes her head and bites out, "Men. Let's go. We're to meet them in the lobby."

"Rafael?" She can't mean it's Fisher. He's indestructible.

"Honey, it's Damian. But he's okay."

We trudge over icy, packed snow, slipping and sliding on the way. We're both wearing snow boots designed for these conditions, but as the temperature falls, more ice forms, creating a precarious path. I pepper her with questions until she stops so suddenly the person walking behind her slams into her back.

"Sophia." She grips my arm and jiggles my coat. "Listen. He's okay. Some sort of idiot injury. Rafael would insist on a doctor if he was seriously injured. My Rafe is a good man. He takes care of his own. If he's letting him be an imbecile and return to the lobby, he is mostly okay. Understand?"

"Yes." She tilts her head as if she's not believing me. So I nod, emphasizing I understand. My nerves are disarmed and off-kilter. When she took that call, my expectation had been that it would be anyone but Fisher. But he said it had been years since he'd gone heli-skiing.

Gemma jerks my jacket, and I focus on her. "And before we get back. Before I forget. Thank you. Back there." She jerks her head in the direction we came from. "For listening to me. But say nothing, okay? Rafe would be..."

"Gemma. No worries. I won't say anything. Promise."

Satisfied, she releases my arm, and we continue around the bend. Three different SUVs are parked in front of the resort entrance. Stacked luggage blocks the view of the license plates on the Black Chevrolet SUV closest to us.

Five uniformed employees circulate through the front entrance, performing duties like talking to guests, stacking luggage onto push carts, and managing the valet system.

Inside the lobby, Gemma removes her gloves and taps away on her phone. When I approach, she slides her sunglasses on top of her head. "They're five minutes out."

She and I choose to remain bundled up and stand just inside the lobby entrance doors. Fisher is obviously fine. There's nothing to be worked up over. If he's being an idiot, I'll insist he goes to a doctor. A heli-skiing accident could've been a lot worse.

These are all things I repeat to myself on a loop for much longer than five minutes. Gemma's incessant tapping on her phone eventually jars my awareness that I too have a phone. I pull it out and text Fisher. I probably should've done that earlier. The men might think it's odd Damian's wife hasn't texted, but me and phones... There's no response.

I hold the phone out, alternating between scanning the road out in front of the hotel and the absence of three dots on my screen.

Two white SUVs turn on the road in front of the hotel, and instantly I know it's them. They would've hired drivers from the same company to take them to the heli-skiing company. Or maybe the heli-skiing company provides transportation for its customers. I never thought to ask this morning.

God, if he'd been seriously injured... it's unfathomable. He's a force. A wall of impenetrable muscle and skill. A CIA legend. But people die heli-skiing. He's a badass, but he's not infallible.

Wheels crunch over ice as the lead SUV pulls to a stop in front of the lobby entrance. Black glass conceals the backseat passengers from view. A bellman rushes to the driver, attempting to tell him he can't park in that location. The passenger door opens, and Ivan jumps out and opens the passenger side back door.

Ivan offers his arm to Fisher, and he puts weight on it, sliding out of the vehicle. The second his feet hit the ground, he grimaces.

"What did you do?" I rush to him, searching for an injury. His coat lies across his shoulders, but neither arm is in the sleeves. His left arm is at an angle, and he's holding it with his right arm.

Fisher's lips are tight with strain. He grits out, "Old injury. Stupid."

Like a good wife, I sidle up beside him. "Do you need to put weight on my shoulder?"

"It's my shoulder that's injured. I can walk fine." He plows forward without a second glance my way.

"You're in for a fun night," Ivan jokes. "He's a pissy patient."

"Ah." I'm not sure pissy is a word, but I get Ivan's meaning.

"Guess you guys won't be joining us for dinner?" Gemma asks. She made reservations for all of us to eat dinner together in the village tonight. I study Fisher's retreating rear. Even if we wanted to, it would look odd if I cajoled my pissy husband to go out.

I give Gemma a quick hug and tell her I'll text her to let her know how he's doing. She nods and pats my back.

When I catch up to Fisher, he's stepping into an elevator.

"You okay?" It's a stupid question, but it's the one that rolls out.

He presses his back against the elevator wall and closes his eyes. "Just need some pain meds. I'll be fine."

"They didn't have anything to give you?"

"Didn't trust anything they'd give me." I nod, knowing where he's coming from, but in this case, his paranoia probably cost him in pain.

Back in the room, he ducks directly into the bathroom and opens his travel bag and a pill container. He pops four white pills.

When he sits down on the sofa, I kneel before him.

"What're you doing?" His cheekbones above the line on his beard are bright red from either wind or sun burn. The creases around his blue eyes deepen through his scowl.

"Helping you." I tap his boot. He obediently lifts his leg, and I remove the boot, then do the other one. He never flinches. "What, exactly, is injured?"

He points to his shoulder. His head rests against the wall, and he closes his eyes. "I took a cliff and, like a dumbass, tried to do a flip. Landed right on my shoulder."

I straddle his lap, and his eyelids snap open.

"I'm taking this shirt off," I say before he can ask the question. I start with the uninjured arm and shoulder. His skin is cool to the touch. Heat builds around my neck and face, reminding me I'm still in a wool sweater.

Leaving his thermal top half-on, I shrug out of my thick sweater, then focus on the patient again. With care, I lift his thermal over his head. As tenderly as possible, I glide the shirt over his shoulder and down the arm he's keeping close to his side.

A bright white scar traverses his shoulder. There's no bruising...yet. My fingers brush the skin, and he flinches.

"Hurts?" I ask. He doesn't respond. "What's the scar from?"

"Old surgery."

"Rotator cuff?"

"Yep."

I press my thumbs over the scar tissue, and his neck muscles strain. A vein running down his throat pulses. If he's injured

himself, all the surrounding muscles are going to tighten. I tap his arm and climb off his lap.

"Go lie down on my bed."

"What?"

"Pants off. Just briefs. Face down."

"Excuse me?"

"You need a massage. There's no way we'll get you an appointment this late in the day. Go."

"Sophia...you don't need to."

"Go. Do what your wife says."

That comment earns an amused smirk, and he begrudgingly obeys. Only when he reaches the bed, he hesitates.

Jesus, he must be in so much pain. "Here, let me."

My fingers tug at the button on his pants. I flick the snap open, and he sucks in air, and the loud breathy sound catches my attention. I pull down on the zipper, clutch each side of his ski pants, and bend my knees, bringing his pants with me. The sizable erection captured by the black cotton briefs reveals all.

His heady scent and heat surround me as I remove his socks, one by one, brushing my hand over his muscular calf, roughened with dark twists of hair. My throat tightens and my heart reverberates against my breastbone. My head feels lighter, dizzy.

CHAPTER 16
FISHER

Sophia kneeling before me, her mouth inches from my aching erection, sufficiently distracts me from my busted shoulder. I can barely breathe as her fingers travel from my thighs, over my knees, and down to my calves. My thought process slows, as if all my blood has traveled from my injury to my engorged, needy dick.

"Sophia." Her name comes out as a heady groan. This isn't right. It's the exact opposite of right, which is wrong.

The points of her nipples push against the barely there Thinsulate fabric top. My breaths are shallow and rapid.

Deep inside me, I know it's wrong. On the surface, it's innocent enough. But the desire crashing over me, what I'm wanting her to do, what I want to do to her, it's all wrong.

Avoiding my gaze, she gestures to the bed. "Get on," she says, her voice strained. "Face down."

The mattress sinks under my weight. I shove the stack of pillows out of the way and stretch across the bed from corner to corner. A sharp pain sears from my shoulder, up my neck, and down my arm.

"Easy," she coaxes.

I try again, lying down on the bed, face turned to the side. The

pain's what I deserve. You're not supposed to want your friend's daughter. Or the young girl you watched over and kept safe. Especially the young girl who was likely raped by sick, twisted men. That last thought eliminates my hard-on. *Good.*

She crawls over me, slinging a thigh over my back. Heat sears my lower back and the base of my spine. Her weight presses my groin into the mattress and my semi twitches, coming back to life. I open my mouth to protest, but her fingers dig into me, and a groan escapes.

She shifts, jostling my body, dragging her leg across me as she leans toward the side table. She grabs a bottle and repositions herself. I hear a snap, and then liquid pours down the length of my spine.

"What is that?"

"Oil."

"Why do you have it?"

"A girl has her reasons." I close my eyelids, attempting to force my brain to not think about any of those reasons. Her fingers. A toy. Thighs spread. Shut it down.

She palms my back on both sides of my spine, up and down. She uses her body to deepen the pressure. With each push forward, her crotch grinds against the top of my ass, pressing me down into the downy comforter. My dick aches, but as she kneads my back, stopping just shy of my shoulder bones, I give in to her touch.

As the tension eases, she bypasses my shoulders and digs into my tight neck. With a little more oil, her frosty fingers smoothly glide over my heated skin. The contrast in temperature, after a brutal day on the mountain, is transcendent.

The pads of her fingers lightly brush over my abused shoulder with unmistakable tenderness. The heat of her body warms my spine as she lowers herself, cocooning me. A warm softness lightly brushes over my scar. Her lips. Fuck. Those soft lips.

"Sophia." Her name is a warning.

"Flip over." Her words heat my ear, and her breath tickles. The side of her face grazes mine. "I need to work on your front."

She lifts off me, and cold air circulates around my exposed skin. This has *bad idea* written all over it. But with closed eyes, I comply, gritting against the pain in my shoulder.

Velvety liquid coats my chest. The bed dips, and she slings a leg over the tops of my legs, settling her center over my strained erection. With both palms, she repeats her actions from earlier, this time stroking from my abdomen over my chest. Her nail scrapes a nipple as her hips undulate over me, coaxing my dick.

Fuck. She knows exactly what she's doing.

I press up off the mattress with my good arm. This can't happen.

But her fingers dip into my shoulder, and the pain has me crashing back against the mattress.

"That hurts, doesn't it?" Sophia sounds compassionate.

"It's an old injury." About fifteen years old. It flares up, especially when abused. Her tender touch eases me back into a lull, as do her slow, rhythmic movements over my groin.

I shouldn't be doing this. Lying here, with her over me. The sexual energy between us is palpable. My fingers twitch, aching to grip her, flip her over and drive into her. To punish her for teasing me, for tempting me. Because she knows exactly what she's doing. And she's fully aware I'm friends with her father. Not to mention Ryan, the man she considers a surrogate uncle. A man who threw me a lifeline when I needed one most.

Those nails scrape my shoulder, my throat, and into my scalp. Sensual tendrils spread down my spine and across my limbs. *God, this feels good.*

"That's it. Relax." Her hips grind over me, and Jesus, it's conceivable I could come just from this slow, erotic, semi-clothed massage. "What pills did you take?"

"Aleve."

"You didn't want prescription strength?"

"Four pills should do the trick."

Her fingers prod and burrow into my sore shoulder muscles. With deep, probing strokes, she manipulates those tight muscles into putty. Much like me.

Once again, she flattens her warm body over mine, only this time, it's my front. And god, she feels divine. Smooth softness blanketing me. Her breath brushes over my ear, and the sensation somehow makes my erection even harder.

"Is this what you want, Sophia?" I ask the question with my eyes closed, my lungs still, and my heart racing.

She places open-mouthed kisses along my neck, sucking along the way. "What do you want?"

It's rather obvious what I want. There's no way she's not aware of what she's been grinding on. "We shouldn't do this, Sophia."

She smiles against my skin, then maneuvers down my body. Her fingers clasp the band of my briefs, and she tugs, freeing my erection. It bobs in the air as she tugs the briefs down my legs.

I close my eyes and swallow. This is wrong. "Sophia. What're you doing?"

"I'd think it's obvious." She climbs back on the bed, but she lifts the bottom of her Thinsulate shirt up her waist, whips it over her head, and tosses it to the floor.

Those melon-colored nipples with hardened peaks sit atop sweetly curved mounds, begging to be fondled, nibbled, kissed, and sucked. My hand reaches out, but I'm too slow. She's down, over me again, pressing her sweet lips all over my abdomen.

"Oh, shit. Sophia."

She raises up, and wild, tangled, crazy, crimson hair falls all around her shoulders. "Fisher," she says in a stern tone, mocking me.

Fuck me. Consequences be damned, I want her.

Her fingers wrap around my dick, lightly at first, and my head tilts and my eyes roll back. "Jesus, Sophia."

The pad of her thumb circles my tip, smearing the pre-cum over the crown. The base of my spine flexes, as do my balls.

She lets me go and straddles me again, only this time, when she captures my dick between her thighs, her silk panties are the only thing separating us.

My fingers tangle with those unruly locks and I tug, pulling her up to my lips. Obediently, her mouth covers mine. Her tongue thrusts in, and I take her. There's nothing timid or unsure about this kiss. No, it's molten-hot, undeniably sinful, hungry, and mind-numbing.

My hands roam her back, and down, over that fine, perfect ass.

She dips her head, and her teeth clasp my nipple. Pain sears into my chest.

"Hey." I palm her ass, then smack. She grins an evil, sexy-as-fuck grin and nips her way down my chest, over my abdomen, and lower.

Her tongue flattens against my shaft and climbs. "Fuck, Sophia."

I can't raise my head to watch, so I lie back, blink at the ceiling, and absorb all the sensations. The hot warmth, the wetness of her mouth. The pull, the suction, the too-fucking-good sensation of those teeth lightly brushing over my sensitive tip. She cups my balls and nearly chokes on my dick, then rises. She does it all over and over, sending me hurling to the brink.

"Sophia," I gasp. I grip her hair and tug. "It's..."

But I'm too late. I spasm uncontrollably, releasing everything.

She swallows some of it, but some spurts across my abdomen. She presses her lips to my side, squeezes me, and hops off the bed. The sink turns on, then off. She pads barefoot to the bed wearing only a silk thong.

The memory of the taste of her nipple hits me so strong my dick twitches. A warm cloth presses down on my abdomen.

"Sophia, that was…" I really am at a loss for words. It was amazing. Mind-blowing. And wrong. So wrong.

She beams. Her coquettish grin says she doesn't share in the regret.

After cleaning me up, she climbs on the bed beside me, reaches for the edge of the comforter, tugs it over us, and curls into my side uninjured side.

I'm not typically a snuggler, but after what she did for me, to me, I'm not about to protest.

"What was that?" I ask.

"You were in pain. Adrenaline helps with that."

It's a sweet thought, but it doesn't make it right.

"Did you not want me to do that?" She sounds unsure, which isn't what I want. But my head swirls. I shouldn't have done that. I should've stopped her.

"Fisher?"

I swipe my brow with my good hand. "It felt very one-sided."

"If you wish, when you're feeling up to it, you can even things out."

Her nose scrunches, and she grins. It's a very Sophia-like grin. A very familiar Sophia grin.

I groan, and she laughs. But when she nestles beside me, I curl my good arm around her. A mistake. I should get up and go out to the sofa.

My eyelids grow heavy. The warmth of her body next to mine and the comforter over us has a sedative effect. Outside, the sun has set, and the room darkens. She lays her head down on my chest, and her heartbeat thuds against my ribs.

CHAPTER 17
SOPHIA

I don't regret what I did. But I'm mystified by my actions. That's not like me. Or it's not like the old me. This is actually what I've been working for in therapy for years. For the ability to take pleasure from sexual interaction.

Never have I been the aggressor. The seducer. Sure, I can be aggressive in defensive maneuvers. In a boxing ring or on the mat. But for the longest time, sex brought unpleasant ideas and physical reactions. And I've hated those residual side effects.

Against my therapist's advice, I forced myself to have sex my senior year of college. My lack of sexual desire, or asexual preference, felt like an injury I carried around that wasn't healing. And I wanted to heal. To put it all behind me.

It worked. More or less. Mechanical sex helped to launch me past a gaping divide between me and my friends and other healthy individuals my age.

But what I did to Fisher, that wasn't mechanical. The area below my waist tingled, my muscles quivered—hell, I wanted him deep inside me. I wanted to touch him and taste him. Maybe a part of me wanted to tease him, to force him to see me as the woman I am, not the girl I was. But that wasn't all there was.

The subtle pounding of his heart beneath my ear soothes. One of my legs drifts over his. A tremor courses through my sex. I still want him.

He's a good-looking guy. But it's not like I haven't been around those before. Could it be the fake marriage scenario? The sparkling ring on my finger? Is that what's turning me on? An underlying subliminal need to conform to society's standards?

Once, in college, on a drunken night, Lauren rambled on about how she just wanted Christian's dick. She was so drunk I interpreted her ramblings as someone repeating what she thought she should feel.

The thing is...what I did to Fisher turned me on. But it didn't relieve me. I still feel that need between my legs. A carnal need. A pulsing desire. My fingers slip down to the gap between my pelvis and Fisher's sleeping form. I clasp my fingers over myself and close my eyes, letting the added heat build around my sensitive, thrumming parts. My hips, ever so slowly, rock against my hand. My fingers press against my mound, nudging and kneading, much like I did to Fisher's tight muscles. But it's not enough, and my finger slips inside.

This right here, getting myself off, is something I've been doing more frequently in recent years. It's as if my body has been slowly coming out of dormancy, awakening to sexual pleasure. That has to be it. It's all timing. Fisher is the first male I've been around, that I've kissed and touched, in years. And then he was there, his erection straining beneath my sex, the buzz between us visceral.

The phrase from one of my prior therapists comes to mind as wisps of pleasure build. Sex is a natural, physical need. My fingers gently tap, massaging myself, mixing light and hard pressure. A calloused hand covers mine, halting my movements.

"What're you doing?" He deftly replaces my hand with his, and the tip of his finger explores. "Hmmm." The low, guttural

noise vibrates through my core, and my hips rock against him. "I passed out without taking care of you."

"You're injured." But not so injured that his left hand can't pick up the slack. His fingers plunge deeper while his thumb caresses my clit.

He maneuvers me onto my back, and I spread my legs, willing him to continue building me up with his long, agile fingers. His hot breath coaxes my throat, and his lips tenderly tease my skin, kissing his way down my body, to my breasts.

His tongue laps around my swollen, eager nipple, eliciting a near purr from somewhere deep within. He withdraws his hand from my center, and I whimper at the loss, but his rough skin glides up my body, over my stomach, to circle my breast. He adjusts his body, positioning himself between my spread legs. He winces. It's obvious he's protective of his right shoulder, keeping his arm clasped against his side.

"You don't need to." I shift, moving away, and he growls.

Slowly, his left hand skims down my side and rests on my hip. He pulls on my thong.

"Close your legs." My eyes flutter open, and he gazes down at me with a look that reassures me my legs won't be closed for long. I do as he instructs, lifting my feet into the air, and he leans forward and nibbles on my ankle as the silk rises over my legs, ankles, and feet. He rests my ankles on his uninjured shoulder and presses soft kisses, a sharp contrast to his rough beard, to my shin and calf. "Your skin is so smooth, so soft."

His straining erection juts out above his thighs as he sits on bended knees, and I bend sideways, reaching for him. He clicks his tongue, and in a restrained, throaty, foreign tone, he says, "No, baby. Not yet. Now, spread those legs."

I do as he instructs, and he trails kisses along the sensitive skin of my inner thighs. He pauses, and those dark, hooded eyes meet mine. "I'm going to hell for this."

I can't help but snicker. Then he kisses me. There. His tongue dips inside, and my body melts, relaxing against the comforter. Spreadeagle, open for him to devour. He licks and laps, and his fingers join in. My skin tingles and my muscles tense and my fingers tousle with his hair, directing him as his tongue circles my clit and sucks. His rough beard against my sensitive skin has me pushing and pulling. It's the bite that does me in, and I let go, back arched, toes curled, shouting out a semblance of the word "Fish."

He presses his lips to my inner thigh, kissing me. It feels like he's thanking me, but damn, he's the one deserving of thanks.

He crawls up over me, hovering lower, his weight on his knees and one arm. His thick, engorged shaft prods my belly, and he places a soft, strained kiss over my heart.

"It was worth it," he says. He carefully positions himself down on the bed and pulls me back against him in a blissful, comforting cloud.

"What was?"

"This. You. You're worth going to hell for."

A sated, happy smile slowly spreads across my lips, and I reach for him, careful of injury. He kisses me, and I taste myself on his lips. Salty, intimate, an aphrodisiac.

I push against his chest, and he breaks our kiss. The tip of his nose brushes my cheek. "What is it?"

"Flat on your back," I direct. "Relax."

With hooded eyes, he lies back, flat against the bed. He splays out his fingers, holding up those strong, capable hands, and I reach for them as I straddle him. I bend over him and kiss him once more, groaning into him. And then I push up, using his chest for balance. I rise and reach for his shaft. I run his crown back and forth, through my slit.

"Jesus," he grits out. "You are so goddamn sexy."

"And lucky you...you're married to me."

He narrows his eyes as if he's going to reprimand me, but then

I take him, sliding down his shaft, letting his length slowly stretch and fill me. Fuck. He feels every bit as good as I thought he would.

"Condom?" He clasps my thigh, holding me still.

"I'm clean. Are you?"

He gives a barely perceptible nod.

I'm not really down with the condom lingo. My experience is limited. "You okay? I have an IUD."

His hand slides over my hip, to my waist, and those dark blue orbs infiltrate deep within my chest. The intensity forces my eyes closed.

My thighs squeeze, lifting me up and down. His thumb presses against me, giving me more, and my hips take over, grinding against him.

"Damian," I gasp. Every time I take him as deep as I can, he hits me deep inside, rippling shockwaves through my core.

"Yeah, baby." He's breathless. I don't think I've ever felt more powerful than I do at this moment, riding him. I hold all the power. His expression is one of ecstasy. I feel like a goddess. Like a queen. I'm in control.

My muscles tense. Pleasure vibrates. His thumb coaxes me, right where I need it, building me up.

"You..." It's all I can get out. And then I'm quivering over him, unable to move, gasping for air.

His hands grip my hips, and his biceps flex as he takes over, moving me back and forth. His hips rise, hitting that one spot, milking my orgasm for all it's worth. Our rhythm speeds out of control, growing sporadic, and as I collapse on his chest, I feel him thickening within me, and pulsing deep inside.

I press wet, sloppy kisses against his neck, and his arm wraps around my back, holding me close to his damp, slick skin. His heart thuds against me at a rapid pace.

"We should've done that sooner," I whisper against his throat.

His arms tighten around me. "Hell awaits. So worth it."

I push up off him, just enough to gaze into those deep, sated, blue eyes. "Can you stop it?" I squeeze my inner muscles, tightening around him. "When you're still inside me?"

He grins and reaches up and brushes his thumb back and forth over my cheek, then pulls me down to his lips. We're still kissing when I shift and he slips out of my hold. I roll off him, onto my side, and my breasts press against the hard muscles of his chest.

It's exquisite and sweet. But there's a pressure in my chest that's uncomfortable. So, I push up, climb over him, and head to the bathroom. When I come out of the bathroom, he's lying on his side, waiting.

"Come back here," he says.

I hesitate. He lets out a huff.

"Sophia. Come back here."

I don't have a good reason not to. Gemma and Rafael don't expect to see us until tomorrow. So, head down, naked, I stride to the bed. My thigh presses against the edge of the mattress.

"Want to climb between the sheets?" I ask. Everything we've done has been above the covers.

"Not yet. Lie here beside me. In a bit, we'll order room service."

I climb up next to him, resuming my position draped over him. It feels oddly natural, as if we've been doing this for a while. This obviously wasn't part of our cover. But no, it was us acting on escalating attraction. Just sex. At our age, in our professions, it doesn't need to mean anything.

My gaze travels up the valley of his well-defined chest to the faint scar. "Tell me about your injury."

"I already told you. I tried to do a three sixty—"

"Not that." I dip my head and nip his salty skin. The friendly teasing eases some of the discomfort in my chest.

"Hey," he halfheartedly protests.

"How'd you injure it the first time?"

He brushes his hand over his forehead and rubs his eyes. "It was a long time ago."

"You clearly had surgery."

"Have you heard of BUD/s?"

"Well, yeah. I grew up in San Diego." He was in the Navy, like my dad. "Were you a SEAL?"

"Didn't make it through. Two days to go. Tore my rotator cuff. Couldn't move my arm. Worst pain of my life."

His eyes are closed. The hard set of his jowl says it's a painful memory.

"An injury like that isn't your fault."

"I still could've made it." Leaning over him, I press a tender kiss over his heart. "I also got pneumonia. High fever. Chills. Medics might've let me continue, but someone died the round before us, from pneumonia complications, of all things, and it had gotten some bad press. They weren't taking chances. They pulled me."

"You say that like you don't think they did the right thing?"

"I could've made it." He lets out a heavy sigh. "I was so close."

I rest my ear against his chest. His heartbeat thuds, slow and rhythmic now. "I'm glad they pulled you."

"That's a shitty thing to say."

"No, it's not. You might not be here otherwise."

"Hmmm." His answer vibrates through his chest cavity.

"How'd you end up working for my dad?"

"Ryan heard about me. I was a mess. Needed surgery, physical therapy. Was in the hospital for over a week with pneumonia. Emotionally, I was in a bad place. Didn't re-up when my time came due. Ryan actually showed up at my apartment door. Told me he had something else he wanted me to consider. Trevor finished out my physical therapy, got me back on my feet, so to speak. I'd been working for them for a while when your dad hired Arrow to handle his security."

"That's right. That's when he became a partner."

"I don't know where I'd be if it weren't for Ryan."

"You would've landed on your feet."

"You think?" He sounds amused, but I wasn't aiming for humor.

"I know." I lift my head and push myself forward until my lips press against the corner of his. He shifts away from my kiss, and his gaze shoots off to the wall.

"What they did for me, though. Makes what's going on here doubly despicable."

"Going on?" My fingers lightly tap over his chest. "So, this is going to keep happening?"

His palm flattens over my ass. Reticent eyes return to me. "As long as you want it to. I mean, at least while we're married."

That makes me laugh.

CHAPTER 18
FISHER

I wake with Sophia's back to me. She's curled onto her side, and I'm draped over her, clinging. The drapes are open, as we didn't let housekeeping prepare the room for the night, and outside the dim glow of a sun hidden by snow clouds brightens the room.

I lie there with her, breathing in her heady, floral scent, in the room's quiet, and recognize the situation. This moment, this second in time, is bliss. Perfection. But much like the eye of a hurricane, this serenity won't last. What I've done here is wrong on so many levels.

I should be stricken with guilt. Not luxuriating in peaceful tranquility. My shoulder aches, but it's a manageable pain. It's not the first time it's taken a beating. I stretch my legs out, straightening, separating our bodies slowly, so as not to wake her. Her fingers curl against my hip, and I still.

She rolls over, and her soft breasts press against my ribcage and her thigh rises over mine. She nips at my chest, and her fingers comb through my chest hair and trail lower. My lungs contract as my body subliminally wills her to continue.

"Sophia," I groan, her name a warning and a wish.

"You're hard." Those long fingers wrap around the evidence, stroking me.

Fuck it. I'm already going to hell.

With that thought, I gently push her onto her back and administer light kisses, starting at the base of her neck, across her clavicle, and down to her breasts as I shift to position myself between her legs. My fingers sweep over her, through her trimmed patch of curls, and into her hot heat. And yes, she is so fucking wet.

"Looks like I'm not the only one who woke up eager."

I watch her closely as my fingers plunge into her, knead, and rub. Her eyelids close and her lips pucker. I listen closely to her little mewls and purrs, learning what she likes, what she needs. She's close. As I apply more pressure to her clit with my thumb, I suck her nipple, teasing the tender peak with my tongue and teeth, and her channel tightens around my fingers as she curls forward.

That's what I wanted. Right there.

She presses on my hip, and her eyelashes flutter. "I want you."

Not one to deny her, I position myself at her entrance and sink deeper into bliss. Because that's what she is. This is. And as fantastic as her tight pussy is, as perfect as her little moans are, as right as her legs feel wrapped tight around me, that's not bliss in its entirety. For me, being inside her is the nirvana I didn't know I'd been seeking. By definition, bliss is fleeting, and the recognition of a blissful moment bittersweet.

With my good arm, I lift her ass higher, plunging deeper, and she chants the words *yes* and broken fragments of my name mixed with gods. I'm so close, on the verge of falling, losing myself within her, but it's not until she quivers around me that I succumb and my orgasm rips through me with the force of a Category Five hurricane. I collapse over her, gasping for air. "Holy fuck, Sophia."

She wraps her arms and legs around me, holding me close as our breathing slows. Bliss.

"That's what I call a good morning wake up." With a coquettish wiggle of her eyebrows, she presses a quick kiss to the side of my neck and caresses my sore shoulder.

With great effort, I push up off the mattress, and she slides out from under me. The bathroom door clicks shut, and I rub my eyes. The day has begun.

I stumble into the hall bathroom, brush my teeth, pop four more pills, get presentable, then work the magic of the Nespresso, which to me is basically a fancy-looking Keurig. I re-enter the bedroom with two coffees.

Sophia sits back on stacked pillows, her work phone in hand. She glances up at me, and a sweet smile slowly spreads. "Coffee. My hero."

I hand her the white mug, then walk around to the other side of the bed.

"What're you reading?"

"Nothing much. An article about Colombia preparing for tourism. Guatemala and Belize have booming tourism. If Colombia can maintain stability, there's no reason the tourism industry won't thrive. Well, drugs." Her eyebrows rise, but her gaze remains focused, reading the article.

"Mexico has drugs and tourism." My black coffee is a tad stronger than I like, so I chug it.

"It does. But they aren't getting it into the States on their own. They've got Stateside resources. Distributors. Crime enterprises these days are international conglomerates."

Her personal phone vibrates beside her. When she picks it up, I glimpse pretty boy Zane's name before she presses it to her ear and answers.

I pick up her work phone to read the article she was referencing. Colombian tourism doesn't interest me, but I need a distraction so I don't stare at her too possessively while she's on the phone. I never particularly liked Zane. He always checked out, so I

chalked up my distaste being because of his rich, spoiled boy status. When the kid turned sixteen, his father bought him a red Ferrari. It's as if good old dad wanted to ensure his son grew into an asshole of gargantuan proportions.

A text comes through on Sophia's work phone from Gemma.

GEMMA TORO:

How's Damian? Want to meet us downstairs for breakfast?

The text is peppered with girlie emojis. I hold the phone screen up for Sophia to read. Her eyes flash with eagerness and excitement. I remember my first few CIA ops. I'd had that same fire. The same thrill at the promise of a mission.

"Zane, that all sounds fabulous. Look, I'm sorry, but I've got to run." There's a pause. "East Coast, remember? This is the middle of my workday." She gives me an amused, slightly naughty smile, and I resist the urge to push the phone aside and claim those lips. "I promise, I'll check the dates and get back to you."

She clicks off the phone and swings her legs off the bed. "I've got to get a quick shower. Can you text Gemma back and ask if we can meet in thirty?"

"Thirty minutes. Copy that." She opens the closet and flicks through hanging clothes while I fixate on her seductive backside. "What's Zane up to?"

"He wants me to go to this thing with him. Just giving me some additional info. But I don't know what I can commit to, you know?" She unfolds a sweater from a stack in the suitcase and holds it out, as if considering if it will do. "How do you make

plans? I mean, I don't know what country I'll be in a month from now, and he thinks I work at a bank."

"I don't make commitments." Those youthful blue eyes look straight into mine, and an understanding passes between us. This is the life we have chosen.

Fingers linked, Sophia and I weave through the lobby guests to the restaurant in the back. At the hostess stand, a bright-eyed young woman with her hair pulled back and a name tag that lists her home country as New Zealand greets us with a smile.

"Our friends might already be here," I tell her. "The Toros?"

"Ah. Mr. And Mrs. Garcia?"

My gaze flits to Sophia, and the blooming warmth in my chest irritates me. Her hold on my hand tightens ever so slightly, and I wonder if she's feeling it, too. We've crossed lines that place me on thin ice that I have insufficient experience navigating.

We follow the bouncy hostess to the back of the restaurant. The window we are seated by should offer an expansive view of the mountain range, but gray, foreboding clouds obscure the peaks.

After the women hug and all the cordial greetings are out of the way, Gemma points to the landscape. "Have you been checking the weather?"

Sophia answers with a slight shake of her head as she stirs her coffee. *No, we've been busy doing other things.*

"The system's coming in faster than predicted. It's hitting this evening. We were supposed to fly out in the morning, but we're heading out after this."

"After breakfast? Really?" Sophia picks up her phone and turns a concerned expression on me. "Do you think we should try to move up our flight?"

Rafael chuckles. "Good luck with that. You guys flew commercial?"

I grimace and nod. Sure, I'm playing the part, but after observing the ultra-wealthy for nearly eight years as an invisible worker bee in the background, I've grown to loathe the entitled, out-of-touch one-percenters. Or maybe it's the point-two-percenters.

"Man, you gotta fly private. You'll be stuck here for days."

"Thank you," Sophia gushes. "That's what I'm always telling him. He thinks first is okay," she flutters those eyelashes and touches my forearm, "but you know, first in the US is really just business. Growing up, we never had to fly commercial."

I sip my water and look across the restaurant at the extensive buffet, pretending to be annoyed. And in truth, it's not much of an act. She's relayed the agreed-on backstory for her character, but there's a lot of accuracy in it. The Sullivans don't own just one private jet, they own multiples, plus two helicopters. She flew commercial from time to time, but only to fit in with her college friends, who were also privileged, just not of the same caliber as the Sullivans.

Rafael pushes back his sleeve and checks the time on a diamond rimmed gold Rolex. He juts his chin, gesturing to the bar area. "Let's get a drink."

"Rafe, we have wait service," Gemma says. She raises her hand and snaps her fingers.

"Baby, we're going to give you two a few moments to talk about lady things."

Gemma lets out an exaggerated, pouty sigh, and she flicks her long nails, dismissing us. "Go. Go. Go talk business." Her emphasis on the last word amuses me. It also shows she's excluded from even the most mundane of business discussions.

As Rafael and I push out our chairs to head to the bar, Gemma latches on to Sophia's arm. "That's fine, baby. I'm going to take this

time to chat with my friend here about that gorgeous mink stole. We might even go buy it."

"I already told you to buy it if you want it," he grunts.

As we head toward the bar, I catch Sophia gushing over the merits of the forty-thousand-dollar jacket. It's a good thing Bauer paired me with Sophia on this, because I sure as hell couldn't have a serious conversation about a forty-thousand-dollar jacket.

"Do you like Bloody Marys? Or do you do the mimosa thing?" Rafael asks. The bartender works double-time behind the counter fulfilling orders from diners, but he's keeping an eye on us, should Rafael say the word.

"Not sure I need any alcohol," I say, gesturing to my shoulder. It's the truth. I'm not a heavy drinker and don't usually start in the morning. He raises an eyebrow. "But a bloody works. Spicy."

He grins. "Heat. I like it."

"Where are the guys?" I ask as the bartender jumps to our order. My guess is Rafael tips well and his reputation precedes him.

"Headed out for one last run since we're packing up early."

"You must be looking forward to getting back to warm temperatures." We've lucked out as far as snow conditions, but the temperature has been notably frigid for spring skiing, dropping to minus fifteen at night.

"I like it all." He grins wide and passes me my drink. "*Salut.*"

I return the greeting, and our glasses clink.

"So, I looked into your businesses."

"You did?" I rest my good elbow on the bar and lean against it, intrigued to learn what he discovered.

"You're doing okay, but you've got a lot of debt."

I glance over my shoulder at the women gabbing away at our table. "My wife," I say with a shrug. "Your wife doesn't help going on about mink coats."

He tosses his head back with a laugh. "The ladies are..." He

rubs his thumb against his fingers as substitution for the word money. "We might have a chance to work together." He scans the room, and, curiously, I do the same. There are two exit points, the side door to the patio is locked, and all the patrons match tourist profiles. No one appears to be watching us. "I've got a trip planned to the States in two weeks. Will you be around?"

"Yeah. I should be. You coming to Santa Barbara?" His expression is unreadable. "Or I could meet you."

"I have meetings in LA, but I'd like to swing up to Santa Barbara. Gemma would love it. In the meantime, consider if you're open to outside investors."

"You interested in brokerage services?" I pointedly push in my eyebrows, going for an inquisitive, surprised expression.

"Always. And a man with your knowledge of the system... There's opportunity. Maybe." He taps my arm. "Let's go back to the ladies before they bankrupt both of us."

"They definitely like to shop."

"Ah, you think Gemma's bad? You should have met my second wife. Rosie." He dramatically shudders. Rosie hasn't come across our surveillance in well over a decade.

"Well, if she's anything like my ex, she's still shopping." I expect him to laugh loudly at that, in a kind of brother bond, but he's solemn. It's unnerving. If the wives off our radar are no longer alive, then he's not happy about that fact.

CHAPTER 19
SOPHIA

Sometimes the unexpected comes in with the strength of a tornado, altering the world and leaving a path of destruction behind. Experience taught me this. When life feels too good, too right, it's time to brace.

An assignment ending a day early is hardly earth-shattering. Yet there's a sinking disappointment pushing down on me. An irrational reaction to otherwise good news. My first CIA assignment is concluding, and the mission accomplished. A calmness falls over me as Gemma babbles about how disappointed she is her travel plans have imploded. The wise accept the unexpected and move forward.

When I give her a hug and beg to stay in touch, I mean it. I like her. She's young and not like the real me at all, but that doesn't mean I don't like her as a person. That's one of the things they teach you about undercover assignments. It doesn't matter if your target is a murderer or a smuggler, if you're successful in your role, you're probably going to like them. If you can't stomach them, if there's no connection at all, you probably won't get far with your target. But you have to stay true to your purpose, not to your newfound friend. In the FBI, we met officers who spent so many

years undercover they were invited to their targets' family weddings. And when the time came, those same officers had to testify against this person, or people, who trusted them.

Fisher and I pause outside the elevators. There's a closeness between us now. An intimacy that didn't exist yesterday. As we wait for the elevator, I lean into him, and his hand brushes against mine. The small contact burns and ripples along my skin with lightning-fast intensity. I glance up at him, searching his face, but I'm not sure what I'm searching for.

Will he want to see me again? Will I ever see him again after we go our separate ways?

The faint lines around his eyes deepen and his jaw muscles flex. He hasn't trimmed his beard in the last few days, and the uneven growth gives him a rugged appearance. When I look at him, I see strength and reliability. Determination. Tenderness. He's a protector. My protector. For a fleeting moment, he was more. Someone who opened up a new side of myself. Those deep blue eyes are introspective and thoughtful. What does he see when he looks at me?

"I'm going down to the business center."

I nod. "I'll check for earlier flights."

It's a typical marital interaction, but there's a bothersome underlying coldness to it. But should any of the Toros be watching, the interaction fits our roles.

Back in the room, a winter storm warning flashes on my phone. The only rescheduling options on the airline app are for later dates. I could get one of the Sullivan jets here before the storm hits, assuming we can get a route cleared, but getting out before the storm hits is iffy. Even private jets have to succumb to the weather gods.

Based on the forecast, we'll be here for at least another twenty-four hours. It's not the worst thing. Fisher and I will have one more night before we go our separate ways. And I should be able to

spend the afternoon doing research. I'd like to follow up with Erik and see if he's got any information on how Killington has been spending his time since being released.

The laptop sits securely behind the vent, but the inexplicable disappointment weighs me down and I quite simply don't feel like digging into work. When I open the wall vent, instead of my laptop, I grab my personal phone and dial Lauren. Her voicemail picks up, and I end the call, saying nothing. She'll see I called.

Then I shoot Zane a text letting him know I called her. As annoying as his reminders are, his efforts at keeping the three of us close are endearing. After the abduction, he was one of my few friends who kept coming around. He's good like that. Persistent.

The battery on the phone is low, so I plug it in to charge by the bedside table.

When I was in the FBI, Lauren and Zane were pretty understanding when I'd get slammed and go MIA. But Lauren's been more sensitive about it now that I theoretically work in finance. And with her recent engagement, there's no doubt she's been venting to Zane. Really, he should be her bridesmaid.

Given the unpredictable nature of my job, maybe I should back out, or offer up Zane as a back-up option. There's a CIA time-off request form, but it's my understanding the company needs could always override a vacation request. Lauren deserves a reliable maid of honor. When I'm back in DC, I'll speak to Bauer about it. Get his take on how unreliable vacation time is in our department.

The CIA now has Gemma's cell number, which means, thanks to no-click tracking infiltration technology, they have everything about her. But I can't imagine they are going to learn anything. There are wives who are highly involved in their husband's business, but Gemma isn't one of them. If anything, Rafael actively works to keep her out of his business. The CIA analysts are probably reading through scores of promotional emails

and intense conversations with personal shoppers. They might be digging through correspondence with family too. My sense is Gemma is close to her mother.

She and I are alike that way. Or at least, at one time, I was close to my mother. I counted her as my best friend.

Her sudden death changed everything for me. I found myself living with a father who up until that point I'd spent little time with. And none of it made sense.

A car slammed into her at an intersection. She died instantaneously, the driver shortly after. At twelve, I was too young to be suspicious. But I discovered a file on my dad's computer. He'd been suspicious. Arrow still tracks the wife of the driver. For years, they've been monitoring her financial activity. She currently lives a quiet life in Guatemala.

An electronic click sounds, announcing Fisher's return before the door opens. I listen to heavy footfalls and call, "Damian?"

He comes into view and sits to undo the laces of his leather boots, wincing as he does so.

"Shoulder hurt?"

"Sore." He rubs it. "I'm probably going to schedule an appointment with the masseuse. We're gonna be here through the snowstorm."

"Did you not like the service I gave you yesterday?"

He pauses, bent over one knee. He looks me over like he's remembering exactly what we did yesterday, last night, and this morning. My breath hitches, but I strive to appear aloof.

"I think you know I loved that." His gaze travels slowly up and down my body, warming every inch in the path of his perusal. I swear it's like he can see right through my clothes. "Best massage of my life."

He drops his gaze to his shoes and finishes removing them. His shift in attitude has me thinking I misread the heat from seconds

earlier. At the very least, his stoic expression communicates dry business.

"Spoke to the office."

"Yeah?"

"Ivan isn't going back with the rest."

"How do they know?" Is there a video feed on the tarmac?

With both shoes off and set to the side, he sits back in the armchair. "He's booked on a commercial flight into the United States. The reservation triggered the watch list."

"Where's he flying into?"

"Los Angeles." His gaze meets mine. "Rafael said he has meetings in LA in two weeks. My bet is Ivan is doing some precursory work."

"They think he's staying behind to check us out?"

"It's possible. Rafael might be fleshing out a potential new business resource Stateside. He wants to visit us in Santa Barbara."

"Is that what he spoke to you about?"

"No specifics. But yes, he and Gemma will be coming back."

My gaze meets his. "So, you think he's already working closely with his family?"

"My guess is yes. His playboy status works well as a cover."

"Then why Canada? We didn't see him do anything remotely work-like."

"This might have really been a vacation. Or..." He shrugs. "He spent three days heli-skiing. That's a shit ton of exercise. He didn't seem sore or tired. Conceivable he flew into Vancouver or elsewhere. There could've been a meeting nearby."

"But you went skiing?"

With a raised eyebrow, he silently asks how I could forget his injury. "Yes, we went skiing."

And if Fisher's theory is correct, and he's held some business meetings out here, or furthered personal connections, he wouldn't

invite a stranger to those meetings. But there's no harm in bringing him along on a fun day skiing through untracked powder.

My personal phone vibrates on the bedside table. I get up to check it. Fisher follows and leans against the doorjamb.

ZANE:

> March 15. It's a Friday. We can leave Saturday morning and spend the weekend in Laguna. You could head back to the East Coast Sunday end of day. R u game? Pls say yes.

ME:

> What's the event again? Can you take Lauren?

"What's wrong?" Fisher asks.

"Nothing." I set the phone down then flip it over. I don't really want to see Zane's response. "Zane's pushing for..." I cross my arms over my chest and rest my bum on the bedside table, while I try to come up with a way to explain it. "Zane and I dated in college. You know that, right?"

Fisher gives a quick jerk of his head. Of course he knows. He probably knows more about me from my college days than my dad or stepmom. Admittedly, he wasn't always the one lurking, but if it wasn't him, someone from his staff was and undoubtedly reported back.

"Well, we ended things with the agreement that one day, when it made sense, we might get together again." The thing is,

there's really no attraction between Zane and me. But I can't deny he's pushing for something when he texts things like spending the rest of the weekend in Laguna. It's conceivable his father, Congressman Oglethorpe, has convinced him he has a better chance of making DA if he's not single. But that's a load of crap. This day in age, no one expects a twenty-something to be married.

"Why did things end with you two?" Fisher draws me out of my head.

"We weren't really together-together." Fisher's brows draw together. "We were more friends who..." In some ways, I used Zane as a means to an end, as my last step in my, quote-unquote, recovery. "We were kind of together, but it didn't go anywhere. Classic case of friends being better off as friends. Which makes it odd that he keeps pushing for us to spend time together. Maybe it's because he lives down the street from my dad once again, but he's spending more time with him too." I meet Fisher's gaze. His expression is unreadable. But there's something about him, the familiarity, perhaps, the fact he's one of the few people who already knows so many of my secrets, including my current job, that I open up to him. "I'm sure Zane has a reason, and it's not really to do with me. Pressure from his dad, something like that." Fisher remains stoic. It's a bit like talking to a wall. "Keep in mind, Zane thinks I'm working for a bank right now. He once told me his dad provided him with a list of women he thought would help his political career. I saw the list. I'm on it. Maybe he's working his way down the list."

"Seriously?" Fisher's expression is no longer stoic. No, he's looking at me like I have descended from Venus.

"Yeah." Fisher isn't a part of that world, but he lived on the fringes of it long enough this really shouldn't surprise him. "Mostly women with trust funds large enough to bolster his political ambitions. Women without aspirations of influencer

status, in our age bracket. The list had been well-researched, like he hired someone on staff to do the legwork."

"I'm sure he did." Fisher stares out the window, contemplative once again. Outside, snowflakes swirl.

"Well, I made the list. But I don't think I'm his dad's favorite. I just think Zane's too lazy to pursue the others. I mean, the women listed weren't exactly desperate. He'd need to woo."

"Zane's too self-centered to spend effort on someone else."

"He's not that bad."

The barest hint of a skeptical smirk crosses his lips. "If you say so." He straightens and shifts to press his back against the wall. He's far enough away that what his dark blue irises lack in color, they gain in depth. "He always struck me as an entitled prick."

"Zane's a good friend." He's entitled, certainly, but that could be said about almost anyone from my high school.

"The guy's a fool. He had you, and he let you go."

I pull my legs up against me and wrap my arms around them. Yes, he ended things with us, but it was completely understandable.

"How much do you know?"

"Enough," he says.

I rub my forehead, trying to think back to what a security officer would have overheard.

"I was very careful." I narrow my eyes, searching Fisher for answers. "Did you have listening devices in my apartment? Dad swore..." I can't continue. Memories of my college apartments, all places picked out with precision by his precious security team short-circuit my thought processes.

"We had video at the entrance, not inside. Your father protected your privacy."

"Then how?"

"Zane wasn't as careful."

"You watched Zane too?"

"Not much." His lower lip protrudes. "Some."

Unbelievable. "That's overreaching." I glare at Fisher, even though it's not his fault. He was hired.

"The guy did coke all through his last two years of college." Fisher shrugs like it's no big deal. "He was one of your friends. He was interacting with high-risk profiles."

He's talking about Zane's fraternity brothers. They weren't the most upstanding citizens. I didn't care for most of them, and I get what Fisher's saying. My father always worried I'd come across someone else wanting to kidnap me for a ransom payment, so they checked out anyone I interacted with. That knowledge contributed to my desire to keep my circle of friends small.

"Well, Zane was patient with me." I was probably the least ideal girl on campus for him to date. I hated parties, had security tailing me anywhere I went, and I lost count of how many times we started to have sex and I backed out. But he was patient. "He put up with a lot." I peer up at Fisher, but he's not looking at me. He's tracking the storm rolling in across the range. "I'd go hot. Cold. Emotional."

I shudder, possibly from the wintry scene outside, possibly from the memory of pushing myself over the last hurdle. All those years of therapy, and I should've been fine. I'd gotten to the point I was angry at myself for not being fine, and Zane helped. The sex wasn't fantastic. I probably bored Zane. It's probably why he didn't want a relationship with me back then.

A weighted silence descends. I should get my laptop. Do some work. But I don't. I rub the heel of my hand hard against my sternum and twist to ease the discomfort.

With the stealth of a well-trained soldier, Fisher's beside me. He cups my chin and gently pulls me up off the chair. My palms fall to his chest. His heart thuds beneath my hands. My lungs tighten and my core pulses. My lips pucker, waiting. I want him to kiss me, to push me back against the bed, to take me.

"Zane didn't do you a favor. You trusted him with something precious and sacred. And if he was too arrogant or selfish to see that, it's his loss, not yours."

I blink in confusion. What is he talking about? "He's not... I don't know what it looked like back then, but it doesn't matter. It's history. He's a good guy. And he's my friend. That's it."

Fisher's lips brush across my brow, and I close my eyelids as my flesh prickles from the softest of touches. His fingers cup my elbows and lightly brush my arms, my shoulders and back.

"Look at me, Sophia." I blink my eyes open obediently. "I get he's your friend. But to me, he'll always be the entitled prick who didn't value what he had, and who somehow made you believe you were at fault. What you've given me? I don't deserve it, but as long as you choose to give it to me, you'd better believe I'll value it. Value you. Because, Sophia, you are precious."

The heat passing between us melts barriers. Those probing, deep blue eyes are too intense. My gaze drops to our socked feet. His thumb strokes my chin as his other hand cups my ass. "Look at me." I endure one last, penetrating view of deep blue, and then his lips cover mine.

I push back against the firm wall of muscle. "Shouldn't we be doing work?" It's a half-baked question spurred by duty.

The rough growth along his jaw scratches the tender skin of my throat, and his fingers find their way beneath my sweater, his touch hot, the pads of his fingers rough.

"This is work. We're doing what married couples do."

I laugh, but ever so briefly. His tongue, his hot mouth, and his hands explore, spiking my arousal and obliterating thought.

CHAPTER 20
SOPHIA

For years, I worked at sex, not out of enjoyment but because I needed to recover. Or, more accurately, I needed to feel like I had recovered. I strove for normalcy. Recovery. But physical intimacy isn't work with Fisher.

My skin tingles from his touch, and I swear, when I gaze into his eyes, there's a connection. Simultaneously familiar and new, the sensation both exhilarates and terrifies.

My palm glides along rippling, toned muscle. His hot mouth sucks and nips. The potency of his touch ratchets up a need so intense my pulse roars. My sex clenches. I paw at his clothes, losing any bit of calm. But thank god, I seem to have the same effect on him.

He tugs my sweater off my head. Palms my breasts. I strain for his belt buckle as he sucks and nips. My pants fall to my ankles. My panties join them.

"Please, hurry." It's both demand and prayer. I'm half on the bed, half off, his feet planted on the floor when he thrusts inside. A sigh of relief pours out. His forehead falls, and he stills.

"God, you feel good." I cradle his jaw in my hands, and his gaze meets mine.

Slowly, he begins to move, alternating between slow, tender movements and hard, pounding, possessive thrusts. Little foreplay. We went from zero to eighty in the blink of an eye. He's a master. Doing exactly what I need.

But it's those deep blue eyes, the care washing over me, that tenderizes my heart through the searing heat. Logically, there's a physical explanation for the emotional build-up. Endorphins and a release of hormones that accompany sex. But this emotional build-up, it's new to me, and that's where the terror comes in. Because I'm feeling all these things. I care for him, but we're not real.

This is what I tell myself as he pulses inside me, skin flushed and damp, biceps bulging. I tighten my thighs and arms around him, holding on as he crashes down over me. I bury my face into the curve of his neck, breathing in his addictive musky scent. His hard chest crushes my breasts. As our breathing slows, his heartbeat thuds against mine.

The sex is real. But it's temporary. I can't hold on to this or become attached. Fisher doesn't make plans, not because he's emotionally stunted, but because he can't. He chose a career that doesn't easily allow a personal life. And I chose the same career.

The CIA would frown on this. On relationships. Fraternization. In fact, there's a form we have to complete for approval for any relationship. Whether the person is in the CIA or outside of it, the relationship must be approved, in theory, before it begins. I'm breaking rules.

From our employer's perspective, what we are doing is wrong, yet nothing has ever felt so right. Just as I honed my marksmanship skills, I must learn how to manage the tangle of emotions sex with Fisher delivers.

Fisher's quiet, slow perusal is unnerving. Am I transparent? But his lips fall to mine, and he gives me the sweetest, most tender kiss. He's still inside me, and my body clenches around him. My fervent wish is that I could hold on, just like this, forever. And

there it is, the terror. The double-edged knife blade Fisher presents.

A subdued whirring noise sounds. Fisher rolls to his side. I sit up and bound to the bathroom. Fisher's deep timbre drifts through the closed door.

"Yep.... She's not with me right now.... Gym... Ten minutes?... Copy that."

I pull a towel off the roll bar and wrap it around me before exiting the bathroom. Fisher's jeans are back on, as is a fresh long sleeve heathered navy t-shirt. He holds a black baseball cap in his hand, and he's bending the brim.

"Who was that?" The Toros should've already left. If they didn't get away earlier as planned, they're not getting out of here for at least twenty-four hours, judging from the limited visibility out the window.

"Aunt Rita." His penetrating gaze travels to my towel. "Told her you went to the gym. You ah, might want to change."

"We're doing a video call?"

"Yep. They have confirmation the Toros are no longer in Canada. I imagine she wants to recap this op and review next steps."

Fisher leaves me in the bedroom, and I get dressed quickly, putting on a gym outfit of leggings, a jog bra and sweatshirt. I gather my hair into a ponytail, combing out the frazzled knots on the back of my scalp.

In the den, Fisher has his laptop set up on the small dining table. Two resort water bottles sit beside it.

"Ready?" The position of his shoulders, the straight lips, and his upright posture are all indicative of work-mode. It's good he easily falls into work mode, because I feed off his energy, and by the time I'm in the chair he's pulled out for me, my focus has returned.

Since it's his government issued laptop, he handles going

through the CIA portal and setting up our video meeting. Rita appears on screen. I've never met her in person before, and she's not at all what I expected. Her black, coiffed hair looks like she took it out of rollers, teased it, and hair sprayed it in place. Narrow spectacles hang down her neck, and square glasses with rounded edges in a blue plastic frame perch on her nose. The skin below her chin dangles, and she puckers her lips as she presses buttons. When the camera opens on her end, we can tell instantly because those puckered lips relax into a grandmotherly smile.

"Hi, you two. Having a good vacation?"

I slide my hands beneath my thighs and smile back at her. One thing they teach us is to lead every conversation with care, and I wonder if that's why she's kicking off our session like this. But we called her from the privacy of our suite. It's not like we'd call her if housekeeping was in the room with us.

"All good," Fisher answers.

"How's the storm there?"

"It's picking up." Snowflakes blow both vertically and horizontally out the window, and thick, hazy clouds obliterate the mountain peaks.

"Here too." Rita's comment leaves me wondering where she is, but that's not my business. "So, here's the plan. When you can get back out, catch a flight to Los Angeles. Then head home to Santa Barbara. I might even come out to visit you both."

"Will we be on a tight schedule?" Fisher's frown lines deepen. An uneasy feeling surfaces.

"My plans are up in the air," Rita answers. "Might be a week or two, maybe more."

"Rita, we're in our suite. Not the conference center." Fisher's dry response is all-work, although there is a hint of exasperation.

"Okay. Here's the deal, kids. On the off chance our friend Ivan checks out your home in Santa Barbara, or your offices, we have a team setting up both locations for you. Go pretend to be a happy

couple. Try to avoid anyone who knows you. Right now, the plan is if he contacts you in Santa Barbara, this operation will get rolled up into an intra-agency task force with the FBI and DEA."

"How long are they giving this?"

"My bet is a few weeks. Or until Ivan returns home. We'll keep it open, give you both a reason to leave the country at some point, just in case months from now he reaches out."

"By chance, did anything happen with their current money laundering conduit?"

"We don't know. That's one reason the continuation of this op has been authorized. Burgeoning interest from multiple parties on this one."

It's official. This operation is continued, I'll be in Southern California, but Sophia Garcia can't be seen as Sophia Sullivan. With wigs and make-up, I can play both roles as it suits me, if I do so carefully.

"When you get your flight rescheduled, I'll get alerted. When you land, give your Aunt Rita a call. I'll tell you where I parked the rental car."

"We'll have two cars, right?" Aunt Rita's expression is the opposite of pleased. "I mean, Damian and Sophia Garcia wouldn't share a car."

"But you would drive together to the airport," Rita says. "And your home will be fully stocked."

I assume she means that includes a car for me. But, if it doesn't, I can borrow a car from Aunt Alex easily enough. When the call ends, Fisher crosses his arms over his chest and cocks his head with a mock-fierce scowl. At least, I think it's mock.

"What was that?"

"What was what?" I rise off my seat. It's time for me to power up my laptop.

"What were you getting at with her?"

"Nothing."

"What do you want to do?" His eyebrows nearly touch each other. I recognize that look. He thinks I'm up to something. "Why do you want a car?"

"Fisher." I say his name with distinct authority, but my smiling lips tease.

"Sullivan." He says my name with a smirk and crowds my space. "I watched you throughout high school. You think I don't know when you're up to—"

My calves hit the front of the sofa and I tumble back onto it, laughing.

He stands before me and runs his fingers through his hair. "Ah, hell." He mumbles something that sounds like he knows exactly what I'm doing. "Two cars." He pinches the bridge of his nose. "I guess it makes sense." He steps away, flicks on the fireplace, and heads to the kitchenette. "Pick a movie. Get comfortable."

"You want to watch a movie?"

"No. We're going to play the role of a married couple. Snuggle on the sofa during a blizzard. And do other things married couples do." With a devilish smirk, he adds, "Got to enjoy the perks of the job."

The job. It is a job. A job that was just extended for only a few weeks. But that's okay. Better than okay. Southern California is exactly where I need to be.

CHAPTER 21
FISHER

Two days later, our rescheduled flight and the journey through customs pass uneventfully. As promised, inside the glove box of the rental car I find house keys and an address.

"Ready to head home, Mrs. Garcia?"

She lowers the back of her seat and stretches, closing her eyes. She spent most of the flight on her computer. When I glanced at the screen, she was offline, reviewing a spreadsheet. "Wake me when we're there."

Given I kept her up last night, her exhaustion today is understandable. If I'm going to hell anyway, I should get as much out of the crime as possible. My philosophy is similar to the adage, "If you're going to steal, steal a lot." Of course, when I first headed down this path, I thought we'd be done with this ruse, back on the east coast, unlikely to cross paths again. What happened in Canada would stay in Canada. A momentary lapse in judgment. But here we are with an extended covert operation. And it's probably going to bore her. If she got bored in the FBI analysis unit, the next stage of this operation will lead her to consider yet another career change.

That's one thing about the CIA that so many don't

understand, thanks to Hollywood. A lot of the jobs within the CIA are mundane. Because of my military background, I've had assignments with more action than most. But I've kept in touch with a few from my Langley class. One woman said she meets the informant she cultivated once a month. The rest of her time is spent at her cover job in the US Embassy.

There is an elite group within the CIA that handles covert operations. Those operations are more of the in-and-out variety, and all highly confidential. From what I understand, they're the kinds of ops that our government will always deny. But you can't apply to be in that group. They come to you. They're the equivalent of the SEALs in the Navy, or the Green Berets in the Army.

The streetlights diminish as I turn onto the 101. It's late, and traffic is light. Sophia's auburn hair sets off her milky white skin. If she hadn't dyed her hair for this assignment, if she'd kept it blonde, would I have been able to cross that line? Would the attraction have been the same? Did my mind require the physical change for attraction to take root?

With her blonde hair, there's so much I remember from over seven years of overseeing her personal security detail. But with her crimson mane, she transformed from young woman to temptress.

Temptress? I wish I could lay the blame at her feet. I'm a dirty fucking old man in his forties who has no business being with her, and if her father, Ryan, or Trevor find out, I'll be dead to them all.

The closer I get to Santa Barbara and to Arrow's home base, the more sobering my thoughts become. How ironic is it that the safe house the CIA assigned to use for our cover story is near Santa Barbara? I understand the logic. Neither Sophia nor I have ever lived in this town, but we've been here enough that we know it well. We could carry on conversations about our home city if asked.

We hit Montecito before Santa Barbara. I double-check the

address. The winding road leading us to our temporary home snakes up slowly. All the homes lining the road face west, across the valley to the ocean. The yards appear to be mostly pebbles with scant vegetation. The higher we climb in elevation, the yards increase in size. My headlights flicker on the occasional fruit or olive tree in tamped dirt yards.

At the end of a steep climb, we arrive at a gate. The paperwork didn't give me a code. There's a keypad surrounded by a slightly rusted beige metal box. Instructions above the box state to enter the four-digit code followed by pound. I enter the personal code assigned to me by the CIA, and the gate swings wide, opening into a wide swath of dusty pavers.

Two wooden garage doors are on the side, but I pull up to the front of the house, framed by mahogany wood columns. Lights flicker below us, ceasing in the distance before a sheen of black. My guess is the view in the morning will be mostly valley, a mix of houses, shrubbery and winding roads, with the ocean far on the horizon.

Given this house is in Montecito, and not Santa Barbara, there's a good chance we can avoid running into our friends in the area. As I approach the front door, I scan the area. As the highest house on the street, there are no neighbors above us, or beside us. The gate provides additional protection. But, if someone wanted to approach by land, there's no barrier. No fence.

The prime security of the location is in that it's not easily observed. I pop the trunk and open the case with my Glock, check to ensure it's loaded, then approach the front door. The passenger car door opens, and Sophia calls, "Wait. I'll clear it with you."

"Stay here. Watch the back."

Motion flood lights flick on when I'm three feet from the front door. A little delayed for my taste, but they flood the carport area in light, as well as the garage side of the house and a portion of the

back yard. The windows near the front door open into an expansive interior with windows on the back wall.

Once inside, I flick on the lights beside the door, Glock raised, on the ready. One living area with an exit to the back door, one kitchen with an exit by a laundry room and a side door, a hallway with three bedrooms. Only the master bathroom has an exit door. The kitchen has one window with cranks to open it, but all other windows are stationary.

"This place is nice," she says from behind me. "Does the CIA always put us up in places this nice?"

"No. But they have a fair amount of real estate, and the locations typically match the cover profile. My guess is this isn't CIA owned. Maybe FBI. CIA rarely places officers in the US. This is an exception." She nods, and I point down the hall. "Three bedrooms. They use one as an office."

The wheels of Sophia's suitcase whir over the tile floor. The sound lessens when the floor transitions to wood. I follow Sophia, my breath light, as faint as if aiming for silence in the dark of night.

She flicks on the light to the master bedroom. Light wood planks cover the ceiling, and the walls are painted white. In the bathroom, there's a white marble shower. A glass door opens onto a private walled area with an outdoor soaking tub. There are three wooden interior doors. One to a toilet room, the other two are closets.

Sophia tilts her head, examining the outdoor soaking tub. With her gaze fixed outside, she says, "Pick a closet."

As I unpack my clothes in the smaller closet, it's clear I'll need to go shopping. I packed for a vacation to Whistler, and now I'll have a prolonged stay in Southern California. I sense Sophia in the doorway.

"You need more clothes," she says.

"Was just thinking that," I admit.

"I'm going to go home tomorrow." Her statement grabs my

attention. "I cleared it with Aunt Rita. I'll drive out of here in the car that's in the garage for me to use. She gave me an address of a parking garage where I can switch cars, and I'll leave as myself. Blonde wig." She points to her auburn strands. "And I'll be back sometime tomorrow. Maybe late."

"That's a pretty long drive," I say, stating the obvious.

"Not that bad. I thought about asking Ryan to fly me down but decided against it."

"What're you going down for?"

"Clothes." She gestures to my mostly empty rack of hanging clothes. "I can see about getting you some clothes too. Dad's about your size."

"That's okay." I'm already with Jack's daughter, I don't need to ransack his closet too.

"Don't like his style?"

"It's not that—"

"Well, I need clothes, and I'll take the time off to visit. If you have to explain my absence to anyone, tell them your wife went away to visit a friend."

"Easy enough."

"Do you have anything that needs to go to the dry cleaners?" Her gaze falls pointedly to the pile of ski clothes on the floor.

"Are you going to do my dry cleaning for me?"

"Wouldn't a good wife do her husband's dry cleaning?"

"I wouldn't know. Never had one."

"Well, you strike me as the kind of man who would want his wife to handle the dry cleaning." She peeks up at me through her lashes. There's invitation written from her flirtatious smile down to the tips of her hot pink toenails.

"Do I, now?" My throat tightens as another body part twitches to life.

"Yeah, you're like a military guy, right? Bed corners should be

folded in tight. Everything ironed." She pauses, peering up at me with a grin that's full of innuendo. "Did I get that wrong?"

"Yeah, I'd say so." In a flash, I have her in her arms. She squeals as I walk her backward, hands on her ass. She bounces on the bed. "Let me show you exactly what I want from a wife, Mrs. Garcia."

In the morning, I take off on a morning run, eager to scout our new neighborhood by foot. When I return, the house is silent.

"Sophia?" I call.

In the kitchen, there's a note on the pristine counter.

D- Be back tomorrow. Will drop dry cleaning off. Love, S.

The note follows CIA protocols. It fits with our character profiles. If anyone broke into our house, or followed me in after my run, the note supports our covers. Yet, my thumb brushes over the word *love*. Idiotic.

I'm in the back of the house, about to shower, when my phone vibrates. The number is Rita's.

"Aunt Rita?"

"Is this a good time to talk?"

"Shoot."

"You've got a meeting in one hour with the cross-agency task force. You'll get briefed on Operation CalTan. FBI is technically lead. They pulled in an external resource about a month ago after we busted several DEA agents in a sting."

"I read about that." The agency did a good job of keeping it mostly out of the media, but within the intelligence community, that kind of sting spreads fast.

"You shouldn't have any issue working with them. Since you're based near Santa Barbara, we've pulled in a local resource. The man you'll be meeting with is your former employer. Goes by Wolf?"

"Yep." I have a lot of respect for Ryan. Working with him won't be a problem.

"He's going to lead the meeting. You can brief Sophia when she returns tomorrow night."

"Copy that."

"We have offices set up for you. Ryan's going to come in as a client interested in your services. Your assistant will be FBI. She'll be working reception."

"Gotcha." I'm hit with a vision of weeks spent sitting around our fake office. "Will I take on other clients?"

"Very well could have some real ones come through the door. If you do, service them. You'll be able to access instructions later on."

In Mexico City, my cover was a banker, so I'm already familiar with the lingo. She gives me the address for my offices. After showering, with one glance in my closet, it's clear I do not have an adequate wardrobe for this op.

I put on dark jeans, a light, long sleeve, crewneck sweater, which will probably be far too warm for Santa Barbara, and the brown leather loafers I wore in the airport. After this meeting, I'll need to go shopping.

An hour later, I'm unlocking the key to Sunset Brokerage. The office is small with an entry room and a reception desk, and one door to an office in the back. The plaque in the hallway reads Sunset Brokerage, as does the outside listing of businesses inside the building. It's a testament to how quickly the CIA can work.

I flick on the lights and leave my office door open. Blinds cover the one window in the office. The view is of the building across the street. When standing next to the window, I can see the corner of the intersection of the office building.

There's a hard rap on the outside door, and the door opens before I get to it. A tall man with broad shoulders and piercing light blue eyes enters.

"Ryan," I say, grinning at my old friend. Yeah, in the past he was technically my boss, but he's a hell of a lot more than that now. He clasps my hand, and we go in for a man hug and a brisk clap on the back.

He's in cargo shorts and an untucked button down with the sleeves rolled halfway up his forearms. His outfit makes me feel overdressed.

"Imagine my surprise when I heard you're on CalTan."

"Eh, could be a boring few weeks." As far as I can tell, unless Rafael Toro does indeed contact me, there'll be jack shit for me to do. "Are you guys tracking Ivan?"

"FBI has surveillance on him. He met with one guy on the docks in LA. He's partied. Driving around in a rental car. I'd say there's a fifty-fifty chance he'll make his way up to Santa Barbara. Someone pulled a full background report on Damian Garcia."

"Probably Rafael. He seemed to know about the debt."

"Also pulled a credit report on Sunset Brokerage." Rafael's been busy.

We each take seats in the front entry room. He gestures to the empty receptionist desk. "Shelly Patel will be here tomorrow."

"She's Arrow, right?"

"Yes. FBI would've been at least a week getting someone to cover, so we plugged our own. She's good."

"I remember her. She has young kids." Former military, jet black hair, olive skin, about five foot five.

"Not so young anymore. Approaching high school now."

I blink and inhale, not liking the brutal passage of time.

"Yeah. Imagine my surprise when I heard Sophia's your partner on this."

"Small world, right?" I study Ryan for any hint of anger, but there wouldn't be. There's no way he could know what's been going on between Sophia and me.

"Where is she?"

"Two days' leave. San Diego. Left this morning."

He checks his wrist. "Let's get to it. Operation CalTan ramped up after we busted two DEA agents in San Diego. One agreed to be an informant."

"You trust him?" Lots of cases gain traction when one guilty party agrees to play nice with law enforcement in hopes of a more lenient sentencing or impunity, but there's always a trust component.

Ryan's expression is blank. "Haven't met him. The Toro cartel typically transports drugs into the US through Miami, Delaware, and more recently Los Angeles. The LA port is a recent acquisition. We think since their volume has increased substantially over the last year, he's looking for additional launderers. That's where you could come in. Maybe."

"How is Arrow involved?"

"Doing some monitoring on the Colombia side that the US doesn't want to be tied to."

"Only in Colombia?" I ask.

"On this project, for right now. Mexico, Colombia, China... same side of different coins. Tensions are rising between countries because we're decades into this so-called drug war, and things are worse than they've ever been. Everybody's pointing fingers. But, like anything, it's a matter of who's profiting."

"You getting a better idea of who's profiting from the US side?"

"Usual suspects." His lips purse thoughtfully. "Not much

changes. Your buddy, Toro, he's got contacts here. He could be valuable since he's a relatively new player in the US market. Previously, the Toros routed drugs through Mexico, but either those relationships soured or he's looking to cut the middle man. If you can get in with him, we could learn a lot. The stalwarts are too good at covering their tracks."

"You've been watching Toro for a while?"

"Monitoring online behavior and activity. Your CIA buddies believe there might be an uprising brewing inside Colombia."

"I'm familiar with those theories."

"It's all pretty standard stuff. FBI wants to get one of their own in on this, so you'll need to look for an opportunity to bring someone else in." He scratches his jaw and leans forward. "There is someone we're getting closer to. Remember Senator Talbot?"

I narrow my gaze as I nod. The guy has been on our radar for years. We suspect he's taken kickbacks from both cartels and gun manufacturers for years, but we could never prove it. There's no doubt he's in the gun industry's pocket, but that's not illegal. Rumors circulate around him, but he's dismissed it all as fake news and the work of political enemies. He's also old.

"He hasn't retired? Guy has to be..." I try to do some quick math in my head.

"Eight-two," Ryan answers for me. His phone vibrates, and the low hum grows louder as he removes his phone from his shirt pocket. He frowns. "I thought you said Sophia went home?"

"She did. Why?"

"Jack's on his way here."

"Why?"

"Wants to meet. He comes up a couple of times a week, but I'm surprised he'd come if Sophia's down there."

Both Jack and Ryan are rich fuckers who fly their helicopters more than I drive cars, so I'm not surprised to hear Jack flies to

Santa Barbara regularly. But an uneasiness grows within me as I play back my conversation with Sophia.

Ryan texts away on his phone, and the urge to cover for my partner strikes.

"She may have been planning to surprise her family." But even as I cover for her, my gut tells me I need to get the hell out of here and find her.

CHAPTER 22
SOPHIA

A fire ant crawls up my arm, and I flick it away. An ant on the tree disappears beneath a piece of bark. I crouch down, shifting away from the tree, and adjust my night vision binoculars.

Wayne Killington sits in a chair overlooking the pool, drinking what appears to be water. It's hard to see what my mother saw in him. Of course, the years haven't been kind. His once thick brown hair has turned gray and thinned. He's lost his jolly Jimmy Buffett persona. For the last several hours, he's sat in that chair, lost in the vision of his rectangular lap pool, possibly dozing in and out of sleep.

There are no signs of hired security. I located two cameras on the outskirts of his property in the rear, one on each side of his house, and one over the front door. Shortly after dusk, I disengaged the two rear cameras.

Dad mentioned they've been keeping an eye on him, and he's been laying low. There are no signs of an Arrow detail. My guess is one of the cameras is an Arrow camera and they're monitoring remotely.

A slight breeze flutters the palm fronds, and stars glitter in the mostly clear night sky. Killington's property backs up to a golf

course. A section of trees and vegetation separates the pristine golf course from the private yards, and it's in this swatch of sandy earth I sit.

My backpack holds a gun, a syringe, a knife, and pliers. But if I do this correctly, I won't need to threaten. In the words of one of my Quantico instructors, the best way to interrogate someone is to understand them. You get the best results by speaking to them with understanding.

If I go through the front door, he's more likely to see me as a friend. If I come upon him while he's sleeping, I'll startle him. Would a man like Killington ever fear me? Is that a trump card I could ever play?

Probably not. He's too arrogant. Prison hardened him. I read the transcript from his parole hearing and don't believe for a second he found Jesus Christ. No, the man simply fell back on the most reliable way to con a parole board.

I don't know what I expected. Maybe that he'd be meeting with someone, either in person or on the phone. Or he'd be working away on a computer, eager to re-enter the business world. Or that he'd have a woman over. But watching him sit by a pool disappoints. It's too normal.

That man seduced my mother, ruined her marriage, and orchestrated my abduction. His actions prove he never loved my mother. If he had, he wouldn't have upended my life three years after her death. I'd just begun to return to normalcy after my mother's tragic death. The pain and loss had finally subsided. I'd scored a role in the school play and was dreaming of college. All that changed when he hired men to kidnap me. He knew our house well and coached them on how to avoid detection. When I was held captive, and he thought I was too drugged to remember, I observed his friendly, neighborly mask morph into one of an unrecognizable sociopath.

The sociopath won't fear me, but he'll underestimate me.

Decision made, I move out from the cover of shrubbery and trees, backpack slung on one side, gun bound to my leg in a holster, covered by my pants, another gun in a holster on my waist, and a back-up tied securely in my backpack. A stick cracks beneath the weight of my boot, but Killington doesn't so much as flinch. My hands sweat inside the black Thinsulate gloves. I grip the bar on the black metal fence that surrounds his property and hoist myself over.

I glance to the back corner, searching for the camera. The absence of a red light appeases me. The cameras remain disengaged.

The floodlight casts my shadow across the travertine. I step softly, heel to toe, in much the way Trevor and Ryan taught me. What started as self-defense classes at my dad's request expanded into more after my acceptance into the FBI. Trevor said there were things he wanted me to learn, just in case the dipshits at Quantico didn't teach it right.

Wayne's head twitches and his resting arm jerks. His eyelids flutter open and his brow wrinkles. I stand still before him, giving the old man's eyesight time to adjust. I let him take in my outfit of black cargo pants, black boots, and light, form-fitting, long sleeve black top. My auburn hair is pulled back tight, covered by a blonde wig with an angled bob. There's a skull cap in my backpack, but I removed it for this meeting. I need him to recognize me. His eyes rest on my gloves, which I purposefully wear.

"Did you come to kill me?"

I study the man, intrigued by his presumption.

"Why would I want to kill you?"

There's something there in his expression I don't recognize. It's not fear.

"How'd you get in?"

"Came around the side of the house." That's not true at all. I

parked my car outside the neighborhood and hiked through the golf course.

He shifts in his chair. His chest rises and falls, and his facial muscles relax. "Can I get you something to drink?"

"No, thank you."

He points to my backpack. "You always carry a backpack with you when you make house calls?"

The man spent his career in the gun industry. He recognizes backpacks that double as gun cases. He's also leading the interrogation.

"Mind if I sit down?"

"Do I have a choice?" His question concedes weakness. He's fitter than he used to be, but he doesn't have my training. And he's unarmed.

I drag a chair over and position it to his side. He shifts his chair, so he faces me instead of the pool.

"What can I do for you, Sophia?" There's genuine curiosity in his tone, and it's distinctly different from his original greeting. *Did you come to kill me?*

"I'm hoping you'll talk to me."

His gaze pointedly zeroes in on my gloves. "You planning on using some of your fancy government torture techniques?"

"Do I need to?" I wait, watching his eyes dart around the perimeter. "I'm here alone," I say to set him at ease. Plus, it's the truth. The words of an FBI guest instructor come to mind. Set them at ease, work to understand their humanity. "Did you love my mother?"

I don't believe he did, not by my measure of love. But people apply a subjective measurement system to love.

"You know I did." He looks me straight in the eye and his hands remain still. His words are crisp. He believes himself. And he's defensive.

"I believe you loved her." His eyes narrow into a distrustful squint, and I amend my words. "In your own way."

"Why are you here? To talk about your mom?"

"I want the list."

He lifts his glass and sips with a watchful gaze. When he sets the glass back down on the armrest, he asks, "You can't let it go?"

I chose a career in law enforcement. Clearly, I have no intention of letting it go. I inhale deeply to curb my irritation. "When I visited you, you mentioned a list."

"I told you, there's no one else."

I narrow my eyes, mimicking his skeptical expression. "We both know you couldn't talk in prison." Fisher was right. My visit to him in the penitentiary had been a fool's errand. "Someone could've been listening. Out here, it's just us. No one's listening. You can deny anything you say." He blinks, hands folded over his belly. I can't be certain what he's looking at. Maybe the pavers. Maybe my shoes. "Think of my mom. If you loved her, don't you think you owe her?"

He covers his eyes with one hand. My question pains him, and I mentally file that observation. With his eyes still closed, he pinches the bridge of his nose. With a heavy sigh, his hand falls back to the armrest, and his gaze falls to the right of the base of my chair.

"You already know the players. Mark Sullivan." He breathes out deeply, and it sounds like resignation. "He's dead."

"Senator Talbot," I say, prompting him. We all know the senator is a conduit.

"He might've been involved, but I've got no evidence. Nothing for you to use in a court of law."

"Who else?"

"What, exactly, are you interested in, Sophia? The guns? The drugs? What do you want from me? I've been in prison for ten years."

"We know Uncle Mark and Talbot weren't working in a vacuum. But we don't have any evidence. Or leads."

"You'll never find any."

I nod thoughtfully. I've come to the same conclusion. We recently caught the Mexican public security secretary taking bribes from the cartels. It was part of a multi-year cross-agency effort, and he's the highest ranking official to be charged in the history of the drug wars dating back to the eighties. I poured over the transcripts of his interviews, and he didn't out anyone higher up the chain. "So, help me," I plead. "For my mom."

He rubs his sternum with the base of his palm, like it hurts. "Do you remember what I told you when you came to visit me?"

"You tried to warn me away." *If these invisible men exist, you don't want to find them.* "They hire assassins. That's what you meant, right?" I study his features, logging any movement or twitch.

"The witnesses in my case all died." His gaze lifts, and he looks directly at me with intent. "That's not coincidence, Sophia."

"And if you talk, they'll kill you? That's your fear?"

His gaze falls as he shakes his head. "Why would I be afraid of death?" A sad smile briefly flits across his lips. "The life I knew is over."

"Maybe now you know how I felt." I lean forward and let some of the simmering hatred and anger boil and hope he can sense it.

He exhales and gazes up to the sky, as if seeking answers or praying to his newly found god. When he lowers his head, it's with the look of a man facing a firing squad. "If I were you, I'd look at the NRA. They're the linchpin for all the gun manufacturers. And I'd look at politicians who are heavily tied to both the NRA and law enforcement. See if you can find offshore bank accounts. Shell companies. Follow the connections."

"You think the government doesn't already do that?"

"Sophia, I don't know what you want from me. I've been out of it for too long."

"No one's contacted you?"

"I've been home less than a week." He chews on the corner of his lip. "I'm an unemployed felon. I have nothing to offer."

I've given that angle consideration, but my bet is the right criminal enterprise will highly value his smuggling expertise. There's a reason mafia and cartel members easily find employment with their old families once they're released back on the street.

"If someone contacts you, you'll let me know?"

"Sophia…" He shakes his head and crosses his arms behind his head, a position of power.

I stand to look down on him. "There's one more thing." I pause, waiting for those beady eyes to travel up my body to my face. "As you know, I was drugged. Fragments of memories hit me at the damnedest times. And you know what I remember? Your neck. Straining."

He closes his eyes and dips his head. The confirmation slowly wraps its way around me. The effect is dizzying. I've always suspected but never knew for sure. He denied it. The sick bastard raped me. He's one of my rapists.

He lifts his gaze, and I read his expression as ashamed, but I don't trust it. You can't trust a sociopath. Ever.

"Sophia, you have to understand." My fists clench. Trevor taught me how to kill a man with my bare hands. I don't need a gun. "You looked so much like your mother. And…I didn't think you'd remember. I just wanted one more time with your mother. One more," he gasps as if in pain. "One more time with her. It was…in my mind…it was her, not you. She just…they took her before I was ready."

I twist my body, bending my left leg, and swing with all my weight. My boot slams into the sick fuck's face and his chair tips backward. His skull hits the travertine with a sickening crack.

I stand, legs bent, crouched. Movement in the periphery catches my attention. A dark shadow hovers near the base of a palm tree.

Someone is watching. I can take cover by a planter, or I can track the son of a bitch down. If they wanted to shoot, they would've already done so. So, I take off at a run, scanning for objects along the path should I need to drop for cover.

CHAPTER 23
FISHER

With a twist of the binoculars, I zoom in on the unconscious man sprawled by the pool. This is Wayne Killington's property. The man lies still. There are no signs of life. Did she kill him?

Rapid footfalls signal her approach. She saw me in the shadows. Her gun is drawn. I stand still, waiting for her to recognize me. How quickly can I get a cleaner here?

"Fisher?" she hisses through gritted teeth.

Given she's in boots, her quiet approach is commendable. What's not advisable is killing a man out in the open. And the fuck of it is I don't have a phone with me since I saw this as a private observational mission. I'll need to backtrack to the car.

"Did you follow me?" Sophia stops two feet in front of me. There's no mistaking the venom in those stormy eyes.

"What's your plan for the body?" I clench my fist and tighten my grip on the binoculars, all the while maintaining a steely gaze. She can have her brat attack another day. Right now, we need to focus.

Lights are off in the house on the right, but that doesn't mean somcone wasn't in an upstairs window. A blue light in the house

on the left says someone is probably watching television downstairs, and all these houses are far enough apart with a high degree of vegetative insulation, so it's doubtful anyone from the ground level would see.

"What body?" She glances back at the house. "He's not dead."

She snatches the binoculars. From this distance, I can't see features, but an arm flails.

"Should we call an ambulance?"

"He hit his head." She thrusts the binoculars at me. "He'll be fine. Why are you here?"

"He hit his head after your boot hit his jaw." I lift the binoculars back up to check him out. "Is he going to be pressing charges?" Killington's hand covers his face. "Did you break his jaw?"

"Let's go."

She stomps in the direction that leads out of the neighborhood.

"Seriously, Sophia. What kind of issue are we dealing with here?" A guy like Killington could cause serious issues for her. The CIA won't smile on an assault charge. It could be the end of her career before it starts.

She adjusts her backpack on her shoulders as she walks, eyes trained on the houses to our left.

"Sophia. Stop." It's good he's alive, but he's still lying on the ground. "Do we need to call an ambulance?"

She stops but keeps her back to me. "He's not going to be filing charges."

"How do you know?" Her conclusion is presumptive. Being attacked at his home could work to his advantage with his parole.

"He just admitted he raped me."

Her words hit like a sucker punch, knocking oxygen clear out of me. That fucking bastard. I should retrace her steps and kill the lowlife.

She charges forward. Based on the bend of her arms, she must be clutching the straps of her backpack. I speed up but am careful to maintain rear position.

We don't speak the rest of the way through the neighborhood, through a narrow line of woods, and out to a rental car parked on the side of the road. She pops the trunk. Her lips clenched tight. She slings the backpack into the trunk, and it hits with a thud but lands upright.

"You came out here to confront him?" I can understand that. I gathered from bits and pieces of conversation over the years that the gaps in her memory from the time she was abducted haunt her.

"No. I came out here to talk with him." She slams the trunk down, crosses her arms, and glares at me with a fury that would have a smarter man ducking. "Why the fuck are you here?"

Oh, you want to do this, do you?

Headlights approach, and I pause until the two-door coupe passes. Then I cross my arms and glare right back down on her. "I'm here because my partner lied to me about where she was spending her PTO. I'm here because I had a hunch my partner might need backup."

"You're not my fucking bodyguard anymore, Fisher. You had no business tracking me here."

"Oh, don't I? Did you miss the part where I said partner? If you fuck this up, then you fuck up our operation. An operation that I got briefed on today, but you didn't, because theoretically you went home for clothes."

"I did go home for clothes." Her chin rises, defiant.

Her defiance sends my blood pressure through the roof. I have the strongest desire to bend her right over my knee.

"Fuck you did." I grit out. "Don't you lie to me. Ever."

She narrows her eyes. With my face inches from hers, I wait. Is she actually going to lie to my face, again?

"Where's your car?" She breaks away and steps to the driver's side door.

"One mile up." Yes, I am more cautious. I slide into the passenger seat, and she turns on the engine. A pair of headlights light up the road behind us, and she adjusts her rearview, waiting until the van passes to pull out onto the road. "Where are you staying tonight?" I'm guessing that given it's almost eleven, she's not planning on going home to her father's, but it's a possibility.

"I have a hotel room."

The tension in the car palpitates. My blood roars thick and heavy. She lied. Put our mission in jeopardy. But aside from the crap she pulled, you never fucking go solo. You always have backup. She's been through training at both Quantico and Langley. She fucking knows this. Stubborn, spoiled woman. Probably can't fathom anything would go sideways. Experience. That's what she's lacking. Then she'd fucking know everything can go sideways in an instant. She's dressed like a fucking burglar. He could have shot her and called it self-defense.

Wanted to talk to him. Jesus fucking Christ.

She pulls up beside a rental car, one I rented down the street from the airport. Ryan flew me down earlier. I made up an excuse about wanting to get down here without being picked up on CTV. He didn't ask questions after I told him it was a personal matter. He's good like that. But I'm pretty sure he picked up that Sophia wasn't at her father's, where I thought she was.

With one leg out of Sophia's car, I tell her, "I'll follow you."

"What makes you think I won't lose you?" she says, gaze fixed on the brick wall bordering the row of parking spots.

"Just try it."

Ice-blue eyes meet mine head on. She wheels out of the parking lot, tires squealing, and I grit my teeth, jump in the car, and floor it. After an hour of flying down city streets, gunning

through red lights, both begging for a ticket in an egotistical chase, she gives up and pulls into a Residence Inn not too far from the airport.

Her door slams shut, and she grits out, "You're not staying with me."

"Like hell I'm not."

Her icy glare has lost some of her earlier fire, but her chin lifts defiantly. She's still in that damn blonde wig, and I want to rip it off. I settle for pressing her up against the car, trapping her with one arm on each side.

"You're not my bodyguard."

"I will always guard your body." *Because you're mine.*

The unexpected thought railroads me, and when she pushes, I stumble.

"I'm not a kid."

"You think I don't know that?" What the hell does she think we've been doing together this week?

She pulls up the hand extension on her suitcase and releases a pointed huff. "You can stay with me." She narrows her eyes, challenging me. "Husband." She turns, and as she's walking away, adding, "It's probably best, given there are cameras."

I follow her, scanning the parking lot. There's one camera on the streetlight and one on the eaves of the hotel. Probably others. It's simply good business to keep security cameras over parking lots. But she's in her blonde wig.

She checks in while I shoot a text off to Erik. He's my go-to from Arrow on all things tech. Met him when I first joined Arrow ages ago.

> Can you check Residence Inn security camera network? If footage stored on server, can you delete footage from one location for me?

· · ·

It's late, but he's a workhorse. I get confirmation back from him and send him the address and time. It's probably overly cautious, but the CIA excels in caution.

Sophia receives the plastic card and speeds off. The twenty-something woman behind the reception counter looks me over, deems me okay, and turns to step into a hallway. It's late, and the lobby is vacant.

Sophia's boots thud against the tile floor. Her black cargo pants hang loose over her long legs but fit snugly over the curves of her bottom. My hand twitches with the desire to pop her infuriating ass.

The elevator door slides open, and I follow her in.

"We're on the second floor," she says.

I push the number two. Tension tightens across my chest. I grit my teeth and divert my gaze away from the woman driving me insane. I can't decide if I want to strangle her, spank her, scream at her, or just slam her up against a wall and fuck her into submission. Maybe all the above, and not necessarily in that order.

"You had no right to follow me."

"No right?" *She's still on this bullshit?*

The elevator jerks to a stop and the doors slide open. Sophia exits, glancing both ways, and turns right. I follow. Overhead fluorescent lights shine bright over the quiet hall.

She pushes a door open, and I follow her inside. The heavy door automatically closes behind us with a loud click.

I reach for her arm and turn her to face me. "What's with this attitude?"

"I can take care of myself. I need you to respect me."

"Respect you? I think we're a few steps past that, don't you?" She stares at me with open defiance. I step forward. She steps back. "Let me tell you something about the way teams work,

Sophia. Respect. Communication. Trust." I let the last word hang between us and step forward. She steps back.

The energy between us surges to a palpable height. My skin tingles. What's between us might be a game to her. I might be her temporary toy. But none of that matters compared to my need to keep her safe. To protect her. Even if that means protecting her from herself.

"If you go it alone, no one has your six. Do you know what that means?"

She doesn't have military training, but I expect it's covered at Quantico. You always want someone to have your back.

"I'm capable." Those light blue eyes hit me head on, and her tiny hands ball into threatening fists. "I didn't need backup for a conversation."

I step forward. Her back hits the wall. "Do you think any one member of a SEAL team isn't capable?" I can see her thinking it through. Trevor and Ryan trained her. Both former SEALs. "But they don't tackle a mission alone."

Her eyes soften, but those fists remain tightly bound. My words register, but she's still burning with self-righteous anger. I brush my thumb across her cheek and gently lift her chin. Her chest rises as she breathes in heavily.

"The idea of anything happening to you...it scares the hell out of me. You have no idea how hard it was for me to remain calm once I figured it out. All the things that could've gone wrong." My body presses against hers, needing the connection, the confirmation that she's here.

"How'd you figure it out?"

"Had a hunch." Her fists release, and she places a palm softly against my chest. Her touch burns through the fabric. "I remembered how you reacted to finding out Killington was released. Figured you were either there, or you wanted to visit Zane without me knowing." Either way, I needed the truth.

"Zane's just a friend."

"He's also in DC this week."

"How'd you find that out?"

"The guy posts everything on Twitter and Instagram." The kid probably has a TikTok account and whatever else media whores do these days. "Why Killington?"

"Like I said." Her fingers travel up the side of my neck, ratcheting up a different need. "Information. He couldn't speak when others were listening."

"Did you learn anything new?"

Anger flashes. "You interrupted."

"Really?" I question her. "Not sure he was going to tell you much after you knocked him unconscious."

"That wasn't supposed to happen." The rampant defiance dissipates. She wraps her arms around my shoulders and lowers her forehead to the crook of my neck. "He deserved it."

"He more than deserved it."

Her shoulders slightly shake, and she lifts her head, a glimmer of a smile across her lips.

"You would've helped me bury his body."

"Without hesitation." I'd kill him for her too, if that's what she wants. I brush my lips across her cheek. Her fingers caress my jaw. "Let me in, Sophia. Whatever you're up to, let me be on your team."

"As my fake husband?"

"No," I say softly, bending to breathe her in. "As a partner. In all things."

A flash of insecurity strikes. A woman like Sophia can have anyone she desires. But no other man will care for her as much as I do, and that knowledge builds the foundation for me to try. I might fail at winning her over, but it's better to try and fail than to never make the attempt. I can survive failure. If there's one good thing about failure, you learn it's survivable. If she brushes me

away, I won't die. It'll hurt, but I'll still do whatever I can to protect her.

"Damian?" My name from her lips, when it's just the two of us, secures my heart. "Kiss me."

CHAPTER 24
FISHER

"Kiss me." The small, breathless whisper serves as my undoing. Or who am I kidding? She is my undoing. This is wrong. I shouldn't be with her, but I'll never leave her side. Not willingly.

We've had one week together, and my body and mind are hers. I capture her lips with a raw hunger and possessiveness that elicits moans. I grab her ass and lift her, ignoring the stubborn ache in my sore shoulder, crushing her to me. She wraps those legs around me, rubbing her core against me. Her fingers roam the back of my neck while my tongue plunders her mouth. I can't get enough of her.

She breaks the kiss and pants, "Now, Fisher." Her fingers claw at my shirt, tugging, demanding.

I back away from the wall and set her down on the bed. Within seconds, my shirt's off and tossed. I'm so fucking hard, and while I'd like nothing more than to ram myself inside her, this is Sophia. Her chest rises and falls in rapid-fire succession, and her fingers clutch the comforter. She's waiting, letting me lead.

"Strip." The hunger in those baby blues sucks the oxygen clear out of my lungs.

She holds my gaze as she takes off her sweater, then her bra. Her pale, peaked nipples point upward, begging to be nibbled and

sucked. She stands and undoes her pants, wiggling to aid their descent to the floor. They get caught on her boots, and since I'm already on the floor, kneeling to remove my socks and shoes, I tell her, "Let me."

Her black cotton panties are the only clothing item left on her long, lithe body, and as I kneel before her, I'm struck by her beauty. With her boots and socks discarded, I palm the back of her thighs, up to her ass, and bring her sex to my mouth. I kiss her over her panties, then blow over her tender skin.

I grin up at her as I tug down those panties. She steps out and pulls on me, wanting me to stand, but I grip the globes of her ass with both hands and bring her to me, tasting her. She's wet and eager, and my tongue licks over her a handful of times before her back is arching and her thighs squeeze together.

Her fingers play in my hair, directing my mouth, letting me know with little whimpers and moans when I'm right where she needs me. Her thighs flex. Her core tightens. She's close. With a quiver, her weight falls against me, using me for support.

"I want you inside me," she breathes out. "Fuck, Fisher."

"Responsive tonight?" I kiss and suck my way up her body.

"I need... I can't explain it. Just...inside me...now."

I pause on my journey up her body to lash my tongue around the pebble-hard peak of her breast, and she gives my hair a hard pull.

"Now."

She backs up onto the mattress, crawling backward, those brilliant, stubborn eyes locked on mine, her lips wet and swollen, her skin flushed.

I crawl up the bed, positioning myself between her spread thighs. My pulse beats a thousand beats a minute, my breaths are quick, and my cock weeps with need, jutting out, begging to take her. I hold myself up, hovering over her, as I claim her mouth once again, my hardness pressed into her belly.

She squirms, and her fingers wrap around my length, demanding.

I brush her hands away and guide my tip through her wet center, back and forth. She whimpers. "Please."

"Look at me." She raises her gaze from where I tease her. "Eyes on me."

And then I sink into her. She's tight. Glorious. She feels so fucking good. I strain, pulling back and pushing forward until every bit of me is inside her, surrounded by her heat.

"Fuck, Sophia. Damn, you feel good."

And then we find our rhythm. Her thighs press against my hips, and she rocks against me. Captivating me. So many sensations and emotions swirl, it feels like my ribcage will explode. That's when it hits me. I'm making love to her. This is what it's like to make love to someone precious, to someone who has the power to drive you crazy, to make you cast aside reason and logic.

Those swollen, full lips purse, and her eyelids close, and her body quivers around me. I reach between us and tease her nipple, twisting and tweaking, and she releases a series of sexy little sounds that drive me to the brink. Her eyelids flutter open, and my lips fall over hers, kissing her as I thrust into her, lost to her. My orgasm rips through me, surging like an explosion.

I collapse over her, sucking in air. Her hands flatten over my back as her arms tighten around me, holding me close. We lie there like that, our hearts beating wildly, out of control. Once our breathing normalizes, I roll over, pulling her naked, sweaty body against mine. We're on top of the hotel comforter, but I don't have the desire to move us, not yet. I don't want to ever move.

She presses her lips to my chest, and my fingers go to her hair. The hair is coarse, rough, and the scalp unnatural. I tug.

"Ow." She sits up and pulls at the wig, removing it herself. There's a skullcap, and she removes that too, along with clips and a band. Matted auburn hair tumbles down. I reach up to toy with

the ends, but she scoops up her hair gizmos and waltzes naked into the bathroom.

I get up and pull the comforter back and slide between the cool sheets. With one arm resting behind my head, I wait, eyes trained on the bathroom door. The toilet flushes and the sink runs. Minutes tick by.

When the door finally opens, a timid smile plays across her face. I lift the comforter, gesturing for her to join me.

She complies. Her skin is cool, and she wraps around me, seeking warmth. I kiss the top of her head, and she presses her lips to my chest.

I've dated women before, been in the occasional relationship. But never before did it feel like this, this degree of comfort and happiness from a woman curled up beside me. The ease in my chest, the feeling of fullness is something I've never had before, but now that I have it, I never want to let it go. But I'll have to, and soon.

As if she can read my mind, she peers up at me and says, "I've never had that."

"Me neither." Her hair is soft, even the matted sections.

"No, I mean, I've never had that kind of need. It took over me. A pulsing need to have you." She lifts her head, and she shakes it a little. "I've never..."

"It's good with us." The words don't do us justice. We're good together, but I wonder how much experience she has.

"Before, I more or less forced myself to have sex. It was like a part of my recovery."

"You forced yourself to have sex with me?" I pull back, needing to see her for this.

"No, not you. When I first had sex. It was that last step, if you will, to a full recovery. It wasn't something I wanted. I didn't pulse with need. Not like I do with you. I've wanted you. Every time. But that, right there...it was almost torture until you..." I settle back

down into the mattress, and she lies with her ear pressed to me as I weave my fingers through her silken tangles. "I guess this is what attraction is like."

It's more than lust, but there's no point in dissecting it.

"It was hard for me...you know...after."

She's talking about the abduction. About the rape. It's the unsaid word that hung in the air around her for so long. It's years later, and I still can't seem to force it out. But I can hold her. Breathe her in. Care for her. Protect her.

Sophia's grip around my waist tightens. I love this. I love her.

The thought comes out of nowhere, but deep in my soul I know it's true. Lying here like this, the peacefulness surrounds us, and I know if I had the choice, she'd be it for me.

"It took me a long time," she says, her voice soft and scratchy. I press my lips to her soft temple and her pulse reverberates through me. And understanding dawns too.

"Is that why you went to him tonight?"

She draws lazy lines against my chest.

"Sophia?"

"I went to him hoping to use some of the interrogation techniques I'd learned."

"Waterboarding?"

"No, nothing like that. The exact opposite, actually. There was an instructor at Quantico who talked about successful interrogation relying on understanding the person. Understanding what drives them. I thought I might talk about my mom and maybe guilt him into sharing with me more about the people he was involved with."

"You think there are more?"

"Has to be. He was the contact for one gun manufacturer, but it's larger than that."

"Senator Talbot?" The man will take donations from anyone, and it's pretty obvious he sculpts legislation in return for those

donations. But he's smart. Arrow has illegally hacked his communications, and there's never been anything there to lead to a prosecutable crime.

"Well, yeah, but it's pretty common knowledge he's a crook. But people don't care. They vote along party lines. But no, I mean, who is Talbot working with? Who recruited my uncle? There's a history there."

"You sound like you're searching for the wizard behind the curtain. The one pulling all the strings. But I don't think it works like that. It ebbs and flows."

"Oh, I know." She lets out a sigh. "Did you ever hear about Oxi Alley and Florida?"

I search my memory. We go through information overload sometimes in the CIA. It's one reason we rely so heavily on analysts. In my role, I'm focused more on cultivating information resources. But it's still important to remain abreast. "Couple of pill mills, right?"

"The biggest source for opioids on the East Coast. And there were legitimate doctors involved. And why? Because they boosted what would have been around a $300K annual salary to $1.2 million. More than tripled their salaries. I'm sure they had all kinds of justifications for it, from paying off student loans to wanting a bigger house, but one third of their patients died, and they kept doing it. And that's a relatively small amount of money. Someone out there is making a shit ton more than a million a year. I think the ringleaders of that enterprise made around forty or fifty million in two years. One operation in Florida."

"There's a lot of incentive to build a crime business. And like any industry, the participants network. They look for mutually beneficial arrangements. Doesn't mean it's being orchestrated by a cabal."

"Hmmm." Her low rumble sounds like a purr. I close my eyes, reveling in this closeness. "Maybe."

Conjecture is pointless. "You know, you missed the update earlier. We're now a part of Operation CalTan. Cross-agency task force. Arrow's involved. I met with Ryan this morning. He debriefed me."

"Ryan? And Aunt Alex?"

"He didn't mention Alex. They busted two DEA agents who were accomplices with a drug smuggling enterprise, and one of them is now an informant."

"Is Rafael's distribution network compromised?"

"We don't know that yet. The Toros have added additional entry points into the US. He might just be looking to expand his back-end operations."

"Coming to you as a money launderer, right?"

"That's the expectation. The hope. Went to my new offices today. We're set up and ready for business. Have you heard anything from Gemma?"

"No." Her thigh shifts. Her smooth, silky skin rubs up and down over my leg. "I plan to reach out...give it a couple of days but send her something along the lines of we're back home and I'm bored and what is she up to. You know, that kind of thing."

I cup her full ass and caress her curves. "You're bored?"

"Well, you know, I am a housewife." She raises her head and gives me a cheeky grin.

I roll her onto her back. My fingers explore, roaming her soft skin and seductive curves. "If my wife is bored, I think I've got to do something about that. Don't you?"

"Like what?" There's a flush across her skin and an amused look in her eye.

"Well, since there's no urgency this time around, I think I'm going to start with my mouth, tasting every delectable inch of you."

CHAPTER 25

SOPHIA

The last two domestic weeks have left me with far too much time. Each morning, Fisher and I wake early for a grueling run or weight routine, then he leaves for the faux office and I settle into my home office.

Given my CIA workload is light at the moment, I've been able to devote more time to my side project. Killington's release reignited my never-ending research. I spend my days mapping connections and following up on every surveillance report within my reach.

At night, Fisher and I play the role of newlyweds. If anyone is watching us, they're getting quite the show. Any fears I once harbored that I might be sexually ambivalent are a thing of the past.

I've met up with Aunt Alex twice. But I follow all the recommended precautions. I once met a retired FBI agent who said he spent twelve years undercover with the mafia and would go home at night to his wife and kids. In twelve years, his two worlds never overlapped, even though geographically they were around thirty minutes driving distance apart. If he could do it in Boston,

then I can do it in Santa Barbara, or at least, that's the argument I pitched to Fisher.

Gemma has yet to respond to my texts. Pegasus, the system we use for surveillance, shows the number hasn't been used since she left Canada.

Rafael hasn't been in touch with Fisher, but Ivan swung by the brokerage offices. Given he's spent his time Stateside in Los Angeles, we believe he came up specifically to check out Fisher's brokerage on behalf of Rafael. But we could be wrong. He claimed he had business in the area, and surveillance picked him up on CTV near the marina.

My home office overlooks rolling hills dotted with homes, roads, and palm trees. The navy blue stretch of ocean is far off near the horizon, broken only by the occasional splash of white. The arid, sandy earth surrounding the house changes in color based on the location of the sun, transforming throughout the day from shades of rusty browns to terracotta.

There's a quiet to the house. Yes, I fill the time with research and analysis, but there's time in the lengthy days to reflect. My thoughts often stray to Killington.

I've always suspected the bastard raped me; therefore, his confession didn't warrant me losing my cool. I should've capitalized on his admission. But my emotions overpowered reason, and I threw away what could've been a fruitful interrogation.

Failure or not, I recorded our meeting, and I've played the tape repeatedly. "Follow the money." I get that. A derivative of "follow the money" is "follow the connections." I've spent hours reviewing photographs from the CIA, FBI, and social media.

Wayne Killington worked with the Morales cartel. When he got busted, we had nothing to go after them. That fall, my dad got looped into the gun smuggling arrangement Killington coordinated.

They were using luxury yachts, privately owned by different parties to avoid suspicion, to smuggle guns into Mexico and drugs back into the US. The DEA and FBI were involved in that bust, and it led to fracturing the Morales cartel distribution network. The cartel weakened over the years, competitors strengthened, and it's no longer considered one of the major Mexican cartels.

Several employees within Sullivan Arms, my family's gun manufacturing business, got busted in that sting and they are serving time. But my dad always said they were lower-level people. My uncle should've been arrested too.

But my uncle was a smart man, and they didn't have anything concrete to tie the gun smuggling to him. He faced charges for hiring a hitman to kill my dad, but he also hired phenomenal lawyers. His case never saw the inside of a courtroom, thanks to delays. Cancer took him before his case was ever heard.

My father, understandably, cut off all contact with my uncle. Interestingly enough, my uncle still included my dad in his will. He also included my uncle, me, and my cousin, Billy. I refused to go to the reading of the will, but I heard all about it. Billy's always been a wild child, thrown out of multiple boarding schools and a college dropout, so my uncle attached stipulations to him accessing his inheritance and requires that my dad's brother, my Uncle Liam, sign off on him receiving it. Apparently, Billy threw a tantrum when the same restrictions didn't apply to me. Also, I received more than Billy did. Not that I cared. If Billy asked, I'd give him my inheritance, but I haven't heard from him in years.

Family drama aside, I now have a new interest in my uncle's will. Follow the money. Back when Uncle Mark passed, my dad emailed me a copy of the will. During my research over the last two weeks, I found that file and took the time to read it. Two hundred and fifty million went into a trust for my stepmom's drug addiction rehabilitation facility, Nueva Vida. Patrick, my stepmom's best friend, received one hundred million. Over the

years, I've grown to love Patrick. He's a big, burly man with an enormous smile, a fantastic laugh, and a kind soul. I hadn't heard he'd received anything, but I'm glad my uncle didn't forget him. Apparently, the two men were together for a long time. My dad and Uncle Liam received the bulk of their uncle's inheritance, both inheriting three billion in a nontaxable trust, plus the entirety of his stock in Sullivan Arms. And there was a long list of recipients of smaller amounts ranging from five to twenty-five million dollars. I've studied the list extensively.

Wayne Killington received ten. Senator Talbot received twenty-five, plus his political action committee received twenty-five. The head of the NRA and the organization both received twenty-five. Zane's father, Congressman Oglethorpe, received the same distribution to both himself and his political fund.

Other smaller figure recipients included staff at my uncle's properties, his masseuse, the Houston church my family theoretically attends, my uncle's alma mater, and my private school in San Diego. A horticultural society in Houston received ten, as did several art museums in the Houston area.

Photographs of the recipients in my uncle's will line my home office wall. Most are in the NRA or in politics. It's not surprising that the NRA would be well-represented. The NRA is tight with the heads of most major gun manufacturers. And the NRA supports political candidates who support protecting the second amendment.

My wall of photographs of men posing in group shots at charity banquets, hunting, and playing golf, with arrows marking connections, is meaningless. They obviously run in the same circles, work in the same industry, and share the same objectives.

Regardless, I'm curious. I want to know more about Zane's father, who lived in our neighborhood, Wayne Killington's neighborhood, and rose to prominence as a California congressman during the same time period Sullivan Arms went

public and Wayne Killington rose within the company. I grew up thinking of him as Zane's dad, but I'm curious how a public servant became so wealthy.

My phone rings. It's the CIA phone, and the line calling in is from the brokerage front.

"Hello?" One unexpected phone call, and my pulse picks up.

"Sophie, you're not going to believe who I've got here in my office." Fisher's booming voice lets me know he's speaking to others, and I'm probably on speaker.

"Who?"

"It's us!" a female voice screeches.

"Gemma? Is that you?"

"Yes! Come meet us for lunch. Then we'll go shopping while they do man stuff."

"You've got it! I'd been worried. You didn't return any of my texts."

"Oh, I lost my phone. What a disaster. I'll tell you all about it. Get your butt here."

"Hon?" Fisher's voice breaks in.

"Yeah?"

"Meet us at the restaurant, okay? I'll send directions to your car."

"Sure thing. Can't wait to see you, Gemma!"

The call ends, and after concealing my research project behind a tapestry, I rush to get dressed. There's not much I can do to my air-dried hair, so I twist it into a half-knot, find a short skirt that goes well with a pair of surprisingly comfortable Prada heels, and a little top that exposes about an inch of my waistline. Basically, it's an outfit I'd never be caught dead in back in DC, but here I'm Sophia Garcia.

Twenty-five minutes later, I'm pulling the door open to The Lark.

Gemma squeals and stands at the table, hands clenched,

elbows and knees bent, like she's eager to give me a hug and she's just waiting for me to reach her. We throw arms around each other like we're the best of besties.

Rafael stands and offers a much more subdued hug. Before sitting, I lean down and give Fisher a peck on the lips. He reaches up and squeezes my bottom. His fingers linger on my thigh. Of course, I can't possibly know what he's thinking, but the glimmer in his eyes says he likes my short skirt while his possessive touch says it's too short for public consumption.

"So, how long have you both been in the US?" I glance between the two of them, but really, I'm wondering why we didn't get a heads up that they entered through customs.

"Oh, we've been here, what, three days now?" Gemma says to Rafael. "I love LA. I spent an entire day shopping on Santa Monica Boulevard."

"I do love Santa Monica." It's a completely honest assessment. And I'm feeling a little impressed that Gemma didn't gush over Rodeo Drive, since it gets so much attention. Santa Monica has some of the same luxe brands, but it doesn't have the pedigree of Rodeo Drive and therefore isn't quite as pretentious.

She and I devolve into a conversation about boutique shops and her finds. During gaps of conversation, I glean that Rafael and Fisher are discussing windsurfing.

After lunch, we leave separately from the guys, and I drive us over to the section of State Street that's closed off to cars. I figure it's a good place for us to leisurely kill some time while the boys go back to the office to discuss business.

We meander down the sidewalk, popping into stores or galleries. Since separating from Rafael, she's been more muted, less vibrant. We step into a home goods store, and as I pick up a succulent in a pot, I ask, "Are you okay? You seem a little quiet."

She picks up a coffee table book called *Surf Like a Girl* and flips through the pages.

"Jetlag?" I press.

She snorts. "We came on a boat." A touch of alarm crosses her facial features, and for a second, when her gaze locks on me, I sense fear. But, just as quickly, her attention returns to the book's pages. "A friend. I think we'll fly back, though." Her hand rests on her stomach, and my immediate thought is seasickness.

"What kind of boat?" And how did she get by boat from Colombia to the West Coast?

"Yacht." She holds both arms out and laughs. "Monster."

"Super yacht?"

"Yes. Very nice, though."

She sets the book aside and lifts a ceramic conch that could double as a serving bowl. "What's the interior of your house like?"

"Um..."

"Like, would something like this work? I want to get you a gift." Her lips form a pout. "So, what's your style?"

"At our home here?" I think about the house we are currently living in. "It's modern. Light and airy."

"Beachy?" she asks.

"No, not so beachy. More American Southwest. Terracotta tiles, shades of terracotta colors, mixed with wood beams. But you do not need to get us anything."

"Sophia? Is that you?" The voice calls from behind me, and I freeze.

Lauren's hand falls to my shoulder and she tugs to get my attention. "You dyed your hair red! Holy shit. At first I wasn't even sure it was you, but then I heard you and knew it was you." She places her hands on both my shoulders and holds me at arm's length, studying the color. "I really like it. It really makes your eyes pop. I love it."

"It's more auburn than red," I say, gaining my voice and blinking my brain into action. "Ah, Lauren, this is my friend, Gemma." I turn to Gemma, who is watching us closely. "And

Gemma, this is an old friend of mine." I pointedly place a hand on Lauren's hip, so I can dig my nails into her if needed. "What on Earth are you doing in Santa Barbara?"

"Well, I could—" Her speech halts when I dig a nail a little deeper in.

"Lauren, where did you go?"

I spin, searching for Lauren's mom. *Shit.*

"My mom is driving me nuts. We came here to visit a bridal shop she loves. I'd say for you to join us dress shopping, but I'm done. I can't take any more. Not today. Does Zane know you're here?"

"Lauren's getting married," I interject.

"Lauren?" Her mother's voice seems to echo through the store.

I grip her shoulders, much like she did mine when she assessed my hair. "I'm going to duck out before we have to spend hours with your mom. Besides, it's not like I'm her favorite person, right?"

I pinch her shoulder, tilt my head, and almost wink. It's a half-wink, and it's a gesture I'm hoping Lauren will read into enough to understand something is going on. She doesn't know I'm currently CIA, but she knows I used to be FBI.

Please, Lauren, play along.

"Lauren?" Her mom's voice draws nearer.

"Oh." She blinks, her gaze goes behind me, probably on Gemma, then back to me. "Yeah. Get out of here." To Gemma, she says, "You really don't want to get caught in a conversation with my mom after she's had a couple of glasses of vino."

I guide Gemma, my hand on her elbow, out of the store.

Lauren calls after us, "Call me, okay?"

I toss a hand in the air, waving as I walk away.

"There you are," I hear Lauren's mom gush. "I've walked all over this store. You just took off."

Holy shit. That was close. And if they are on State Street, then we need to get off State Street.

"I can't imagine not wanting my mother to be near my friends," Gemma says. "How sad."

"Oh, I love her mom, but she's got a mouth." I motion with my hand, batting my fingers against my thumb to mimic talking.

"She must not be that close to you if she didn't know you dyed your hair." She pauses near an outdoor rack of clothes and lifts a hangar.

"I dyed it recently. Damian loves it." I lift a dress off the same rack and hold it out, pretending to scrutinize it. "At first, he said it was like he was cheating on me. But now he's used to it."

"I could never dye my hair," she says.

We both hang up the dresses and continue down the sidewalk. I glance behind us to the home goods store entrance. Lauren and her mom have yet to step onto the sidewalk.

"You've got gorgeous hair. I'd kill to have that luster."

"Oh, it's not that—"

"Do you want to head back, closer to the boys?"

"Sure. But what I was saying is that dying my hair just doesn't work well. I don't know that I could ever get that kind of color."

As I guide her around the corner, off of State Street, my phone vibrates within my handbag. As I dig around in my Louis Vuitton for it, I can feel her eyes on me, studying me. I hold out my phone for her to see.

"It's Damian," I say, although she can see the name on the screen. "I had a feeling it was him." I press the phone up to my ear. "Damian?"

Aware of the need to put more distance between us and Lauren and her mom, I continue walking, hoping Gemma will stop staring and follow.

"Hey. Where are you guys? Rafael needs to go." *Oh, thank god.*

"We're not far from your office. Should I take her back there now?"

I pause and turn. She's still standing in the same location on the sidewalk, several feet back.

"Rafael needs to go," I tell her. "I'll take you to him."

When the call ends, I dump the phone in my bag. "You ready?" I ask Gemma.

"It's funny," she says.

I pointedly push forward in the direction of my car.

"You don't use video when you speak with Damian. I always answer with video. Rafael wants to see my face. I mean, if we have a connection and it can work."

"I'm not crazy about video."

My car comes into view, and I point in the direction we are heading.

"Do you have any photos of you as a blonde? I'd love to see the difference."

"I'm sure I do."

"Hand me your phone. I'll search for them. I want to see this blonde Sophia. I think I can see it. I think I might like it better."

"Please." We reach my car, pop the trunk, drop my handbag into it, then slam it closed. "Are you going back to LA tonight?"

She slides into the passenger seat. "I'm not sure." She texts away as I back out of the spot.

In my rearview mirror, I see a man in a pickup truck start his car, too. He falls in line behind the car behind me.

"They should be here any minute."

Ivan gives a curt nod and heads outside, presumably to wait for her. He's definitely acting in a security capacity, but it's odd to me he left Rafael here alone. If I were pulling security for two people, I'd insist they stay with me.

Unless someone is with Gemma right now, but is so good at his job, even a trained officer is unaware of his or her presence.

"Your office lacks a little something."

I glance around the paneled walls, attempting to see the space through Rafael's eyes. The team planned for a brokerage space that said moderately successful. The planned message had been one of a brokerage owned by a competent individual yet overextended. A business that would float by below the radar of the public eye.

"What's that?"

If he says diplomas, I actually have two fake ones framed in a closet. The team created them, but whoever hung them didn't nail into a stud and one of the frames crashed down.

"There are no photos of family."

I point to the framed photo of Sophia sitting on my desk. The photo is AI generated, created by some CIA genius, with the use of our two photos and then digitally enhanced with a background at the beach and my arms around her, her red hair blowing in the wind, us both laughing.

"Yes, yes, your wife." He paces back and forth, hands thrust in his slacks pocket. "But your parents? Siblings?"

Ah, and here it is. The conclusion to the interview process. He needs to know if there are people I love who he can hold over my head. He needs insurance.

"No siblings. My mother is in a nursing home."

"You don't take care of your mother?" He practically spits out the words, and I second-guess the wisdom of the team that developed my back story.

"She has Alzheimer's. It was the best place for her."

"My condolences. That must be difficult. Is she nearby?"

"No." I let out a breath of air and furrow my brow. "Research has shown that patients do better with the semblance of freedom. In Europe, they discovered that if you create a village...it's not real, you know? It feels real, though. A grocery where they can buy things without paying, a clothing store, a toy store, that kind of thing. Basically a little town straight out of a Lego village. And she can walk around freely. Nurses dress as people living in the town. It's...experimental, but she's happier there."

This is all made up. My actual parents live in Minnesota for part of the year and will soon winter in Florida when my father finally retires. There's no way I'd let my backstory for my parents match reality.

"So, where is this magical village?"

"In Kentucky."

"Huh. They have horses there, right?"

"You're thinking of the Kentucky Derby. Famous horse race."

"Yes. Your mom...did she ride horses?"

"No, and they don't let...there are dogs and cats in the town, no horses." I smile as if his line of questioning is amusing in a conscious attempt to cover up the uneasy feeling I'm getting at him blatantly digging for someone to use as a threat. Because based on my backstory, the only person he can leverage is Sophia. The CIA brainiacs screwed this up.

He pulls out his phone and reads the screen.

"What about you? Any siblings?"

He glances at me, then back to his phone. "They're here."

He heads out of the building. He passes Patel without so much as offering recognition. I glance back at her, and she gives me a questioning look.

Earlier in the day, he'd been friendly. Borderline flirty.

The bright sunlight blinds me the second I step out of the building, and I pat down my pockets for my sunglasses.

There's an SUV parked illegally on the street. The backseat passenger door is open. A man with a shaved head is driving, and Ivan is in the front passenger seat.

"Hey, Damian," Gemma calls from the back seat.

With my hand sheltering my eyes, I attempt to peer into the backseat, but it's difficult to see into the vehicle.

"Hi. What'd you do with Sophia?"

"Right here," a familiar voice calls. and I turn, scanning the sidewalk. An odd sense of relief washes over me as she approaches, striding down the sidewalk with the confidence of a runway model. "Had to park."

Rafael thrusts his hand in front of me and gives it a firm, quick shake. "I'll be in touch."

He gets into the back seat and the door slams shut. Sophia settles against me, her arm wrapping naturally around my lower back, and we both wave. She's wearing sunglasses, but I squint into

the sun until the SUV turns right at the stop sign and moves out of view.

One car parked on the opposite side of the road peels out, pulls up to the stop sign, and turns right. On a bench, an older man in a fedora reading a book gets up from the bench in front of the dry cleaners and nods, then strolls out of view, around the corner.

I glance up and down the street. Confident that's the last of our CalTan teammates, I gesture to the office door.

"Should we go inside?"

Sophia weaves her fingers through mine and tugs, leading us in the opposite direction of the Toros and the fedora man.

"Everything okay?"

"I think so. Just feeling the need to talk where we won't run a risk of being heard."

Adrenaline surges. It's something I'm fully aware of because the bright light becomes painfully brighter, the sound of passing cars louder, and an irrational desire to wrap Sophia up and haul her behind a bulletproof shield rises.

"Did something happen?"

"Yes."

I scan the street ahead of us. A mother pushing a stroller approaches from the opposite side of the street. Two parked cars line the street, but both are empty. We're the only two pedestrians on this side of the street, although a cyclist approaches up ahead. I scan the roofline.

"Go ahead," I tell her, my grip around her small hand tightening. I'm not carrying, but I crave the comfort of my Glock at my waist.

Of course, she doesn't need my clearance. She's conducted the same risk assessment.

"Lauren ran into us. I played it off. But Gemma might be suspicious. If felt like she was thinking about it on the way to meet you guys."

"Something was off with Rafael when he left too. It could have been a text he received—"

"From Gemma?"

"I couldn't see his phone screen. Or, right before he left, he was digging into my family history. He may have realized I'm not an ideal candidate."

"How did it go before then?"

"Good. Seemed interested in my business. Asked me my views on a few different investment strategies." I think back on our afternoon together. There was also a lot of nothing discussion. Best surfing locations, hang gliding, windsurfing. He struck me as someone who felt much more comfortable shooting the shit than actually discussing business.

"Everything was fine until he got a text?"

"Yeah. He asked Ivan to locate you. Said they needed to go."

Our stroll slows. Up ahead is a busier intersection, and we'll be in the mix of pedestrians.

"I don't think Gemma texted him, but I could've missed her sending a mayday." She's thoughtful.

"Let's head back to your car."

"Isn't it a little early to be calling it a day at the office?" Concern hovers within the question. She's worried we're being watched. And we very well could be.

I lift our linked hands to my mouth and press my lips to her knuckles.

"It's early, but we're newlyweds, remember?" And he spent over an hour in my office. I'm sure he sensed it wasn't a particularly busy business. I'd thought that would make us a more attractive proposition for a money laundering front, but maybe it only served to increase his suspicions.

We could drive ourselves crazy wondering. In a situation like this, it's best to not overthink. Otherwise, we might inadvertently tip our hand.

"We've got to trust the team is all over this, monitoring any communications they can access, and for that matter, them."

"So, we just go back, and what?"

"We play house."

CHAPTER 27
SOPHIA

Playing house with Fisher has undeniable advantages. One, we cook real meals together, eating outside and relaxing. He pulls me away from my Venn diagrams, and since it's in the context of work, guilt lies dormant.

The team agreed we need to stay put, especially while the Toros are Stateside. Yes, they are under surveillance, but there is a low level of confidence we have tagged all members of their team. Plus, if they needed to, they could hire additional resources.

At six in the evening, Fisher enters my office. He looks at my wall of photos and linked connections. There are connections everywhere. Every US politician. Every political cause. If you look deep enough along the paper trail, a connection to every crime organization. We need an inside source who's an instrumental player.

"Let's call it a day," Fisher says. "It will all be there tomorrow."

He helps me hang the wall tapestry over my collection, and like any other married couple, we enter the kitchen together and discuss dinner options. It's the after dinner portion that twists my heart and brain. Because it all feels so right and normal and like something I want to continue. And it can't.

In the morning, I wake before sunrise. He's asleep on his stomach and his head is turned, facing me. As the sun rises, the golden lights flicker on a scattering of gray strands. In the day, his grays aren't particularly noticeable, but in this light, and under this close of an examination, they can be found. His breaths are steady and even. Within me, I feel a pull. As if the atoms that make up my physical form are pulling in his direction, asking to be closer.

The scar on his shoulder is raised slightly. My lips have covered every centimeter of that scar. He favors the shoulder but insists he's fine. There are tattoos on his bicep. A compass with the words *Non sibi sed patriae* in the perimeter. *Not self but country.* It's an unofficial Navy motto. A spear with a strap of leather from the base dangling in the wind.

When I asked him about the spear, he said the tattoo parlor had art examples, and he liked the spear better than the gun. I don't yet have a tattoo, but if I were to get one, I'd want to steal some piece of Fisher's. Something to be close to him that only I would understand. Our secret. Or maybe just my secret.

Early morning light filters through the cracks of the shades. As peaceful and happy as these early morning minutes are, the day shall rise. The pull on my heart is for a life I did not choose. I was never in the Navy, but the saying applies. Before I met Fisher, my motto would've been more along the lines of *Non sibi sed vindicta.* Not self but revenge. Deliverance.

Fisher's eyelashes flutter. He lets out a muffled groan. Before his eyes are open, he reaches for me. In return, I reach for him. The skin along his back is smooth and warm. His fingers brush my hair off my forehead and his lips form a sleepy smile.

"Morning, beautiful."

"Morning."

With slow, lazy movements, he touches me. The inches between us dissipate. My body hums with anticipation. His lips trace a path from along my collarbone to my breasts. He brings me

to an orgasm with his fingers. When he pushes inside, I cling to him, to this feeling of being complete.

In the bathroom, while a toothbrush and toothpaste fill my mouth, Fisher sidles up behind me and kisses my neck. I'm in his T-shirt, and his chest warms my back through the thin cotton. "I love waking up with you."

Our eyes meet in the mirror, and I smile before spitting into the sink. He taps my butt before leaving me to finish in the bathroom alone.

When I enter the kitchen, the smell of coffee greets me. Fisher's dressed in running shorts and a Lycra shirt, but he offers me a mug of steaming joe.

"Where are you off to?" I ask, accepting the coffee after lifting on my tiptoes to brush my nose along his neck. The tip of his beard tickles my nose.

"Running down to the ocean. Meeting Trevor. We're doing an ocean swim."

"Run-swim day?"

"Run-swim-bike. Trevor's loading up bikes for us. I might run back. We'll see."

"Sounds like you'll be out there for hours." I have a pretty stringent routine myself. As a woman, I need to be fit to be adept at hand-to-hand combat. But Trevor, Ryan, my dad, and even Fisher...these former military guys...there's a love there that transcends a need for physical fitness. It's like they get a high from pushing their bodies to the max. All of them are triathletes.

Fisher rinses out the blender while I sip my coffee, watching him.

"Any updates from CalTan?" I assume he would've checked while getting his protein drink together.

"Not this early on a Saturday. Trevor and I will check in after the swim."

"Sounds good." He sets the blender on the drying rack. "I keep

playing my run-in with Lauren over in my mind. If Gemma's aware at all..." At the very least, that run-in would've made her suspicious.

"We play it day by day. You handled it well. That's all we can do."

I follow him to the door, where he bends and ties on his running shoes. He stands, hesitates, then presses his lips to my forehead as his palm cups the side of my face. The warmth of his skin lingers, and my fingers cover the expanse of skin he heated.

There's a brisk coolness in the air. Shrill birds sound off in the nearby trees. I grip my mug with both hands, sipping on the brew, as I watch Fisher jog down the steep decline until he's out of sight.

Back in the house, I return to my office and unplug my phone. There's a text from an unknown number. It came through late last night.

> **UNKNOWN NUMBER:**
>
> Are you around tomorrow? This is Gemma. ;-)

I shoot off an email to the team with the new phone number for Gemma Toro. It's early, so I expect everyone isn't on task quite yet. If anything, a lot of the team is out getting their workouts in. Which is something I also need to do. Although I plan to do yoga and strength training today.

> **ME TO UNKNOWN NUMBER:**
>
> Sorry. Went to bed early last night. Yes, I'm around. Want to hang out?

.   .   .

I set the phone down and stare at the text. This is good. This means that she's not suspecting anything. But I never touched base with Lauren. And she's got to be wondering what the hell is going on. I dig out my personal phone from the safe and turn it on.

As expected, two missed calls and several texts await.

> LAUREN:
>
> What's going on?
>
> Call me when you can. I think I understand things more clearly now. But I won't put anything in writing.
>
> Are you still in SB? I'm here until tomorrow. Breakfast?

God. I really am such a bad friend. It's early, but I dial Lauren anyway. She answers on the first ring.

"Hey," I say as she says, "What the hell is going on?"

I curl my knees up against my chest. "I can't really say, but thank god you were perceptive yesterday."

"So, obviously you're still working for the FBI. And you're undercover or something. Although it's not like red hair makes you unidentifiable."

I'm not authorized to tell Lauren anything, so I just sip my coffee.

"I guess it's good that you finally got into the field. I knew it was just a matter of time. But do they have you working nonstop? Is that why you had to wait until now to call me? Are people listening in on your calls?"

"Lauren, people could always be listening."

There's a pause. "You're getting paranoid."

I'm not quite sure how she came to that conclusion, but... "Lauren, I can't say much. You understand that, right?"

"Wow. I'm right. You're undercover. I'm so proud." Her voice rises several octaves. It could be a play at drama or it could be genuine. "Wait. So...you're going to make my wedding, right? I mean, obviously if you need to thwart an evil empire from a nuclear bomb attack, that will take precedence, but otherwise, you'll be at my wedding, right?"

"Yes." I visualize the vacation request form I submitted prior to leaving for Canada. "In the absence of a nuclear bomb threat, I will be at your wedding. But the events leading up to the wedding..." I let my voice trail.

"Right. I understand."

Does she? I'm not sure she does, but she watches a lot of action movies and *SEAL Team* is one of her favorite TV shows, so maybe she does.

"So, how are the men? Do they look like your old security team? What was that one guy's name? Fisher?"

Fisher's name coming out of her mouth has me grinning. But then I think back to my class at both Quantico and Langley, and yeah, they aren't all like Fisher. It's a mix of aesthetics, because that's what the companies need. The better someone can blend in unnoticed, the better for the company.

"Trust me. They don't all look like Fisher. But enough about that. Tell me all about the life of a fiancée."

She bubbles over with wedding planning ups and downs. They have the most important elements done. The venues, the band, and obviously, each other. But she's struggling with dress, color theme, and menu.

The ringtone from my work phone sounds down the hall.

"Lauren, I've got to run. But just know I love you. And I'm so grateful to you for yesterday. You. Are. Awesome."

"So are you. Call me when you can. And try to visit me before you leave California!"

"Will do! Love you!" And with that, I end the call, throw the phone down on the bed, and rush to my office.

I answer on the fifth ring, barely catching it before voicemail.

"Hello?"

"Hey, girl. Can you be ready in thirty?"

"Minutes?"

"Yep. I've got a surprise."

"Sure. What should I wear?"

"Something comfortable. I'm in leggings, sandals, and a comfortable top."

That sounds like yoga, but something tells me that's not surprise-worthy for someone like Gemma.

"I'll be ready."

In a flash, I dress, then lob a call to my dad on my personal phone. I get his voicemail but leave a message.

"Hey, Dad. Just calling to say hello. Tell Ava and Justin I said hi. I'll try to reach you later. Love you." Justin is my younger half-brother, and if I were to guess, he and Ava are off at a sports event with him this morning. It seems their weekends are becoming all about Justin.

After locking away my personal phone, I shoot off a note to the CalTan team notifying them I'm going to spend the day with Gemma again, then write a note for Fisher.

Leaving with Gemma. She says it's a surprise.
Will have my phone with me.
Love you,
Sophia

CHAPTER 28
FISHER

The last leg of the bike ride home burns my calves and quads. Dried salt rubs below my eyes and along the edge of my hairline. The California sun beats down on my back, and a light, crisp breeze dries the light layer of perspiration. Out on the beach, running in the sand, I'd been sweating. The chill of the Pacific had been welcoming.

I forgot how great life in Southern California can be. I used to have this in San Diego. Trevor and Ryan picked a great place to live. Jack, too. He moved to San Diego to be near his daughter once he and his first wife split, but he mentioned more than once he had no intentions of leaving. Sure, California has its problems, but the palm trees, blue sky, mild temperatures, and ocean create paradise.

The stretch of drive up to the top hits a near vertical, and I push off my seat, digging my heels down, and drive through the burn. The house is quiet, and the garage doors are down. I disengage my shoes from the pedals and walk Trevor's bike up to the house. There are no bike racks inside the garage. I rest it up against the side of the house. I might need to buy a car bike rack to return it to him later today. Adding a bike rack in a temporary

garage doesn't make sense. I could lean it against a wall in the garage, but the space is tight. I wouldn't want to risk one of us dinging his bike. It's an expensive, high-end, lightweight model. Trev invests in his toys.

That thought has me scanning the grounds. Yes, this house is at the top of the hill. It's pretty safe. But to be safe, I should probably put it in the garage until I get it back to Trevor.

Outside the front door, I bend to remove my bike shoes before entering the house. My calf muscle tightens and my back cracks as I stand. Damn, getting old sucks. There was a time when I could follow up a three-hour workout with a few beers. Now I need to stretch in the shower.

Shoes hanging on two fingers, I twist the front door handle. It's locked. I rap my knuckle against the door and wait. Kick an ankle out and lean over, stretching my quads that are getting tighter by the second.

I listen, but I don't hear any movement inside. Maybe she went to the grocery. Or decided to visit her Aunt Alex. Ryan didn't join Trevor and me this morning. Something about a kid's soccer game. Maybe she joined them?

I scrounge through my backpack, searching for the key, find it, and unlock the door.

"Sophia?"

Silence greets me. I move down the side hallway, set my dusty bike shoes down, dig out my running shoes, and set them down too. I open the door that leads to the garage. Both cars are parked inside.

Alex and Ryan wouldn't pick her up from our house, would they? Maybe she went for a walk and they picked her up on another street?

"Sophia?" I call again, scanning the back yard through the open windows that overlook the hillside and the distant ocean.

A piece of paper lies on the counter.

Gemma? She went with Gemma somewhere?

A sense of unease hits. I open the fridge, grab a bottle of water, and drink it down to flush any excess electrolytes. On the way to the bedroom, I check her office. It's in order. Her Venn diagram is covered. Doesn't look like she did any work before heading out.

I pull out the phone I'm using for Damian Garcia, and call Sophia. It goes to voicemail. I shoot off a text, peel off my socks, and stare at the phone. I attempt to track her phone, but nothing comes up. It's the first time I've tried to track the Sophia Garcia phone. She may not have remembered to approve me as one of her friends tracking her. I'm getting uneasy for no reason.

I locate my personal phone, turn it on, and call Erik. It's Saturday. There's no need to bother Ryan or Trevor when I know they'll just turn around and call Erik, Arrow's tech guy. There's a woman who he works with, but her domain is cybercrime. Erik is the surveillance contact.

As I dial his number, it occurs to me there's probably someone on the CalTan team I should call, but calling Erik is easier.

"Fisher. How goes it?"

"Can you track Sophia for me? Let me know where she is?"

"Sophia?" he lets her name drag like he's asking for more information.

"Sophia Sullivan. She's working the CalTan op. She has a CIA tracker on her. Can you just—can you have someone on your team locate her? She left a note that she left with the target, but she didn't say where." I pace the room. The cool wood floor grounds me. "I'm sure it's nothing. I was out with Trevor, and when I got back, she was gone. I'm just—"

"Wouldn't she have checked in with someone on the team? Oh, never mind. I see a notation. Let me call you back."

The line goes dead. I set the phone on the bathroom counter, turn the shower on, and begin to stretch, letting the cool water warm.

Five minutes later, the phone vibrates.

"Where is she?" Steam coats the bathroom mirror.

"Last known location was at a helipad near you."

"Are you fucking kidding me?"

"No. I assume you tried calling her?"

"Voice mail."

"Yeah, I saw the call when I checked her phone records. I'm working now on getting flight records but..."

"But what?"

"Might take me some time. It's a nothing helipad. Might not have even logged a flight plan."

"Fuck."

"Any reason to think the worst?"

I pinch the bridge of my nose, thinking back to yesterday. I'd blown it off. Assumed she was in the clear. "She ran into a friend shopping yesterday. We thought she pulled it off without any suspicion."

I can hear keys clicking in the background.

"Where are you? In the office?"

"No. I'm at a vineyard, but I have a laptop in the car. Let me go. We're working on it. Don't freak out. Could still be nothing."

Right. He's right.

"There's an app that tracks all the birds in the sky, but it doesn't necessarily show occupants. It has registration details. Let me get someone working that angle. Although, this is Northern California."

"What does that mean?"

"Lots of birds in the sky. And a lot of them are registered to corporations."

"The Toros aren't residents. It'll be a hired transport."

"I'll call you back."

In the shower, it hits me how fucked up this situation is. Her last known location isn't in the mountains with bad reception,

indicating they went to an exclusive spa. No, it's at a fucking helipad.

Yes, for Gemma, a helicopter is probably the same as an Uber. They could be in transit going to San Fran for a shopping excursion. Or Los Angeles, for that matter.

This is Gemma. No matter what, she won't go far away from Rafael. And CalTan has surveillance on Rafael and Ivan.

I turn the water off, and as I'm drying, dial Erik.

"Where's Rafael?"

"He and Ivan are in San Diego."

He'd mentioned meetings in LA. "What's in San Diego?"

"Surveillance says they've spent most of the time in the hotel."

"Are we sure they're still in the hotel?"

It wouldn't be surprising at all if they threw surveillance a curveball.

"We're waiting for confirmation."

"Are you fucking kidding me?"

"Arrow's not doing the surveillance. It's FBI."

"And those fuckers can be obvious as fuck."

"Let's not throw our teammates under the bus yet."

I take a breath. Sling open the closet door and grab some clothes. "Fine. Call with any update."

This time, I end the call. Sure, Erik's a partner at Arrow and I'm acting like he works for me, but I don't give a damn.

My next call is to Ryan. Family time be damned.

"Hey. Head to the helipad." The man is succinct.

Every exhausted muscle tightens as if lit by a live wire.

"What'd you find out?" I ask as I rush through the house like I just got an order to be wheels up in thirty.

"Confirmation on hotel location. No sighting of Sophia, but analysts say there's no way Gemma will be acting alone. If they have her, Rafe and his men will be involved."

"So, we're going down to San Diego?"

"Based on the timeline, they're probably still in transit. We won't be far behind."

At the helicopter pad, Ryan asks, "Anyone follow you?"

"No."

He's already got it ready to go, and I jump in. The second our headsets are on, his voice comes through the mic.

"Tell me exactly what happened yesterday."

"We both sent in updates."

"I want to hear it from you."

"I wasn't with her. I was with Rafael. She told me she ran into a friend. Lauren." I stare out ahead of us, trying to calm the rush of adrenaline to remember exactly what she said. "I'm not clear why she was there."

"Should we put surveillance on Lauren?"

I try to remember what I know about Lauren. She was one of Sophia's close friends, so we had a full background on her. More than once my team helped Sophia get a drunken Lauren home. Nothing suspicious. Normal college behavior. What did she major in? English?

But what did Sophia say? She played along?

"I think it's a coincidental run-in." I cringe as I say it, because no one in our line of work thinks much of coincidences. "When Erik checked Sophia's phone log, did he mention if she talked to Lauren?"

"She did. Five minutes and twenty-five seconds. But Lauren called her multiple times last night. Doesn't appear she answered."

I think back on last night with Sophia. No, once we entered the house, we weren't on our phones. A visual of Sophia's flirty smile and her straddling my lap hits hard, and I snap my eyelids closed.

"She probably explained to Lauren what was going on."

"You think she looped her in on this op?"

"No. Nothing like that. Sophia wouldn't break protocol. If

anything, she told her she's UC FBI. Sophia hasn't shared with any of her friends that she's working for the CIA. They think she's in finance." Sophia and I didn't discuss what she'd say to Lauren, and we probably should have. Why the fuck didn't I think about that? But no, Sophia's a professional. "You can set surveillance on Lauren, but I don't think it's necessary."

"We've already got surveillance on her."

"And?"

"She's still in her hotel."

"Back in Santa Barbara?"

"Yep."

We ride in silence the rest of the way. I have my CIA phone out and keep an eye on team updates. Right now, we're operating under yellow status, meaning we're aware and alert, but no definitive danger has been determined. She could simply be out of cell reach.

But we're in California, and the idea that they are in some remote location where a tracker won't work feels highly unlikely. At the same time, a team covered the last location of her tracker and phone and there's nothing there. It's like she vanished.

Ryan takes a call through his headset. I can't tell much about what's being said to him, but I hear his end. It's a lot of grunts, followed by, "About twenty-five minutes out. See you soon." The call ends as we touch ground.

"We're going to the FBI offices?" I ask for clarification as I scan the helipad, searching for our transport, and unbuckle myself.

"I am. You're driving to Jack."

"Why doesn't he just meet us at the offices?"

"He doesn't know yet." He pauses and waits to speak until I've removed my headset. "It's going to hit him hard. You go update him in person. If there's a reason for him to come to the office, I'll let you know. But we're still operating under the assumption

CalTan is a go and everything hasn't gone sideways. Under that assumption—"

"I shouldn't be seen near FBI offices, which are probably monitored via street cams. Gotcha."

"I'd switch with you. Jack's like a brother to me. But this plan makes the most sense. And I need to be with the team."

"Right. I'm the operative, not the strategist."

He gets me. I see it in his pensive expression, even if his ice-cold eyes are covered by shades. "I'll keep you updated."

I glance down at my phone. The trouble is, we don't have any updates.

Déjà vu strikes on the drive through the Sullivans' ritzy, gated, beachfront enclave. The same palm trees flutter in the wind. The green lawns manicured with golf course precision. Shades of pink, red, and white flowers dot the landscape in flowerbeds and pots. Every few houses, there's a gardener out front tending the plants. The mansions are the kind that always made me wonder what career did they choose? The landscape hasn't changed since I stopped working here, but everything in my world has.

As I pull up to the Sullivan gate and buzz for entry, the NPR announcer on the radio catches my attention. "Senator Talbot, the Texas Senator, died earlier today. His wife of forty-one years, Geraldine Talbot, released a statement to AP News. He was eighty-three years old."

A buzz sounds, and the heavy metal gate slides to the right, letting me onto the property. The news segment transitions to an auto insurance commercial. The brief alert didn't include cause of death, but at his age, the cause often doesn't qualify as newsworthy.

The front door opens before I've reached the threshold. Jack Sullivan greets me. He's got the look of a man who is hoping for a pleasant house call but has a gut instinct that's kicked in and set

him on edge. I get that, because my instincts have been on hyperdrive for hours now.

"Did Ryan call ahead?"

"Ryan?" He visibly swallows. "So, you're here on official business?"

"It's okay," I say, scanning the yard behind me.

I step inside, and he closes the heavy iron and glass door. Ava peers out from the kitchen.

"Hey, Fisher. Long time no see." She's got a glass of Perrier clutched in her hand. She holds it up. "Can I get you anything to drink?"

"No, I'm good. Thanks."

"Babe, you want anything?" she asks Jack.

He gives a quick shake of his head and holds his hand out to her, a gesture she clearly understands since she sidles up to his side. I look to Jack, unsure about what I can say in front of Ava.

I scan the living area I know so well, and down the hallway that leads to Sophia's bedroom, expecting her to come out and greet me. But she's not here. My gut roils.

"Can I talk to you in private?"

"Anything you need to say to me you can say in front of Ava."

"What's going on?" Ava looks between me and Jack. Her palm covers Jack's chest.

"She doesn't have clearance." I say it apologetically, because I know Sophia and Ava are close, but she's not a part of Arrow. I didn't delve into it with Ryan, but I assume the only reason Jack has clearance is due to his partnership in Arrow.

Jack lets out a defeated sigh and pierces me with a hardened stare. "I screwed up one marriage with secrets. It's not going to happen with this one."

Annoyance flares that Jack feels emboldened to break the rules, even though I'm well aware there are probably many spouses out there who know more than they should.

"You said Sophia's okay. So you aren't here to tell me she's dead."

His words are like a blast of cold water. "No." I shake my head, as much to emphasize my answer as to wash that horrific notion away. "But..." On the way over, I planned how to tell him, but the phrasing left me.

We're standing just beyond the foyer that's more hotel lobby than home, and Jack asks, "You want to talk in my office or out on the deck?"

"Kitchen." In his office, he's CEO. On the deck, we can be seen from many vantage points. He's got a fucking public beach in front of his estate.

"She called you this morning, right?" I read the team update. It was a brief call to her dad.

"She left a message. Nothing material. What's going on?"

Ava pulls a stool out and pushes it in my direction, offering it to me, but there's too much troubled energy flowing through my veins for me to sit idle. I pace in front of the island, glancing between the view of the ocean and Ava and Jack.

"Fisher? You look frightened. What's going on?" It's Ava's voice that pulls me back into this room with Sophia's parents. I glance down at the phone screen in my hand. Brush up. No updates.

"We don't know anything yet." Jack's expression turns to stone. "As you know, we've been working two targets. We were successful on approach, and our contacts are being leveraged—"

"What the hell is going on with Sophia?" Jack interrupts.

Ava's enormous eyes track both of us.

"We don't know." The words come out rough and thick with emotion. I look to the ceiling. Telling her parents is worse than discovering this fucked-up scenario this morning. Saying it out loud. I grit my teeth. Fuck it. "She's with the target right now. Not answering her cell. Tracker not picking up her location. I left this

morning for a run, came back to a note." I slow myself down and make eye contact with Jack. "Might be nothing. But she ran into a friend." I blink, realization setting in that, of course, Jack and Ava know Lauren. "Lauren. Totally unexpected. But she thought she played it off and our target didn't pick up on it."

Jack's face remains unreadable, but his head nods slightly, like he's adding it up and figuring out where we are and why I'm now at his door.

"Lauren's with her mom, Heather." Jack and I both turn our attention to Ava. She lifts her shoulders in a slight shrug. "Heather told me about it. Mother-daughter spa and shopping trip. They're doing lots of that. Dress shopping. For the wedding. There was some bridal shop she wanted to visit."

That explains why Lauren was in Santa Barbara. I rub my temple, thinking about what would've been said in front of Gemma. Sophia didn't really go into details.

"What spa?"

Ava sucks on the corner of her lip. "I can't remember. I can call and ask. Why, what are you thinking? That maybe Lauren mentioned it?"

"No." My gaze travels over the ceiling and frustration mounts. "Never mind. I was thinking maybe Lauren mentioned it to Gemma, but the last location was a helipad. If she took her to a spa in Santa Barbara, they wouldn't travel via helicopter."

"They took my daughter in a helicopter? And the goddamn motherfucking tracker isn't working?"

Ava holds on to Jack's arm. I pace in front of the window. At this moment, I'd like to pick up a kitchen chair and smash it through the window. We don't know shit, and we're helpless. Colombians are notorious for eliminating leaks. If Gemma got suspicious...

"You're concerned." It's Ava's soft-spoken words that pull me back.

My hand goes to my hairline, and my fingers maneuver the skin on my brow. *Think. Panic serves no one.* If they're on to her, what exactly would they do?

"You love her." It's Ava again, and I spin around, fixing an irate glare on her. This isn't the time to get into that.

But Jack's eyes narrow into a lethal gaze. "Are you dating my daughter? Is that why those bastards set you up as a married couple on this op? I should've fucking known."

Jack's hands ball into fists at his side. If he wants to hit me, I deserve it. He should bludgeon me. Not because I'm dating her. We never talked about anything past this assignment. But he should bludgeon me because I should've protected her. From me. From this.

"You. Sick. Fuck." The stool clatters across the floor as Jack leaps into my perimeter. "I trusted you. She's twenty years younger than you."

His fist collides with my jaw. My head snaps. Pain courses from the side of my face to my neck.

Ava screams, "Jack!"

She's there, pulling on his raised arm.

The bitter taste of blood coats my tongue. I bow my head and stride to the door.

I deserved that. I deserve more. To be kicked in the ribs. Pummeled.

Jack, Trevor, Ryan... The whole Arrow team can batter me to a pulp, after we find Sophia.

CHAPTER 29
SOPHIA

"*Mi valedor*, wakey wakey."

I blink several times into darkness.

The click of a car door and a flood of cool air arouses me.

"We're home," Gemma says. Her eyelids are half-closed.

The driver, a man with a tree trunk body, jet black hair, sleeve tattoos, and a thick gold chain, holds the door open. He introduced himself as Trey, but I think of him as tree.

"Are you sure you don't want to crash here?" I ask.

"No. Rafe wouldn't approve." She says it like she's speaking to Tree. As if he asked her, and not me. "And Trey's at the hotel, too."

Ah. Of course. If she stayed with us, Tree would probably have to spend the night in the car or call for backup with whoever else Rafael has working discreet security.

"Well, thank you for a fantastic day." I lean across the seat and attempt to give Gemma a hug, but she falls against the far door and snuggles into it. I glance back at Tree and envision him getting her into bed on his own. He could undoubtedly do it, but I doubt Rafael would approve.

"Don't forget your wine."

At that, Tree moves to the back of the SUV and opens the hatch.

Floodlights flick on, seemingly all at once, flooding the front of the house in golden light. Tree comes around from the back with a case of wine. My pocketbook sits on top of the wine.

"Where was that?" I ask as I hold out my arms, and he steps past me, dismissing my offer for help.

"In the hold on the helicopter."

The dull throbbing in my head intensifies. I need more water. The front door opens, and Fisher fills the doorway.

"Where the hell have you been?"

"We flew to a vineyard," I say, holding my hands up in a very Gemma-like way. "We drank a lot."

"Where do you want the wine?" Tree asks. "I need to get her back."

Fisher's gaze goes from me to Tree and back to the car.

"Shhh," I say, playing the part, "Gemma's sleeping."

Negative energy rolls off Fisher in waves, and my stomach flips. It's the same oh-shit flip from when I was younger and I did something wrong. And just like back then, I know exactly what he's pissed at. We didn't have a signal in the section of Napa we flew to, and by the time we landed, I was already tipsy, and then we proceeded to drink all afternoon. And I didn't check in.

I follow Tree through the front door where he sets the box down in the foyer.

"Thank you..." I call after him, wiggling my fingers like I'm Gemma.

After I close the door on him, I lean my back against it, tentatively taking in Fisher. The ends of his hair point in a thousand different directions. It's not that late at night, but he looks like he's been up for days.

"Why didn't you reply to my texts?" He's leaning against the

wall, arms crossed, but his muscles are tense, the absolute opposite of relaxed.

"Honestly, I..." I let out a sigh. "We didn't have signal." I actually haven't even looked at my phone. On the way back to the helicopter, I fell asleep in the back seat and woke up when we were in transit.

"And your tracker?"

That question puzzles me. "It should've worked. I had it."

"Last known location was the helipad eight miles away."

"Oh." A visual of the box where he stored my bag has me shifting to my other foot. "The storage box must have blocked signal."

"Storage box?"

"In the helicopter. It was this black bin. I didn't think about it. Tree took our stuff and put it in there before we loaded up. Gemma wanted to pay, so she instructed him to leave my pocketbook back at the helicopter."

"You didn't think I'd worry?" His blazing eyes are a veritable storm cloud threatening lightning bolts.

"I didn't have a signal. But I had my tracker. And I left the note." My gaze tracks to the immaculate kitchen counter. My insides twist. The headache worsens, and my mouth feels like sandpaper.

I bypass him and enter the kitchen, open a cabinet, get a glass out, and run the tap water.

He remains in place, lips in a flat line. "Do you want to hear about my day?"

I swallow about half the glass of water and set it on the counter with a clink. The room shifts, or the floor or the walls do. It's hard to tell, but it's clear I've still got alcohol in my bloodstream. "Not good?" My question comes out high-pitched.

"No, Sophia. Not good doesn't come close. It started with a

note. Then the discovery your last tracked location was at a helipad. Then a gazillion unanswered texts."

My gaze falls to the box of wine and my handbag lying on top of it. I move over to it, a sense of dread filling me. It never occurred to me that the tracker wouldn't work. It's a CIA tracker. I figured they worked anywhere in the world.

"Guess what my first thought was?"

I dig in my bag for my phone. My cheeks burn. I turn on the phone. I let out a breath of air. Only three missed calls and four texts. That's not too bad.

"Sophia? What would my first thought have been?"

I lift my gaze from the phone and cringe under the accusatory glare. Gemma and I were out having fun, drinking the day away, but, yesterday, shit. "You thought she saw through the Lauren thing."

He rubs the back of his neck, and his forearms flex. Aunt Alex would say he's calming himself down. He's bothered. Worked up. Or exhausted.

"What happened?"

"You mean other than me beating myself up for not having been more circumspect about the risk? For not having been here to protect you?"

"Hold on." I step forward, calling out that patriarchal bullshit. "I don't need protection."

"Really, Sophia? How long ago was it you promised you wouldn't go out on your own?" I open my mouth to argue that this is different, but his lips curl into a venomous scowl and I shut my mouth. "There is no I in team? Ever heard that before?"

"I didn't know my tracker wasn't working!" It's not like I set out to do this on my own. Even when I got in the helicopter, I didn't know where we were going. I didn't know she planned on drinking all freaking day.

"Let's go back to my day."

My legs weaken, and my stomach falls. I want to curl up in bed, but instead I pull out a kitchen table chair and sit. He remains standing. Livid. Lividly standing. Is lividly even a word?

"Your father knows about us now."

"What?" I look up at him, completely confused. "Did..." My stomach drops. How the hell would my father get involved? "What did you do? Did the operation get compromised?"

"What did I do?" He pushes off the wall. "What did I do other than prepare to unleash hell to find you?"

"Don't be mad at me!" Yes, I'm shouting, but my head hurts and my stomach is out of sorts, and I should've been tracked.

"Don't be mad at you!"

"Fine. Yell. Repeat my words back at me." Now I'm out of my chair, yelling right back at him, fists at my sides, head pounding. "Did the operation get compromised?"

"No."

I pick up my glass of water and my phone and pad to the back of the house. The most important thing is that the operation isn't compromised. I need some aspirin. It doesn't matter if Dad knows I'm seeing Fisher. He's still alive and—I halt at the entrance to the master bedroom. The king bed is rumpled on one side, with the comforter pulled back and the pillows stacked. Fisher had been in here, lying back on the bed. His phone sits on the dresser.

Fisher follows me down the hall. The overhead light shines on a purplish raised cheekbone.

"He punched you?" He blinks a couple of times in acquiescence. "Why'd you tell him?"

It's hard to fit those pieces together. Going from being worried about where I am to telling my dad about us.

"Ava figured it out."

Ah. She's good at reading people.

"Rafael is in San Diego. We thought if they were torturing you, or..." He runs his hand through his hair, and his pained

expression says he can't go on. My stomach sinks and my chest aches as it hits full force what he feared. "Ryan met up with the surveillance team monitoring Rafael. I went to make your dad aware."

"Oh, shit." I close my eyes, and they burn. I'm bone-tired. "Dad thought I was missing?" My chest quakes thinking about what that must have been like for him. Knowing what he went through before when I was fifteen. "I should call him."

I remember I'm holding a phone and flick it to life.

"He knows you're okay." There's resignation in his tone.

"What do you mean?"

"Rafael finally returned my call. I asked him point blank where Gemma had taken you. Turns out Gemma wasn't returning his texts either."

"We spent the whole day drinking."

"Well, your driver had his head on his shoulders and kept Ivan updated."

My chin itches, and I scratch at it. "He had signal?"

"Apparently. Or he called from another location. Was he with you all the time?"

"I really..." I stop speaking to prevent myself from admitting that I wasn't keeping an eye on Tree the whole time. We went to Opus One, which happens to be my favorite of all the vineyards. "Rafael doesn't suspect anything?"

"No. I think my reaction was in line with what he would expect it to be, given I didn't know where the hell my wife was."

Guilt and exhaustion twirl around me. I head over to the bed, scoot up onto it, and let my feet rest on the footboard below the mattress. Holding my face in my hands, I try to think through it all.

He comes to stand before me, and I raise my gaze to his. The light is dim in the bedroom and there's no color in his irises, leaving only pools of black and gray.

I reach up and gently caress the bruised skin. One bruise. Dad

could've done far worse if he'd wanted. Actually, in that situation, two highly-trained men—it could've been brutal. But neither Dad nor Fisher would go animalistic, especially in front of Ava.

"He'll get over it," I say.

"I didn't plan on telling him." I look up into his eyes and see he's speaking the truth. Of course he is. Why would he tell him the truth when what's going on between us is temporary?

"It's just as well. You don't need to worry. He needs to stop seeing me as a little girl." Perhaps if he sees me as an adult woman, he'll stop manipulating my career.

His hands fall to my shoulders, and he leans closer. His chest rises, and I get the sense he's breathing me in.

I reach for him, wanting to hold him. He respects my dad. It must've crushed him for my father to lash out at him. And if anyone had been with my dad other than Ava, a woman who is insanely intuitive and hears what's unsaid, he probably could have informed my dad and never had to come clean. And shit. Arrow was his transition plan out of the CIA.

"I'll talk to my dad. This won't block you from getting a job with Arrow if that's what you want."

Fisher's hands leave my shoulders. He steps away, goes into the bathroom, and unzips a small leather bag. He places a toothbrush in it, then steps out of view, but I can hear him in the shower.

"What're you doing?"

"You can have this room. I'm moving to the guest room."

I curl up onto the bed, knees to my stomach. I should probably log on and read through the team record of what happened today. But I don't have the energy.

The confusion is hard to cut through when my mind is loopy. I never wanted to hurt Fisher. Or scare him. I promised him I wouldn't go out on my own, and I didn't. I upheld my promise. I just...that damn tracker. Why didn't it work?

The guest room lies on the opposite end of the one-story home. Ironically, it's the room where Sophia stores her secrets.

In the morning, I'll update her fully on my conversation with Rafael. We fully expect after the Monday meeting he requested, I'll be dealing with the Americans he's recruited. Some will deliver cash in envelopes and have essentially no idea who they're working for. Many will have family in Colombia and will do exactly as told to ensure their loved ones' safety. Special Agent Williams briefed me on what to expect on Monday and how to respond.

The plan is to set up the accounts and conduct trades and purchases long enough to get a grasp on the Toros' preferred money laundering scheme, and someone within the task force will determine when we've gotten as much information as we can, and we'll shut it down.

I'd love to go for a run. My best thinking is done when determination overrides painful knees and stiff muscles. It's one foot after the other, inhale, exhale, in a meditative trance that increases blood flow, loosens my joints, and frees my mind.

Earlier today, I feared the worst. The idea that Sophia might

be hurt, or, god forbid, die, while working this job just about killed me. I'd felt so helpless, and that's not an emotion I handle well.

It occurred to me she didn't have a signal. But if she had any idea how scared I'd been, she would have found a way to call. To get word to me she was okay.

But why would she know how I feel? I don't think I fully realized how deeply I care until faced with the worst. And to her, I'm a part of an operation. A city she's passing through.

This operation could continue for a few more months, but it will end, and when it does, I might not cross paths with her again for years. That's the way it is in our profession.

I pull back the comforter and stare down at the crisp, white linens, remembering what Ava said...that I love Sophia. Love? I've never been in love before. It could be love. There were times today it felt like my life would end if hers did. But if it's love, it's unrequited.

"Is something wrong with those sheets?" Sophia leans against the doorjamb. Her auburn hair is tucked behind her ear, looking as youthful as ever, even if the skin below her eyes is puffy. "You've been staring at them a long time."

"What's up?"

"Why are we...are you..." She sounds unsure of herself, which is a side of Sophia I haven't seen since she was a teenager. She folds her arms over her middle.

"Sleeping here?" I ask for her.

She shrugs.

I pinch the bridge of my nose. How do I explain? What we have isn't just sex. But it's not more either. "Sophia." I breathe out her name, struggling with the right words. "Today, I thought I lost you." Emotion wells up in my throat and my eyes water, evidence I'm not cut out for this. "Tomorrow we can talk about it more. But I think it's better if we keep this, between us, on professional ground moving forward."

"Is this a case of you caring more about what my dad can do for you than what you care for me?"

"What?" How can she say that?

She avoids my gaze, and she damn well should. "Or is this a case of it gets tough, so you quit?"

My head nearly explodes. Any sadness or despair gets blown to smithereens.

"There's nothing here to quit, Sophia!" Those blue eyes widen, and she cowers. I am not a quitter. She's implying I rang the bell willfully, not because I was injured and they thought I might die. I shared with her a story I never talk about, and here she is throwing it back in my face.

"You!" I raise my hand, pointing my index finger directly at her traitorous heart. "Clearly, I mean nothing to you. If I did, you would've gotten word to me. You would've checked in. You wouldn't have scared the living daylights out of me. There's nothing to quit here." Another thought comes to mind, and I point harder. "You said it's just sex. And if it's just sex, then it's not quitting when it ends, is it?"

Holy shit. My blood pulses with rage. How dare she throw my biggest failure back in my face. Something I've never shared with another woman. Something only a handful of men, men I consider brothers, know about me. And that handful of men, Ryan, Trevor, and Jack, they'll probably never speak to me again.

Jesus, I've fucked up.

Out the window, the twinkling lights of homes and streetlights dot the shadowy landscape. The buzz of my phone vibrating has me turning around. She's gone. I'm not surprised. She called me a quitter, but she quit before we even got out of the gate. Which is exactly what I should expect from someone who is so much younger. I don't have any business dating someone in her twenties. Who the fuck am I kidding? I don't even fucking date.

I dig my phone out of the carryall I stuffed with the few things

I grabbed on the way out of the master bedroom. There's a text from Ryan.

RYAN:

R u with Sophia?

ME:

Y

He thumbs-up my response. I wait for anything else. But there's nothing.

I stretch my neck to the left and right, loosening my tight shoulder muscles. Should I approach her? There's really no point.

The dull throb in my head intensifies, and I dig through my toiletries bag for aspirin.

I can't think about this. I don't want to think about this.

Sophia appears at the bathroom door. "Fisher?"

"Yes." I grip the edge of the counter for support.

Through the mirror, I watch as she slides down the wall, onto her butt, and her legs stretch out across the floor. She gestures to the floor across from her, in front of the cabinets. "Sit."

I exhale. Frustration? Bullshit emotion? I'm not sure. It won't kill me to sit, so I do, opposite of her in the spot indicated. "Why are we sitting on the bathroom floor?"

"To talk." She says it matter-of-factly.

I rub my aching head and bend my legs, preparing to stand. This is ridiculous.

"This is how my dad and Ava handle things, when they get

upset with each other. I walked in on them once. Both sitting cross-legged on the floor. Neither looked happy. I walked right out, but asked Ava about it later."

"Logical." She's a therapist, so it's not surprising that she's big into talking.

"I've never been in a relationship before... I mean, not in a mature relationship before. But I thought maybe we should try it."

"Sitting on the floor?" Yes, I'm being a jackass, but I'm probably dehydrated from the long workout this morning followed by a frantic afternoon and one helluva emotional rollercoaster.

"Communicating." Whisper blue eyes flash to mine, and my heart cinches. "Because maybe we weren't in a relationship before. And maybe it's not what either of us wants. But when I walked back into that room, and I thought it was just...whatever we have was just...it hurt way too much for it to just be sex. And if it's a relationship, then our first step would be talking. You know, putting it out there. Talking."

CHAPTER 31
SOPHIA

Somewhere along the way, I mastered locking down emotions. But the last few days busted the locks and chains. The cold tile seeps through my clothes and exacerbates the chill permeating my skin. My fingers tremble, and the slight tremor captures my attention. I wipe one shaky hand across my cheek, to calm the spasms, then pull back and touch my fingers. They're wet.

Crying is not my normal. I am strong, yet here I am breaking down. And he's just sitting there. What are we doing here? I'm an idiot. He didn't dive into this for a relationship. Neither of us did. Who am I kidding? We don't have what my dad and stepmom have. It's not even close. I push up off the ground, needing space.

Warm fingers clutch my cold ones and tug me onto his lap. His thumb strokes my cheek.

"Hey." He draws out the word, and the softness in his deep, comforting tone ratchets up a swirl of feelings that climb my throat, threatening to choke me. "It's okay."

He brushes my hair behind my ear and tilts my chin up.

"I'm not opposed to talking." The pad of his index finger smooths over my lips. Caring, dark eyes pour over me, warming me. "I care about you, Sophia. A lot. Probably too much."

"I care about you, too." *I love you.* The thought wells up unbidden.

"It's in my nature to be protective." His hand cups my chin, and I lift his palm to my lips.

"That's why you were so good in security." If I'm honest, I resented him—or, well, not Fisher, but the entire security requirement. Hated it at times. I still want to believe I don't need protection. Countless hours on the mat, self-defense tactics, knife skills, time on the gun range, all of that was done to eliminate any residual helpless feelings. And I was at the top of my class at Quantico and Langley. Not many can say that.

As if he can read my thoughts, he says, "I trust you can handle yourself now. But it's still in me to want to protect you. Today...I lost it. I went from thinking they had you and were going to contact us with threats, to thinking they would kill you without brokering a deal, to wondering if you staged it all so you could re-visit Killington or that maybe you engineered Talbot's death."

"What?" Absentmindedly, he rubs my back, calming me, but I'm stuck. "Talbot died? How?"

"The news blip I heard didn't say."

That man took campaign contributions from shady sources. Who would—

"He was eighty-three," Fisher says, filling in my thought. Right. It doesn't mean anything. "Getting back to the conversation at hand." He pauses until I return his gaze. "If we're going to be together, I think I need for us to be a team. Not just on this operation, but moving forward. I can't just have you out there, not knowing anything. And I know that's not fair, but—"

"Fisher." My voice has a parental quality to it that surprises me. "Agency first." It's more of an FBI mantra, but a version applies to the CIA, to the military—heck, he's got it tattooed on his body.

He blinks. He glances to his arm, possibly having similar thoughts to mine.

"We're going to need to insert a tracking device in your molar." The warmth of his hand envelops the back of my neck. "Or maybe under your skin."

Now I'm grinning, because he's being silly, but I also kind of love how his silliness makes me feel. Like he needs me. Like maybe he loves me, too, and this isn't temporary at all.

"I'm serious. I'd prefer to be your partner on ops, but if that's not always possible, I need to be able to find you."

I rest my forehead against his and inhale deeply. There's no cologne, not even a trace of soap smell. It's all Fisher. My fingers scrape along his unruly beard as warm sensations unfurl within my chest. And when I pull back and look into his eyes, that thought, "I love you," returns.

"Military couples survive with one person away on a mission. We can, too."

"Mmm...true. But we're not a military couple. The CIA can benefit from couples. They have plenty of officers pose, like us."

"You're serious about this?"

He takes my hand and flattens it against his chest and covers it with his own. "Sophia, I've never been more serious in my life. About this. About you. I love you. And if I've hesitated at all in telling you that, it's only been for self-preservation."

My chest quivers and I suck in air.

"But the only way I can do this is if you're all in. You can't shut me out. If we're going to be together, you've got to let me in. Your side project. Your life. I don't need to run things, but I need to be by your side, as a teammate. Otherwise, I'll go crazy."

"Crazy?" Yes, it's a lame response, but he's taken my breath, my words.

His lips press against mine. Softly, once, twice. Then harder.

His tongue slips between my lips, and I curl against him, welcoming the comfort and the warmth.

He breaks the kiss, and his palm cups my chin. "You are remarkable. Determined, capable, intelligent, driven. You've had my respect since the first month I met you, and you defined your boundaries and worked hard at overcoming the shit that happened to you." His chest rises as he inhales deeply. "I can't tell you exactly when I fell in love, but I can tell you that I've never felt what I feel for you for anyone else. I'm not an expert on relationships. Sure, I've had them before, but never one that lasted. And the cards are stacked against us. Your family, our careers, our backgrounds...none of it's ideal. But I want to be there for you, with you, for as long as I can be. When I met you, my future was my career. You've flipped it. Now, I don't care about a future unless you're in it." He dips his head and presses his forehead against mine, skin to skin, noses side by side. "But you have to let me in. Otherwise, I'll lose my sanity."

I push back, just a few inches, enough that I can look him in the eye, sniffle, and hate that I do, because it comes across as weak. "I don't have a choice about letting you in. You're already in here." I pat my chest, and he raises an eyebrow. An argumentative eyebrow. "I'll tell you everything. All my theories." I let out a sigh. "My work that doesn't seem to be going anywhere. But I don't need for you to protect me."

"I know." He breathes out the admission, but those dark eyes drill deep. "You're skilled. Trained. I get all of that. But sharing the load strengthens us. That's why teams are stronger. It's not that any one man can't do it alone, but we're a helluva lot stronger as a team."

His long fingers curve around the back of my neck, below my hair, and I close my eyes, leaning against him. A calm washes over me, settling the emotional tidal wave. A sense of peace drifts through in its wake.

"I didn't try to do today on my own."

"I know."

"I love you too." Those dark eyes take me in, and I swear, his warmth penetrates my heart. "I've never said that to anyone before." It's something that's probably obvious, but at the same time, I need him to understand I don't say those words lightly.

His large palm cups the side of my head and brings it down to his shoulder. The beat of his heart vibrates through me, soothing me. I nuzzle his neck, breathing in his musky scent, while holding on tight.

He drops his lips to mine. The deep, sensual kiss is like a match to tinder. I twist in his lap to deepen our connection and straddle him. His fingers glide up my back, finding the skin below my shirt, the touch sending the small hairs along my arms rising to the sky. I grind against him, earning a low moan as we kiss. Need grows deep within me. He tugs at my shirt, and I dutifully lift my arms. It's up and over my head, thrown somewhere behind me, and his teeth graze my neck. His hands cup my breasts, lifting them to his mouth, and sucks on my nipple. I let out a loud groan. I tug on his shirt, wanting it off, needing skin on skin.

My bra tightens around my ribcage, then it's loose, unsnapped, and somehow, I'm in the air, up off the floor. Fisher stumbles, hits the counter, and sets me on it. He stands between my legs. My fingers comb through his hair and along his shoulders. He drags his shirt hem over his torso, and my hands flatten over his firm abdomen and up the planes of his chest. The smooth skin covering taut, firm muscle, down to his narrow waist and his pajama bottoms, where I grip the band and shove down. His thick, hard cock springs free, and I grip his width.

He tilts his head back, groaning, as I tighten my grasp. I slide down to the ground and flatten my tongue against the base of his shaft and lick up.

"Fuuuck," he groans.

I circle my tongue along his tip, lapping his saltiness, then dip my head, opening my mouth wide, taking as much of him as I can. He lifts my hair, holding it out of the way. I cup his balls and massage, earning another uncontrolled groan and a pump of his hips. He thickens in my mouth as I work him over, and then there's a loud pop when he pulls me up by the arms and sets me on the counter.

"I need to look at you." He grips the waistband of my tights and tugs. I squirm on the counter, helping him. He pulls at each leg, and it's awkward, but then he maneuvers them over each ankle and they're gone.

I'm left with an emptiness and an ache that only he can fill. His mouth covers mine in a sloppy, wet, kiss. A kiss nearing desperation. I squeeze my thighs, attempting to soothe the aching need.

"Please," I moan. "Now."

I spread my legs, and he steps between them. I watch as he runs his tip through my center.

"God, you're so wet," he breathes out, voice husky in the semblance of prayer.

"Please." I sound needy, and it's as if I'm praying, too.

I watch as he pushes inside and whimper.

"Look at me." I tear my gaze away from where we're joining and look straight into his dark blue irises. "God, you feel good. So right."

"Please," I beg, but I don't have any idea what I'm begging for.

His thumb circles my clit as his hips pump, penetrating deeper with each thrust.

The edge of the counter bites into the backs of my thighs, and I raise my knees, lifting to better meet him, to take him. Sweat breaks out across his skin, and I smear it with my fingers on his back. And then his thumb presses down as his angle hits a spot somewhere deep within me and I arch forward, screaming out,

toes curled. My head tilts back, and I chant senseless words as the most intense orgasm of my life crashes through me. His thrusts become erratic and his head dips, and his mouth plunders mine. He flattens against me, as close as two humans can be, and he pulses his release.

"I love doing that with you," I say as soon as my breath catches up and I possess the power of speech.

He brushes his lips against my forehead. "Not as much as I love doing that with you." He slaps my ass playfully. "Let's get to bed. It's time to show you just how much I love you."

The click of heels against terra cotta tile echoes through the open floor plan. Sophia sweeps through, triple-checking all is in order.

It's Monday, and Gemma and Rafael are stopping by the house. Rafael suggested we meet here instead of at the office. After our meeting, Gemma will return with Rafael to Los Angeles.

Yesterday, Sophia and I visited Ryan and Alex's place and picked up a variety of clothes to fill our closets to ensure that to the casual observer, our closets appear full and lived in.

The precaution might be overkill, but if you have any suspicions someone is staying in a staged home, checking the closets is a smart thing to do. Luckily, our profiles are affluent individuals, recently married without children, so it's completely believable we would live in a modern clutter-free environment.

Click. Click. Click. Click.

Constant clicks.

"Come sit," I tell her.

The request is selfish. Her heels are sky high, and they define every muscular curve along her calves and thighs. She's wearing a short, sparkly, purple dress that barely covers her ass and scoops down in the front, pulling the eye to the valley between her

breasts. With each step, her crimson tresses, curled in loose waves, bounce and her posterior muscles flex.

Outside surveillance waits. Arrow has someone parked near the bottom of our drive, prepared to follow Rafael after he leaves. Plus, for extra safety, we have two men hidden about two hundred yards out in steep, undeveloped land. Normally, we wouldn't take those kinds of precautions, but given it's Sophia, and her father doesn't give a fuck about the profitability of this operation, and he is newly engaged in this endeavor, we have backup.

It's overkill, mainly because if Rafael decided to take us out, he wouldn't do it himself, especially on US soil. He'd send someone else to do it. My gut tells me this house visit is part of Rafael's system. If he hires the wrong people, money goes missing. Intelligence sources believe he's still proving himself to his family, hoping one day to take over. What's not clear is if he'll follow his father in a public-facing legitimate role as a diplomat, or if he'll follow in his uncle's path.

Sophia places one hand on the wall, above her head. Her other hand rests on her jutted out hip. The hem of her dress lifts higher up her thigh, and she bends one long, lean, creamy leg. She's stunning.

"I don't have a place to hide a weapon."

"I can see that." The hemline on that dress provides no cover, but I approve.

"My heels." She shrugs.

"Come. Sit." I command.

"Should I change?"

"No." My answer is quick and firm, like another part of my anatomy.

Her glossy, full lips curve up into a teasing smile. She pushes off the wall and saunters to me, dramatically lifting one foot in front of the other like a runway model. Her bright blue eyes

sparkle more brightly than the cloudless sky shining through the glass panes.

She stops before me and bends until her hands rest on the armrests, giving me a clear view of her perky, unrestrained breasts. My mouth waters and my cock strains against my pants, begging to be freed.

With one quick movement, I catch her, spin her around, and have her squirming on my lap as I tickle her.

"Teasing me? Is that how you want to play it?" Her head tilts back, laughing.

I caress her skin, silky smooth, stroking my way to the apex. I clamp my palm over the thin strip of fabric, and she stills.

Those blue eyes lock with mine, and I shift to reach those luscious lips.

"No kissing." She shakes her head with a look of regret. "Took me forever to get this lip liner and gloss just right."

I slide the fabric to the side. "You're wet."

She blinks rapidly, and her chest rises when my finger dips inside. My thumb covers her clit and massages the nub, earning a mewling sound.

"Feel good, baby?"

"Mm-hmm."

Her fingers tighten on the back of my neck.

"Lower your dress."

If I can't kiss her, I want to taste her, to suck in one of her sweet nipples and feel her tighten around my fingers as I scrape my teeth over her sensitized flesh.

She struggles, squirming in my lap, attempting to maneuver the thin strap on her shoulder off. She gives up and moves the fabric on the front to one side, exposing one lone, perfectly shaped, rose-tipped breast. I suck it into my mouth and roll the nipple between my teeth. My fingers are soaked in her juices. Her body tenses and her spine straightens, and my thumb pulses over her.

Knock. Knock.

There's a glazed, faraway look to Sophia's eyes. Her chest rises and falls rapidly. I want so much to claim those lips, but I settle for leaning into her, breathing her in and kissing her neck as I remove my hand.

"You okay?" I ask softly.

She whimpers and gives me the softest of smiles before pushing up off the armrest and straightening her panties and dress. I stand up, too, holding out my wet hand. There's a noticeable wet spot in my slacks from where my dick leaked pre-cum. *Great.*

On my way to the kitchen, I glance to the left. There's a large pane of glass the length of the front door, and Rafael stands in front of it smirking.

I hold up my hand, still walking to the kitchen, and shout, "Be right there."

As I wash my hands, I struggle to remember if someone can see the armchair from the front door. I'm almost certain the most he could've seen would've been her heels hanging awkwardly.

As I squirt hand soap into my palm, I hear Sophia open the door.

"Rafael, hi. It's so good to see you."

"I see my timing is impeccable."

I can't hear Sophia's response, but I'm guessing she said something funny because I hear boisterous laughter.

I finish washing and drying my hands.

Sophia asks, "Where's Gemma?"

"She's not feeling too great. She sends her apologies. But she's hoping I can convince you to come down and visit her in L.A."

"Rafael," I say, holding my arms open as I enter the foyer, "so good to see you."

There's a man beside him I recognize. I've seen him before on the street in front of our business.

"And this is Enrique. He's a good friend. Good man." Rafael

claps Enrique on the back. "I needed him to meet you, as he's going to be working with you."

"Nice to meet you." I extend my arm. He hesitates, glancing between me and Rafael.

"He washed it," Rafael says.

"Oh, my god," Sophia says, placing a hand over face. Her cheeks blush a bright shade of pink I've never seen before.

Rafael, Enrique, and I chuckle.

"Don't worry, Sophia. You're newlyweds. When the husband comes home early, this is a good thing to do."

She just shakes her head, looking completely adorable. I tug her to me and cup her ass with my palm as my lips smack against her juicy ones.

"Ah," she complains, but she's wearing a bright smile that shows off her pearly white teeth and lets us all know she's joking. "Now you've got gloss all over you." She puckers her lips, and her teasing look earns her butt another firm squeeze. She sidles against me, much the way Gemma always did with Rafael, and asks the men, "Can I get you anything to drink?"

"Thank you, Sophia. Ah, maybe water? We can't stay long. I've got a meeting to get to."

"Enrique?" she asks.

"Water would be great. And, ah, do you have a restroom?"

"Certainly. Right down that hall and to your left."

I lead Rafael outside onto the back patio. It's a perfect seventy-two degrees outside, and the view from the back is impressive. There's a slight breeze, and a potted palm flutters.

"So, what's wrong with Gemma?" I ask as we select seats facing across the valley to the ocean. Along the horizon, specks of white dot a navy canvas.

"She thinks she had some bad sushi. She's disappointed she couldn't come today. I'm hoping she'll be okay to make it back to LA

this afternoon." He grimaces, and I get the feeling he's remembering her back at the hotel. "She is really hoping I can convince Sophia to visit her in LA. I've got meetings, and she gets bored on her own."

"I'm sure Sophia will jump at the chance to visit."

He grows serious and glances over his shoulder, as if checking for someone. "Things...I don't know...Do you follow the news in Colombia?"

"Not really," I lie.

"It's fractious right now. People..." He holds up his fists and acts like he's slamming them together. "There's...how do you say... collateral damage. If she comes to LA, I don't want to scare your Sophia, but I'll have security with Gemma. I don't worry as much up here, but LA, San Diego...I worry more. There are those who might recognize Gemma."

Sophia slides the glass door open with her elbow, and I jump up to help her. She's carrying three glasses of water with cucumber slices in them.

"Are you hungry at all?" she asks Rafael. He barely looks her way.

"Why don't you bring out the charcuterie you prepared?" I suggest.

"I'm really not—" Rafael begins.

"She already prepared it. It's light. You can pick at it."

He smiles and smoothes over his shirt with his palm after setting the glass of water onto the coffee table in front of him.

When Sophia slides the door closed behind her, Rafael says, "I really don't have long. There's a meeting tonight in LA I need to get back for, and I hear the traffic is..."

"Temperamental," I supply.

"Yes. But I wanted you to meet Enrique. He lives here." He pauses and gestures out to the neighborhood below us. "In this area. He'll be bringing you cash deposits. I want it deposited and

invested. Then periodically we'll sell stock, or I'll have you purchase equity in specific Brazilian entities."

I stretch one arm out across the outdoor sofa cushion and cross one ankle over my thigh, glancing back at the house, remembering Enrique is still in the restroom. The sun reflects on the glass, making the panes more of a mirror than a window.

"Are you sure you want me to invest? You know, any stock purchases could decline in value."

"You would only pick winners, *sí*?"

I chuckle. "I'm not a magician. If I were, you wouldn't be offering to invest in my company. If we're...if the goal is to cycle money and remain off any radar, I'd recommend safe investments, not stock. I could send you a list of easily convertible assets to acquire."

"You turning away business?"

"Just giving advice." I shrug nonchalantly. "It's what you want, right?"

He grins and points at me. "That's why I like you. You're not a kiss ass." Then he grins wide. "Unless it's your lady." He glances over his shoulder, back at the house. "Looks like things are going well with you two."

"Indeed. I'm a lucky man." I say, smiling as Enrique slides the door open.

"I can tell." He nods thoughtfully. "And it's not just the..." He holds up his hand and shakes it. "It's the way you look at each other. There's something different now."

"We're in a good place."

Enrique steps out on the patio, and Sophia follows, holding a tray in front of her. Enrique stands awkwardly beside Rafael's chair.

"Rafe, I got an alert that there's a wreck on the 101. We should probably head."

Rafael lets out a groan. "I'm sorry, you two. I thought we

could have a nice afternoon catching up. But..." He lets out a sigh. "Next time, you and me, we'll go windsurfing." He points to the Pacific. "Sophia, have you got plans for the next couple of days? Gemma gave me a job, and that's to convince you to come visit her. Please? Gemma will not be a happy woman unless I sell you on this."

Sophia glances at me, as if she's asking permission. Of course, she's playing a role. And, I have to admit, I rather like this bit of the role-playing.

"I can't think of any reason you can't get away for a couple of days, can you?"

She squeals, like I've granted her permission for something she so very much wants to do and bounces a bit in her heels.

"Sounds like she's in. I have some business in LA, too. Maybe I'll drive her down."

"Great. We're staying at..." His brow crinkles and he looks to Enrique. "Let me ask Ivan."

We all follow Rafael as he traverses the house and exits through the front door. Ivan leans against a car, a phone in his hand.

"Ivan, I didn't know you were here. You didn't want to come inside?" Sophia asks.

"He's a slave driver," Ivan jokes, gesturing to Rafael. "I had some emails to take care of. You all done?"

"Yes." He snaps his fingers. "Where are we staying in LA?"

Ivan looks between us and Rafael. He appears hesitant to answer.

"Sophia's coming down to do things with Gemma. You know how she's been bored."

"Chateau Marmont. When?" Ivan doesn't sound happy, but if he's in charge of security for Rafael, having been in his position in the past, I imagine he is mentally reconfiguring personnel assignments.

Rafael turns to us. "Tomorrow? I'm sure Gemma will be feeling better, but she'll call if she's not."

"That sounds like a plan," Sophia says, softly clapping her hands and beaming at me. She deserves an Oscar, because I knew her at fifteen, and even back then she didn't clap her hands and bounce.

"Next time, we're staying longer," Rafael announces.

He shakes my hand and pulls me in for a brief man hug. Enrique gives me a stern nod. And Ivan taps away on his phone as he moves to the driver's side of the car.

Sophia sidles up to me, playing the good wife. She rests her head against my shoulder, and her hand slides from my waist down to cup my ass. I squeeze her up against me, and she grins. Ivan does a three-point turn to exit our driveway. We both wave until the car is out of sight.

Two men up on the cliff rise, one with a faux bush attached to his shoulders. They hustle down, knees bent, hands out for balance on the steep descent. The first one to the patio speaks. He's in full desert camo, and he's carrying binoculars and a backpack.

"Guy outside did a quick tour of the grounds but never stooped or stopped in any location. Looked like his purpose was to secure their automobile. We lost sight of the one roaming inside your house. You need to check for bugs."

"Got it," I say.

Sophia steps away from my side as if it just occurred to her we should no longer be pretending to be a couple.

The man holds his hand to his ear, as if comm is coming through. He glances at his colleague.

"Phantom is on the go."

"Good. Will be useful to learn who all he's meeting with in L.A."

CHAPTER 33
SOPHIA

"Do you want to come in and get something to drink?"

The two men in camouflage have all the markings of former military. The camouflage pants hide their legs, and the shirts they wear hang loose, but based on their strong jawlines and general build, they're fit. A sandy layer coats their hiking boots. Their expressions are stern. If I met them on campus, I'd expect they were teaching self-defense tactics or shooting skills.

The guy closest to me, possibly two inches shorter and with a scar above his right eyebrow, takes off his hat and rubs the side of his fist against his brow. "Thanks, but we better get going. Besides, safest if we don't enter. Don't forget we lost sight on the one guy."

"I was in the kitchen." His stony gaze stops me short. The man's correct. To be safe, we need to check the space.

"I'm Sophia," I hold my hand out.

"Felix," he says, then jerks his head toward his partner. "Knox."

"This is Fisher," I say.

"We know Fish," he says with a wry grin. "How you doin', man?"

Fisher looks up from his phone. He's been reading something

while I attempted to be cordial with our Arrow teammates. He appears oblivious that Felix greeted him. "Alejandro Toro cleared customs at LAX."

"Rafael's dad is here?" The elder Toro travels to the US periodically. "That's probably the meeting Rafael needed to get to. But Alejandro usually goes to Miami or DC."

As an analyst, I studied the high-level political leaders for all the South American countries. Alejandro Toro is one we all studied, given his suspected ties to the Toro cartel, led by his brother.

Felix checks his wrist. "Well, I've got to get out of here. My daughter's soccer game starts in less than an hour. I'm scorekeeper."

"You need a ride to your car?" I ask.

"Nah. Just a short hike away. Hey, just so you know, there are coyote tracks up there."

"Interesting," I say, not sure what else to say to that. I suppose if I had a cat or a dog, that would be important information to know. But Felix knows the score. This isn't our real home.

After saying goodbyes, Fisher and I head inside. I jump on my laptop, while Fisher scans the rooms, searching for anything Rafael and his henchman might've left behind.

He comes into the office and says, "Clean. What're you working on?"

"I wanted to review my file on Alejandro. Found a news alert that last week there was a raid on the Bay Clan cartel. Twenty-four dead. Two being extradited to the United States." I search for the Toro cartel. "No history of raids on the Toro cartel."

"Supports the theories that Alejandro helps his brother out."

"I'm going to look through the photos on file of Alejandro. Check his Stateside connections."

"He's a politician. Was an ambassador. A photograph is meaningless."

"True, I suppose." That theory completely negates my last couple of weeks pouring through old photographs. He's right. The connections are endless. "Do you have anything else you want me to do?"

"Can't think of anything. I'm heading to the office. Ryan or someone from the team will stop by as a client, and I'll update them on today and our trip to LA."

"Want me to come with you?"

"No. I doubt he's got anyone watching us, but it'll be suspicious if you join me."

"I'll call Gemma. Check in on her."

"Good idea." He steps closer, kisses me, then strides out of the office. My fingers go to my lips. The soft brush of lips was in many ways a perfunctory kiss, but it also felt natural and sweet. That was the kind of kiss my dad would give Ava if he was heading out of the house. Warmth unfurls. We're real.

I give Gemma a call and get voice mail, so I send her a text.

ME:

> Gemma, so sorry you're not feeling well! (sad face emoji) But can't wait to hang in LA! What all do you want to do? What should I wear? (champagne toast emoji) (confetti emoji) (red high heels emoji)

Deciding that's a sufficient number of emojis, I hit send.

Then I get to work diving into Colombian cartel intelligence. Or at least the files my security clearance level grants me access to. Most of the intel is pointless. It's truly amazing how much the CIA gathers and tracks.

The front door clicks open, and I call out, "Hun? You home?"

I slam down the laptop, push out of the office chair, and release the tapestry that covers my wall of photos and notes. Steps draw closer, and I scan the room.

"Sophia? Where are you?"

My muscles relax as Fisher comes into view.

"You scared me."

"Sorry. I was wrapping up a call. What're you doing?"

"Just research." He's tense. I can see it in his lips, the deeper wrinkles present along his eyes and brows. The depths of blue seem deeper. "What's going on?"

He leans against a doorframe and holds a hand out to me. I take it, and he pulls me against him.

"We've got to pack. Alejandro Toro checked into the Chateau Marmont. The team is reviewing all the reservations. In the meantime, they've decided we should go ahead on down to LA. We'll play it off like once we decided to go, I scheduled some meetings and we decided we didn't want to drive during Monday morning rush hour."

"Okay. Makes sense." I pop up on my heels and press my lips to his, then step past him into the hall. He clings to my hand, holding me back.

"Have you talked to your dad?"

"No." The slight bruise on his cheekbone is barely noticeable, but it is visible. "I was waiting."

I'm not quite sure for what. Maybe waiting isn't the best word. Procrastinating is probably more accurate.

"Ryan suggested you call him."

"Has Dad been calling him?"

He toys with my fingers thoughtfully.

"What is it?" I prompt.

"Ryan suggested we clear the air before we go down. I plan to talk to him further."

"He doesn't get a say in this."

His dark eyes flash to mine. "I agree. You're mine. No matter what he says, I'm not giving you up. But he loves you. And you love him. There's no reason us being together should cause a rift."

He's right, but there has to be more to it. "He's coming to LA, isn't he? He's involved now, right?" Of course he is. He got scared about me, and now he's inserting himself into an operation he wasn't involved in before.

"Ryan said there's a good chance he'll show up in LA."

I let out a sigh. I love my dad, but he can be a bit much. "So, is Ryan flying us down?"

"No. He and Trevor are flying down to be closer to the LA FBI office. We're going to drive." I roll my eyes, mainly because I'm feeling bratty and I'd much rather take the helicopter. "It's a safety precaution. It's clear the Toros have resources Stateside. On the off chance someone is watching us, we don't want to tip them off by showing up to a helipad owned by Arrow Tactical Services."

"Right," I say, pulling my fingers from his and heading down the hall.

"You can call your dad from the car," he calls after me.

I end up packing a big suitcase. The official story is we'll stay for a couple of days, but realistically, I don't know how long we'll be there. I throw in several of my newly acquired Gemma-worthy outfits, a Balenciaga logo track suit, Gucci print heels, and a couple of Prada dresses. Then I catch sight of the Lanvin sneakers I purchased for Fisher.

"Here you go."

"What are these?" His suitcase is half the size of mine and he's already zipping it up.

"Shoes for you to wear today. Oh, and here's a baseball cap."

He glances at the cap. "Seven hundred and fifty dollars?"

"Take the price tag out before you wear it," I say, returning to my closet.

"What is it made of?"

"Cashmere."

"It's soft. But for that much, I'd expect it to make your dick bigger."

"Very funny."

"Seriously. Do you normally spend this much?" He holds up one of the t-shirts I added to his wardrobe when we were in Whistler. "Two thousand dollars? I mean, I'll admit, it's nice to touch, but..."

"If you want to look the part..." I shrug. Two other officers failed at getting close to the Toros. He can mock me all he wants, but I understand this world.

"But you don't normally wear these clothes?" He seems flustered. It's cute.

"No. I don't," I admit. "One, you'd never catch me in head-to-toe logos. Two, on a day-to-day basis, I'm working with paycheck-to-paycheck people. I don't know if you've ever looked around Langley, but they aren't the most fashion forward crew. I dress the part."

"Huh." He leans against the doorframe as I fill a second suitcase with shoes and handbags. "What does the real Sophia choose to wear? When she's at home, all by herself, not trying to blend in with anyone else?"

I pause, thinking about that. I've been dressing to blend in with others since my mom died and my dad hired a personal shopper. Lorraine gave me the foundational logic for what to wear in every conceivable situation.

"At home, I'm probably in something soft and comfortable."

"Like sweats and a tee?"

I laugh. "Like loose cashmere pants and a long sleeve tee or tank. If it's winter, then a light cashmere sweater." I have a winter white and a heather gray set I wear a lot, but both are back in my townhome in Virginia.

He nods like that's acceptable.

"My tees probably cost around six or seven hundred dollars. It's men's tees that run a couple grand."

His eyes widen, and I laugh. "It's just stuff. Costumes."

"Then why do you spend so much on a t-shirt?"

"It's higher quality. Better construction. Softer to the touch." I pause, kneeling before the suitcase. "And when you don't have to worry about money, why not buy the best?"

It feels a little callous to say it, but I overheard my dad one time making that exact argument to Ava when she flipped out over the prices on some of the items the personal shopper bought for her.

"Seems to me there's a better way to spend that money."

I glance up at him. Given I'm fairly certain a significant percentage of his wardrobe was purchased at a sporting goods store, I don't doubt his sincerity. I zip the suitcase and stand. "Just don't read the price tags. You ready?"

He grumbles on the way to the car. I snag some waters, lock up, and we hit the road. I leave my personal electronic devices behind at the rental, as does Fisher.

"Grab that bag in the back."

I reach behind us and grab a small white bag with the Apple logo. "What is this?"

"Some AirTags. I want you to put one in your wallet, one in your handbag, and one somewhere on your body. If they find it, it won't seem suspicious. After what happened at the vineyard, I want as many tracking devices on you as possible."

He turns out of our neighborhood, and I set about opening up the packaging.

"You know, I've been thinking about that. The black box that he had on the helicopter. Do you think that was planned? Like they specifically brought a metal storage box that would block all signals?"

"Did he make a big deal about putting your stuff in it?"

"No. I mean, as you know, there's not a lot of space for extra stuff. It felt completely normal. Gemma gave him her handbag and phone, too."

"And she kept it in there when you landed?"

"I think so." I think back to us walking away from the helicopter, and me saying that I forgot my handbag. She'd said, *No, ma'am. Your money is no good today. This is on me.* And we'd walked off arm in arm to a waiting car. She did have her handbag with her. "She gave me my phone. It just didn't have cell service."

"If they suspected anything, you wouldn't have made it home. If it was a test, we passed." He flicks his signal to turn onto the freeway. "Did you figure anything out today?"

"With my research?" He nods and accelerates to pass a car.

"No. Not really."

"What're you searching for?"

"That's the problem. I don't really know. I keep thinking about what Killington said. To follow the connections."

"And?"

"I think I'm looking too closely. Everyone's connected. Through professional organizations, political parties, business connections. I think I'm going to step back and instead of focusing on how they're connected, think about what each person gets from it."

"What do you mean?"

"Well, take a politician. They raise money. In return for support, they vote a certain way on a bill. Or they might convince a DA or law enforcement to look the other way. Those are just players, right? Pawns, maybe knights on a chessboard. A company like, well, let's say Sullivan Arms. My family's company. They just want to sell more guns. Deliver to shareholders by increasing profit. They're more of a resource. A part that feeds a larger machine."

"Crime organizations?"

"Yes. Crime organizations."

"Are you a cabal conspiracist?"

"As in there's a group at the very top, pulling all the strings?" He nods with a grin. "I used to think that. But, no, now I think they probably do know each other, but the organization between organizations would be looser. They would only collaborate if it's beneficial. Like legitimate businesses do."

"And so your goal is to take them apart? One by one?"

"Climb the ladder." That's what we do in all of our stings. Start with the worker bees and hope to find the person in charge. It's what makes the Toro operation a success, no matter what happens. We've got an inside connection high up the ladder. "To go back to the chess analogy, it's nabbing the pawns, the knights, the queen, until you uncover the king."

"It's amazing to me," Fisher says.

"What?" Nothing I have said is amazing. It's basic criminal justice strategy.

"You could've easily ended up just like your friends Lauren or Zane. Spending your days shopping and living off your parents. Clothes could've been your nirvana. Or travel. Or whatever the rich kids are into these days. But you're not like that at all. You're on a mission."

"I guess I am." I pull my leg up onto the seat. He's right. Before the abduction, I'd been just like Lauren. The most important thing in my life had been the upcoming Taylor Swift concert. "Before the abduction, I knew crime existed. But in a tangential way."

"Becoming a victim changes you."

"I'm not a victim." My muscles tense at the use of that word. "I'm a survivor."

"Yes, you are. Strongest woman I've ever met." There's respect in his tone and those blue eyes. It makes me love him more. "And you'll get them."

"Whoever them is," I say, thinking back to my board of white string connections. I need an in.

My CIA phone vibrates, and I pick it up and check it.

GEMMA TORO:

> I'm so sorry about today! Feeling better. (celebrate emoji) And so excited you're coming. Wish you were here now. Rafael is going to be locked in meetings. (sad face emoji) What shall we do tomorrow? (high heel emoji) (champagne emoji) (beach umbrella emoji)

I tap out a message to her and read it to Fisher before sending.

ME:

> So glad you're feeling better! (celebrate emoji) We're driving down now. Decided to avoid the morning rush hour. Want to meet up for dinner? (wine emoji)

"Tell her it can be a girl's dinner if she wants. Tell her I need to prepare for a client meeting tomorrow."

"Good idea. She might not want to eat with both of us."

He clucks his tongue and winks, and I alter the text. After that's sent, I call my dad. He's not in my phone directory, but I have his number memorized. And it's an unknown number to his cell, so of course he doesn't answer. I leave a message.

"Dad, this is Sophia. Give me a call when you can. This is my work number. I love you."

"Knocking it all out, huh?"

"Might as well use the drive time productively, right?"

"I can think of some other ways we could use the time."

"Is that right?"

I lean across the seat and rub his thigh. His grin is devilish.

He says, "You've got the right idea," as my phone vibrates.

I sit back and check the number.

"Dad," I say, and he nods, eyes on the road. I answer the phone with, "Dad?"

"Sophia. Everything okay?"

"Yeah. We're driving—"

"Down to LA, I know."

Of course he does. "Right. So, listen. You owe Fisher an apology."

"Excuse me?"

Fisher casts a side glance my way and shakes his head three times quickly, telling me no.

"You punched him."

"Sophia." It's the dad voice.

"Dad."

"He's significantly older than you."

"You're getting morally righteous now? The man who dated my therapist?"

"Don't talk to me like that. Fisher looked out for you when you were a child. It's sick. He has no business dating you. You deserve better."

"Dad." This time I soften his name. He may never understand, but he doesn't have to. "I love him. And he loves me. We're going to be together whether you approve or not." I glance to Fisher. He's gripping the steering wheel so hard his fingers are turning white. "But I'd rather this not cause a rift between us." Fisher glances at me when I use his word. "But it's in your court."

"Fisher's with you now?"

"Yes."

"Tell him I'll see him when he gets to LA."

"Dad." I say his name with an authoritative, warning tone.

"I've got to run. I'm about to land. I love you, sweet pea. Be safe. Be smart."

A dial tone sounds. I check, and yes, he ended the call. *And there you have it, ladies and gentleman, Mr. Jack Sullivan.*

"He hung up."

Fisher reaches for my hand and intertwines his fingers with mine. "I'll talk to him."

I don't tell him that that's exactly what Dad said. I'm twenty-five years old and both my father and Fisher are acting like I'm not the key player here, when in actuality, this is my life. Dad doesn't get a say. And Fisher...it's frustrating. He should just back me. He should fight for us.

"Just give him time, Sophia. He'll come around."

"And if he doesn't?"

He turns those dark blue eyes on me, darker in the cabin of the vehicle, and turns the world to rights. "He doesn't have a choice."

FISHER

The only room available on short notice is a bungalow on the edge of the property. It's actually ideal for us, as there's an exit to the street. It also cost a small fortune, but my partner doesn't care if Uncle Sam covers the expenditures.

I'm a saver and an investor. I've done well, partially due to a lifestyle where I hoarded pay and spent little for years. But, as she pays cash for the room, it occurs to me I'll need to perfect the blind eye when it comes to her spending. We might be able to justify reserving a room here given our targets are here, but something tells me she won't submit the expense. She does hand over the credit card that's in Sophia Garcia's name but gives specific instructions that she'd rather pay in cash.

In the room, she makes contact with Gemma. The plan is for them to meet for a drink in the lobby, then go to some exclusive restaurant where Gemma managed to get reservations. She's already sent the name of the restaurant to the team. We'll have surveillance on them, but we're most interested in Rafael and who he's meeting with.

"How do I look?"

She's wearing sky-high heels and a red dress that's somehow

classy and leaves little to the imagination. Her crimson hair falls around her shoulders in a smooth, shiny drape. She's applied more eye makeup. It's not too much, but it makes her light blue eyes pop, and there's a light pink blush along her cheekbones that exudes youthful innocence.

"Gorgeous." The dress is short, but it's not so short she can't sit comfortably. Still, it exposes plenty of creamy white thigh, and those long, lean legs are spectacular. "Are you carrying?"

"I can't fit a gun in this dress." She looks down at herself wistfully and lifts the hem of the dress as if double-checking her conclusion. But she's right. She might be able to secure a small blade, but if she sat wrong, it might be detectable. And she and Gemma will be drinking. After the vineyard incident, lower risk is better.

"What about your handbag?"

"I have a Sig in it. But I'm debating taking it out. I'm worried that when I go to pay, she may see it."

For what she has planned this evening, many CIA officers wouldn't carry. One could argue she's bringing more risk on herself by carrying a weapon.

"If Gemma sees it, tell her that after seeing you in that dress, I insisted you carry it."

Her glossy lips curve into a pleased smile. "Good idea. I'll play it off like I hate guns, but my overprotective husband feels better if I carry one."

"You've got your earpiece in?"

She nods.

"And your trackers?"

"Yes..." Her mouth opens and she snaps it closed, like she was going to say more but she decided against it. "I have a tag in my clutch, and there's a tracker on this bracelet." She points at one of the gold bracelets on her wrist. It's stacked with two tennis bracelets that glitter and scream money.

"If she talks you into going clubbing, you just remember you're coming home to me."

A wicked smile plays across her lips. I think she likes my protective side. "I don't think she's going to feel like hitting night clubs when she's recovering from food poisoning. But, if I'm wrong, trust me when I say you don't have anything to worry about."

She sidles up to me. The tips of those nails circle the back of my neck, twisting the hair. Her velvety, hot kiss has me wanting to push her up against the wall, lift that scrap of material higher, and take her. I'm hard as rock at the thought, and the tease backs away, taking my breath with her. She wipes my lips with her fingers.

"If you don't get out that door in the next thirty seconds, I can't be held accountable for what happens."

She gives me a coy smile, triple-checks the contents of the bag she's carrying, and heads out. It's a smaller bag, so small it's surprising to me she can pull off carrying a handgun in it. The door closes behind her, and I stare at it, willing my erection down.

The plan is for her to tell Gemma I'm meeting up with a friend. That way, if I'm seen out and about, no one will think much of it. I check my Glock, slide it into the holster at my waist, put on a jacket that sufficiently covers it, insert my earpiece, and head out the back way, onto the street.

Twenty minutes later, after I'm certain no one is trailing me, I knock on the door of a utility van. Jack Sullivan pushes the door open, and I step inside. He glances behind me, then closes us in.

"You've got eyes on Sophia?" I ask, stepping into the van.

Ryan and Trevor are crowded on the far end. A woman with blue hair and a headset sits at a computer. I lean over to see her screen. She's tapped into the hotel's security system, and the view is of the entrance to the lobby bar. I can make out the back of Sophia's dress.

"We've got two women in the bar. Monitoring."

"Good. Any word on where Rafael is?"

"We're thinking he's in the suite. Sent turndown service up, but Gemma turned it away, so we haven't been able to get in the room."

"Now that she's away, you going to try again?"

Jack answers my question. "We have another team in a food service truck two blocks away. Staging for operatives in hotel employee attire. Once they leave for the restaurant, they'll send someone else back in. If the room's vacant, we'll get it wired." I give a quick nod. "Can we chat for a minute?"

At the front of the van, there's a door to the portion of the van where the driver sits. He gestures to it. I don't bother answering, but head to the private area he seems to have commandeered. Might as well get this over with.

The thin door closes with a click. There's no way the others won't hear what we say, but the section has the semblance of privacy. The space is crowded.

This has to be done, but I want to get back to the op. I'm particularly curious who Alejandro is meeting with here in LA. Or, more particularly, who he's introducing his son to.

"Jack." I say his name the way I'd greet someone I didn't particularly care for but held a rank higher than mine. "I love your daughter." I look head-on into his menacing eyes. "I understand I'm not your first choice for her. I promise you, I didn't plan this. But I love her. And I'm not leaving her. Ever." If the CIA doesn't let us work as joint operatives, I'll step away from the CIA. I'd been thinking about doing that anyway.

"She's so young."

"She's twenty-five, Jack. Fully capable of making her own decisions."

"I know that." He spews the words. "But how could you?"

I could ask him if he planned on falling for Ava, his wife, but this isn't a tit for tat. It's not about him. It's about me. It's about

Sophia. It's about us. "Your daughter is amazing." She's intelligent, cunning, driven." I leave off sexy as hell, but his fists clench all the same, and it's as if he can read my mind. "She's many things, Jack, but one thing she's not is a little girl. Not anymore. And I've fallen in love with her. We went into this pretending to be married. You're correct, I don't deserve her. But if I have my way, one day we'll be married legally. I'll live the rest of my days working to keep her safe." A visual of Sophia's wall of connections flashes before me. "I'll back her. Support her. And die keeping her safe."

"Damn right, you will."

The only light comes from a streetlight fifteen feet outside. Jack's lips are in a flat line. His eyes unreadable in the dimness. He raises his arm, and I instinctively flinch but hold in place. If he needs to punch me again, so be it.

But he clasps my arm. "Not thrilled about it. But there's no one out there who would thrill me. She could do worse."

The door slings open.

"Gemma forgot something back in the room. Sophia's joining her to pick it up."

Jack and I both push through the narrow alley to the computer and the blue-haired woman, but the screen still shows the lobby.

"Shit. We don't have eyes?" I snap my fingers. "Can I get in on the audio?"

The blue haired woman clicks away, and static comes through my audio feed.

"Can you hear her?" I look to Ryan and Trevor.

"It's coming in and out. They're in the elevator."

This is fucked up. She's entering a suite with god knows who, and we don't have visuals or men close by. One quick scan of the van and it's clear I'm not the only one thinking of this.

But she and Gemma are friends. There's no reason to panic. Alejandro is a diplomat. It's all going to be kosher. They'll pop in, pop out, go to dinner.

"Wait, hold on." It's Gemma's voice. "I can't take another step in this shoe. It's cutting into me."

"Here, hold. I've got you." That's Sophia.

There's giggling. I press my hand over my ear, straining to hear better.

Knock. Knock.

Gemma must be knocking on the suite door. That means someone is inside. My heart rate kicks up a notch. I hate this. I far prefer to be in the field, in the moment. My palms sweat. There's no reason for this reaction. Gemma will change shoes, Sophia will say hello to whoever is in there, and they'll leave and be on their way to dinner.

"Hi, Ivan." That's Sophia.

There's a shuffling noise. Steps on a floor. Carpeted.

An audible gasp. Close by.

Shit. That's Sophia.

"You?"

CHAPTER 35
SOPHIA

"Sophia?"

Wayne Killington looks as confused as I am. He's sitting on one side of the sofa. His skin has more color since I saw him last, but his off-white Tommy Bahama shirt with brown and green palm fronds across the front highlights his wrinkles and sallow complexion.

A dignified older man with a shock of white hair on top of weathered brown skin sits in an armchair to the right of Killington. I recognize him as Alejandro Toro.

Rafael sits in the armchair across from his father, his back to me, but he turns when Killington addresses me.

"You know Sophia?" Rafael asks.

Gemma steps past me, shoes in her hand. "We just stopped by for me to change my shoes. We'll be gone in just a minute." She rushes down the hall to what is presumably a bedroom.

Ivan is to my back, near the door of the suite. I don't see any of the other members of Rafael's entourage, but they must be near.

One man behind me. Three in front. The three in front don't appear to be armed. Ivan is.

"Why is she here?" Killington asks. He sinks into the cushion

on the couch, making him appear lower. A subservient player on the chessboard.

"Why are you here?" I direct the question to Killington, ignoring all others in the room.

My senses elevate. Awareness piques. I hear the air conditioning. See the red dot of a plane light passing in the distance through the window. My fingers tense. Ready.

Confusion crosses his expression. He's looking between me and the Toros. He gives a half-laugh. "I'm guessing you guys don't know she's FBI?"

In my periphery I see Gemma appear in the hallway, sparkly platform Golden Gooses on her feet.

Alejandro sits like a king on a throne. Calm. Dark brown eyes taking it all in.

"We met her in Canada." I can't see Rafael's face, but his tone sounds skeptical.

The CalTan team has to be hearing this. No one wants a shootout. Voices from the courtyard waft in through the window.

"Sophia Garcia." Rafael turns his questioning gaze my way.

"Hate to break it to you guys, but this is Sophia Sullivan."

Alejandro's eyes narrow. "Why is that name familiar?"

"Cassandra Sullivan. Remember her?"

Killington has the Toros' attention. An object presses against my spine. Ivan's spicy cologne fills my nostrils.

He's standing too close. I can take him. When I need to.

"What does my mother have to do with this?"

Killington's smile falls. He looks to Alejandro, then to me.

Recognition lights Alejandro's face. "She's the woman who knew too much."

My mouth opens. It's an involuntary reaction. I need to breathe, and my lungs are contracting.

Slowly, I open my clutch. The movements are tiny, so as not to

alert Ivan. My fingers wrap around the smooth handle, the index finger around the trigger. The clutch falls to the floor.

Gemma gasps. "Sophia, what're you doing?"

I point my gun at the back of Rafael's head. If Ivan shoots, I'll take Rafael with me.

This doesn't add up. There's no reason for Killington to hold back now, so it's question time. "I thought you worked for the Moreno cartel?"

"The Morenos worked for us," Rafael says.

Alejandro shoots him a look that I interpret as telling his son to keep quiet.

"I hired a few of the Morenos. Sold to them. But I never worked for them." Killington's looking at me with mournful eyes. I recognize the expression because it's the one he wore at my mother's funeral.

"And now you're back in the game."

He shakes his head. "This is a meeting with old friends. We haven't broken any laws, Sophia. There's nothing you can arrest us for."

"Is that why there's a gun pointed at my spine?"

"This is the girl you abducted," Alejandro says matter-of-factly. He's put it all together now.

"And raped," I add. I hold Killington's gaze, waiting for him to deny it. Out of the corner of my eye, I see a flash of coral nails cover Gemma's bright red lips.

"Only because I loved your mother," Wayne says.

"Say that again?" The gun in my hand quivers. The muscles in my forearms strain.

"I loved your mother. Missed her. You looked so much like her." His hands are still. He looks me in the eye. The sick fuck believes this clears him.

"You loved her so much you had her killed?"

"Not me." His gaze cuts to Alejandro. So does my gun.

"Do you have a silencer on that gun?" Alejandro asks the man behind me.

I drop to the floor, roll, and shoot.

Pow.

Ivan's head splatters against the wall.

My hands are ice. Training kicks in. Overrides. Gun raised. Finger curved behind the trigger.

Killington rises off the sofa. One hand is up, defensively. One hand comes around from behind his back. A flash of metal.

Pull.

The bullet hits his sternum. Below his gold chain.

I direct my gun between Rafael and Alejandro. Alejandro's hands are on the armrests. Rafael's left hand is near me. I can't see his right.

My eyes burn. I blink. *Breathe. Focus.*

There's a click of a gun. Close to my ear.

"Put the gun down, Sophia."

I keep my gun trained on Rafael. "Gemma, don't do this. There's a SWAT team approaching. They'll be here any minute. Don't do this. You haven't broken any laws. Not yet. You aren't a part of this."

"Put the gun down," she repeats. But her voice cracks. This isn't her scene.

Glass shatters. Alejandro's head falls forward, the back of his scalp a mix of red and creamy white.

A green dot lights Rafael's forehead and travels down.

"Surrender." It comes out as a whisper.

The dull *pop, pop, pop* of guns with silencers rings nearby. They're in the hallway.

"Gemma. Rafael. You can work with us. We'll take care of you."

The door slams open. "FBI!"

CHAPTER 36
SOPHIA

The acrid smell of gun residue and blood taints the air. I direct my gun at Rafael.

"Gemma. Put your gun down." It's Fisher. He's here.

She lets out a sob. "You won't kill him?"

"No. Hand me your gun." Fisher holds his hand out. "No one else has to get hurt." Out of the corner of my eye, I see Gemma's hands cover her face.

Fisher stands behind me. To my frozen skin, he's hot. He presses his ear. "We've got her. All clear."

My gaze tracks to the hole in the glass. A web of cracks. Alejandro's gaping head.

"Baby, it's okay. It's over."

In training, they talk about an out-of-body experience. I lived it once. But it was hazy. I was drugged. There are no drugs in my system now. And I feel like my soul has departed my body and I'm taking in the room. Blood stains the carpet. Blood spray covers the walls, the coffee table, the sofa.

Three men in SWAT gear and AR rifles line up in the hall. One man latches handcuffs on Gemma. Out the window, across

the courtyard, I swear I think I see the shadow of my father, putting away his long gun.

Killington's eyes are open. His fingers still clutch his handgun. It has a walnut handle. One from the Sullivan Arms custom collection. He's dead. A corpse.

And behind me, my first kill. Ivan. A hired man.

"Sophia, babe." Fisher's hand covers my wrist. The touch kicks off a chain of reactions. I blink. Swallow. "It's okay."

I meet Rafael's gaze. "You'll work with us?"

He gives a slight nod, and I lower my gun.

There's a flurry of activity. Everything had gone quiet. But now I hear police sirens and the whir of a helicopter. A floodlight shines over the courtyard.

My hand muscles cramp, and I pass the gun to my other hand and stretch out the fingers.

Fisher wraps his arm around me. He pulls me into his chest. He's wearing a vest, and the rough edges cut into my skin, but relief he's wearing one surfaces.

"You okay?" Ryan stands in front of me. A flashback to him standing there, years ago, when I was rescued, hits me. He'd stood off in the distance as my father carried me away from a nightmare.

"I'm good."

My dad pushes through the line of agents and officers, Trevor following him. "You okay?"

My gaze falls to Ivan on the ground. Part of his skull is missing.

"You dropped to the ground like we taught you," Trevor says, pride evident. He's a coach, through and through.

"Thought I was going to have a heart attack when you did that. We weren't quite set up yet." Dad's a sniper, but he's careful. He doesn't take a shot unless he's sure.

"You were on the roof?" I glance out the shattered window, to the building across the courtyard.

"We didn't know if we might have a hostage situation," he

explains unnecessarily. I'm sure when they heard what was going on, they jumped to cover all possible events. "What was Killington doing here?"

Gemma and Rafael are no longer in the room. They've been escorted out.

"I'm not one hundred percent," I say, "but I think he was here to get initiated. Again. Did you hear? Alejandro had Mom killed."

"I heard." He squeezes my shoulder, his gaze on me. He doesn't need to tell me he's the one who took Alejandro out.

"Where'd they take Gemma and Rafael?"

"CIA, FBI, and DEA are all going to want a turn at them," Ryan says.

I lean into Fisher. His arm is around me. Sensation creeps back into my skin. "We should be there first," I say to him. "They're our contacts." Gemma might've known what she was marrying into, but she didn't know it all. "Gemma's going to need me."

"We'll get to them. It's a madhouse outside. They're getting them away. Officially, this will be an FBI operation," Ryan says. "I've got orders to get you both out of here without being photographed."

The fog lifts. My body's still ice cold, and my fingers quiver, but a sense of urgency rises. "We need to get the word out that Alejandro died from..." I glance over at his lifeless body and exploded skull, "an aneurysm."

I push away from Fisher, needing space to think. "We'll say he died suddenly and unexpectedly. There will be an autopsy that determines cause of death as an aneurysm. You'll fix the body so when they request the body be returned to Colombia, no one will suspect anything."

"Outside, news stations are everywhere," Ryan says, clearly questioning me.

"No. This is a huge win if we can get Rafael back into

Colombia without anyone knowing he's been compromised. He'd be an incredible source."

"You think you can get him on your side?" Ryan asks.

"Let me try." I look to Fisher. "Let us try. He said he'd work with us." All the pieces fall into place. "Look at it this way. If what really happened comes out, this will be an international incident. You'll never get the evidence to convict him in a US court, much less an international court. This is our best bet. If we support him taking over his father's position in the Colombian government, we'll have an inside source at the highest levels."

"What's in it for him?" Fisher's dark blue eyes support me, he's simply asking the right questions.

"He's an international playboy. That's the life he loves. If what really happened here comes out, there's a good chance it won't play out well for him back home. All he needs is one enemy to start rumors that work against him. If he plays this with us, he gets to return home gaining the sympathy of his country, a role that will allow him to continue to travel internationally and do all the crazy sport shit he likes, and it's less likely he'll be caught in cartel crossfire. It's a safer life for his wife than trying to take over the cartel side of the business."

"But we'll be taking the information he gives us and effectively shutting down the trafficking business. His father literally leveraged his role to build those channels," Trevor argues.

"True. But let us talk to him. According to our intelligence, he's new to this side of the family business. There's a good chance he's not crazy about it. And his father accumulated a significant amount of wealth over the last several decades. He doesn't need the money. He might welcome this. And even if he only agrees to share information related to other crime businesses, not his family's, it's invaluable information. It'll be the highest-ranking source within a crime organization." My skin tingles with excitement at the thought. There's so much to learn about how

these organizations interact with each other and with powers within the US. And Rafael will be in the perfect position to question and acquire information, because he can claim his father didn't have time to teach him everything.

"People heard gunfire. There's a news helicopter outside," Trevor says, pointing.

"Right. Dad, you've got to get your best PR team on this." He blinks his agreement. "Make up a story. Freeway chase. Guy got out of his car, on foot. Something." I look around the blood splattered suite. "This is the Chateau Marmont. Tons of shit happens here. This will add to the mystique. Just get someone covering the tapes to ensure the story matches what any cell phones out there might've picked up."

Dad pulls out a phone from his back pocket and heads out.

"Ryan, can you run point with the CalTan team? Sell them on this plan?" He nods. "Fisher and I need to get to Rafael and Gemma ASAP."

Trevor crosses his arms and gestures to Ivan. "What about this guy?"

"I'm not sure. We need a story that sounds right to the Colombians. We can ask Rafael for his suggestions. If no one's looking for him, maybe we can just say he chose to stay in the US." A low-level nausea stirs as I take in his still warm form. But it's good he died. I'd never trust him to not rat out Rafael.

Fisher grimaces. "He's Colombian. He's probably got a family."

"Right." I bet the CIA has a full rundown of his family in our database. "Well, he also has a gun, and the FBI stormed the hotel looking for a suspect. If we have to work that angle, we can."

Ryan pulls out his phone and dials, walking in the direction my dad went.

"Where are the other guys? It was more than Ivan."

"FBI pulled them. They were eating dinner at the bar when

everything went FUBAR." *Fucked up beyond all recognition. Right.*

"Okay. Trevor, when a story is finalized, be sure to apologize to them. Tell them they were mistakenly pulled aside."

"Wait. One other guy is dead. He was manning the hall," Trevor says.

"Okay. Work it into the Ivan story. Ideally, we can play this as a chase off the freeway. That's a Tuesday in LA. Panic ensued when a Colombian official lost consciousness. That's the reason for the ambulance."

"And Killington?" Trevor asks.

Killington. A man I hated. Despised. The man who should've been my first kill. "I visited him at his house recently. He appeared depressed. The CIA has people we can call. Let's have them move him to his house and make it look like suicide. He won't be the first guy to get out of prison and not be able to handle it."

I look to Trevor and Fisher. "Have we got a plan?"

They glance at each other, and both men nod. Wordsmiths, these two.

"All right. Let's go find Rafael and Gemma."

Trevor leads us through a maze of FBI and LAPD. He's worked enough cases, and been to enough Operation CalTan meetings, he's recognized. Within twenty minutes, we're escorted through a private entrance away from the press commotion and driven to the holding facility where Gemma and Rafael are being kept for interrogation.

If we can pull this off, it will be an enormous victory. In the back seat of the car, my adrenaline crashes. I lean into Fisher. A deep exhaustion falls over me. It's like nothing I've ever felt before. Fisher might be feeling it, too. He holds me tight, eyes closed as the unmarked car glides through the city streets.

CHAPTER 37
FISHER

It takes hours for the talking heads to duke it out and for the CIA to win the battle for rights to Rafael and Gemma. It's almost four a.m. by the time we're allowed into the interrogation room. Coffee and food helped us through the inevitable adrenaline crash. In the last couple of hours, Sophia worked her magic and located a federal safe house for us to transition Rafael and Gemma to so they won't feel like animals, Sophia's word.

The plan is, if they agree to working with us, we'll transition them to the more comfortable environment where they can shower and sleep. Security is being set up by the location. We'll position it as for Rafael and Gemma's benefit, but it'll be pretty clear that we're keeping an eye on them, at least until they return to Colombia.

We've already spoken with Bauer at length. He's thrilled and is calling this the biggest win of the year. If we can win them over. A lot of times in this kind of situation, it wouldn't be an "if." We'd have prosecutors working with the FBI to ink out a deal for a more lenient sentencing in exchange for working with us. But it's trickier with individuals who are not American citizens.

The FBI agent running point for Operation CalTan exits the

room, along with the DEA officers. One of the women warns us, "They aren't being particularly cooperative."

"You wanted names of anyone within the DEA working with them, right?" Sophia asks.

"We know they've got people on the inside." The woman sounds frustrated, but she also looks exhausted.

"He may not know the names. There are layers," Sophia says. "We'll figure it out."

"Well, they're yours," the FBI agent says. "I'm gonna go get coffee. I'll be here when you're done. You guys get the call on where they head after this, right?"

A holding cell or the safe house. "We do," I tell him.

"Good luck," he says with an expression that reads he's got zero faith we'll get anywhere.

After they leave, Sophia places her hand on the doorknob, and I touch her shoulder, stopping her for a moment.

"Whatever happens in there, this is a victory." Her lashes flutter as she places her hand on mine. "I'll follow your lead." Her lips turn up into an appreciative smile. "I love you."

"I love you, too."

I bend down until my lips hover near her ear. "Now, let's get this done so we can get back to our hotel room and I can show you how much I love you."

It's four a.m., and she's dead on her feet, but a slight blush lights her cheeks. Stunning. Brilliant. Mine.

She turns the knob, and we enter the interrogation room.

Gemma and Rafael sit at a table. They're both handcuffed, and the cuffs are locked to the center of the table.

"What?" Sophia gasps. "Oh, my god." She turns to me. "Damian, can you get the keys?"

"Damian's your real name?" Rafael asks. He's smart enough to suspect aliases.

I look him straight in the eye, man to man. "Damian's my first name. I'll be right back."

Of course, the plan had been for us to be the ones who got them out of handcuffs and brought them comfort. The keys are three feet out of the room, but I pause, giving enough time for it to be believable that I had to go chase them down.

When I return, Sophia has food spread out on the table and her arm is around Gemma. I unlock the cuffs, and Rafael rubs his wrists while Gemma puts her arms around Sophia's neck.

Rafael makes a noise in his throat, and Gemma pulls back, but her gaze remains on Sophia. "That man...he raped you?"

Sophia nods, and my insides burn. It's not news to me, but it feels like it is. Gemma clasps Sophia's hand and turns to Rafael. "Who was he?" He opens his mouth, and in Spanish she adds, "Not his name. Who was he to you?"

In Spanish, he says to her with a fraction of the energy she threw into her question, "They killed my father. Why are you holding her hand?"

"Sophia did not kill your father," Gemma says, but she lets Sophia's hand go and shifts her chair closer to her husband.

Sophia kneels on the ground, positioning herself to address them both. "I'm sorry about your father. My mother was killed. I remember how much it hurts. Still hurts."

Rafael says nothing. His expression is stone. Gemma's mascara stains her cheeks. Most of her eyeshadow is missing, and the area below her eyes appears puffy. Her lips purse, then her lower lip quivers. I get the sense she might cry.

I pull out the chair across from them and sit. "None of this was supposed to happen," I say. "Did they treat you badly before we got here?"

Gemma slowly shakes her head, but it's Rafael who speaks. "What's going to happen to us? I don't have the information they want."

"We have a place we're going to take you. So you can get some sleep."

"Prison?"

"No. A comfortable place," Sophia says.

"I asked to speak to a lawyer. They denied me," Rafael says.

"We're hoping you won't need one," I say, and he raises an eyebrow.

"Are you FBI?" he asks. "FBI has already been in here." His dark eyes narrow with distrust.

"Wayne thought I was FBI. That's what he knew me as. I haven't worked for the FBI in over eighteen months."

"So, how do you fit into this?" He's looking between the two of us, and Gemma's gaze has fallen to the ground. She's going to let Rafael lead this discussion.

"We're CIA," Sophia says.

Rafael almost looks amused. "So that's what you were doing in Canada? Trying to make contact with us. Dad always warned me to be careful. You. Interpol. MI6. Danger everywhere."

Sophia acknowledges his soft accusation with gracious understanding conveyed solely in her expression.

Rafael closes his eyes and tilts his head back.

"We have a proposition for you," Sophia says gently.

He crosses his arms over his chest. Gemma covers one of his forearms with her hand, and something heavy passes between them.

"Sophia, I remember your mother."

Sophia's eyes widen, and while I have an urge to leap across the table and hold her, my woman doesn't need to be held. Not right now. She's strong.

"I didn't know her," Rafael says, clarifying his statement. "But I remember the decision being made. My father. My uncle. More my uncle. She overheard a meeting. One of our security men found her hovering outside. When he opened the door to the

room, she saw all the participants. That man, Wayne Killington, he did try to convince them she didn't know what she saw. They didn't want to take any risk. My father rewarded his loyalty over the years."

"By buying guns?" Sophia asks.

He shrugs. "He rose in the ranks. I remember the decision being made, but I was young. *Fútbol* was my life then." A small smile plays along his lips, as if he's remembering better days. The smile falters, and he addresses Sophia. "I want you to know, I didn't have anything to do with your *madre*. That wasn't me."

Sophia rises and drags a chair over. "You and I are even, Rafael." He lifts an eyebrow in silent question. "My father killed your father. He was the sniper on the roof across the courtyard. He heard him say..." Her voice trails as if she can't bear to finish the sentence. We're all too tired for this. But we have to do this now.

"My father killed your mother, so your father killed my father." Disgust plays across Rafael's features, and he rubs his face with his palm. "This is life in Colombia."

"Well, we'd like to work together to help improve things." Sophia straightens. She's ready to bring it to the table. She's no longer wearing that skimpy red dress and heels. One of the agents lent her a navy sweatshirt and sweats, and white socks. Her crimson hair is pulled back. Tired, but she's determined.

"How, exactly, can you improve life in Colombia?"

"We want to throw support behind you assuming your father's position." He wasn't expecting her to say this, but Sophia pushes forward and explains the entire plan. How the official word will be that his father died unexpectedly. We'll say he's spent the night at the hospital. An autopsy will confirm the aneurysm findings.

"And how will you explain Wayne Killington?"

"How well known is he in Colombia?" Sophia asks.

"Not very." His countenance is both grim and reflective. "He hasn't worked for us in ten years. This meeting you came into, it

was one of many meetings my father lined up. We were going to see if he could resume working with us. Dad was going to try to help him get back on his feet. At one point in time, he managed the relationship with the Morales cartel, but they're..." His fingers flay and he moves them as if to say they're nothing now.

"So our plan will work. We'll make it look like he committed suicide at his home. Chances are no one will discover the body for days, if not weeks. The connection won't be made to your father."

"You can do that?" he asks.

"We've got a team working on it right now. We can do it."

Gemma reaches for him. Her eyes plead with him, but she doesn't speak.

"How will this work?" he asks. "What do you want me to do?"

"You'll take your father's role as a diplomat. You'll still be able to travel. You'll feed us intel as you can."

"You Americans." He shakes his head. "You blame us for your drug problem. But you sell us the guns. You siphon the drugs into your country. Your people get rich and want more. You are the greater problem."

Sophia's quick to respond. "That's true. Which is why we want your help. We're most interested in the structure within the US. You give us names, shipment dates, that kind of intel, and we'll set up stings on our side. It will never trace back to you. With time, we'll destroy the infrastructure." He swallows and his eyes glaze over. I half suspect he might tell us to go to hell. We don't have a case against him, and he has to have figured that out.

"My first three wives were murdered." Gemma swipes at a tear that runs down her cheek, her tearful gaze locked on her husband. "Cartel warfare. I'm not even involved other than as a family member. I leave the country as often as I can. I've refused to have children because it's too dangerous. Targets. I hate my uncle. I hate the destruction. What it's doing to my country. If I can help

you, I will. But I need your word, you're going to help me. Help my people."

Sophia and I exchange a glance, and at the same time, we say, "You've got it."

It takes a couple more hours to get Rafael and Gemma moved into the safe house. The sun has risen and a new day has taken hold by the time we're back in our room.

The chaos outside the hotel has quieted down. I'm sure somewhere within the walls of the hotel, workers are still cleaning. The news hasn't broken yet about Alejandro Toro, but descriptions of a high-speed chase that ended within the venerable walls of Chateau Marmont broke before we left the Toros.

Sophia stumbles to the bed, but I force her into the shower. There are specks of blood near her ear and along her chest that she missed in the bird bath she gave herself when she changed into sweats. I scrub every inch of her, caressing her, massaging her, and showing her in the best way I know how much I care. It's not sexual, but it is sensual and loving. With great care, I dry her, then myself, and carry her into the bedroom.

I draw the curtains and curl up behind her.

"You did it," I whisper softly.

Her eyelids close. "There's more to do," she murmurs.

"We'll do it. You've laid the groundwork."

"With a bang."

"Yes, you could say that."

She rolls onto her side, facing me. Her hands are flat, beneath her face. "I guess this means we're no longer married."

"Mmm." I brush a few red strands away from her face. "We can fix that, you know." This isn't the time for a proposal, but it is the time to make it crystal clear what I'm hoping for. "If I have my way, we'll be partners until the day I die. Partners in every sense of the word."

"Do you think the CIA will let us?" Her eyelashes flutter as sleep looms near.

"We'll ask. But that's not what I'm talking about."

"No?" She yawns, seconds away from sleep.

"You're an amazing woman, Sophia Sullivan. I want you in my bed. In my life. By my side for as long as I live. Think you're game for that?"

Her ruby red lips curve into a smile as she drifts. The pattern of her chest rising and falling evens out as I lie there watching over her, my heart, my soul. Her crimson strands spread across the pillow like a cloak.

She may or may not have heard me, but deep down, I know I'll spend the rest of my life watching over her, by her side, earning her love.

SEVEN YEARS LATER

"How's my favorite Fish?"

"Tired, Frankie. I'm tired." He smiles wide and the thick black moustache above his lip appears to magically lengthen.

"Well, head on up, lovely lady. Grumpy Fish awaits."

"He's not grumpy," I say, defensive of my husband as I wheel my suitcase past Frankie's coffee and newsstand.

"Not when he's with you."

A customer approaches, taking Frankie's attention, and with a wave, I push open the door into our condo. Shortly after returning to DC, Fisher and I moved in together. A luxurious new high-rise on Fisher's street opened up about a year later, and we purchased the penthouse we now live in.

We travel a lot, but there's nothing like coming home. After the CalTan Operation, we were asked to join an elite group within the CIA. Those first few years, we always traveled together. A regular spy team all over Europe and parts of South America. And Fisher was right. There is a plus side to having a couple work together.

Thanks to our Colombian intel source, we've busted hundreds of small-time smugglers and money launderers, senators and

congressman, and discovered more DEA agents in the mix. The small-time wins number in the hundreds. Best of all, we busted two massive international criminal organizations, including five high-powered billionaires who led the conglomerates.

We never learned if Senator Talbot died of natural causes or if he crossed the wrong person. That first year of working off tips from Rafael, we narrowed in on Zane's father, Congressman Oglethorpe. According to Rafael's sources, he acted as a conduit for providing safe harbors for yachts with drug shipments, but before we collected enough evidence to prosecute, he died in a helicopter crash. Zane remains blissfully unaware of his father's misdeeds. After his father's death, Zane joined a private practice as a defense attorney.

Rafael never took over his family's cartel, but he keeps communication channels open and has been an invaluable source of intel. The focus of his life's work has been building up his country. His hope is to help it become less dependent on questionable sources of revenue.

I've been true to my word and have been helping Rafael's people by investing in legitimate revenue sources for Colombia, such as tourism and agriculture, and helping the country to prepare for rising oceans. Rafael and Gemma trust me, and that goes a long way in the intelligence world.

Fisher left the CIA last year. He'll never say it, but I know it's because a leadership spot opened up in our unit, and he believed I earned it. He claims it was all timing. Arrow asked him to open a DC Arrow office.

I've enjoyed the greater responsibility, but I hate spending so much time apart. The new position also has me dividing time between the office and the field, which has given me time to think about what I want from the next chapters in my life.

The elevator door opens, and I hear his footfalls before he comes into view.

"There she is."

He has me in his arms, holding me close, and I breathe him in.

"I've been tracking you. Dinner's ready. You hungry?"

"You cooked?"

"I heated."

He nips at the side of my neck. The faint scent of curry wafts down the hall.

"And I've packed."

I pull back. "You packed for me?"

"I would never," he says dramatically. "But your suitcases are out. The driver's picking us up at nine."

In the morning, we're leaving for vacation. We're spending a few days with my family in San Diego. Ryan, Alex, Trevor, and Stella are coming too. Then we're going on a well-deserved vacation, just the two of us.

Ever the gentleman, he grips the handle on my suitcase to return it to our room for me. I kick off my shoes and pad through our home.

"I'll need for the car to come later. I'll handle rescheduling," I call after him.

"Something come up? You've got to go to the office?"

There's a hint of frustration in his tone, but he's the most supportive spouse in the world.

All along the walls, we have photos we've taken on exotic locations around the world. We've traveled to every single continent in the last five years, with the exception of Antarctica.

"Doctor's appointment," I mumble.

Fisher halts. "Everything okay?"

"Annual appointment."

He deposits my suitcase in our bedroom and returns to the kitchen.

"Heard a rumor," Fisher says, stopping in front of the island.

"What's that?"

"You're being considered for another promotion." His warm, strong hands caress my hips, and I lean back, into him. It feels so good to be home.

"You go to lunch with Bauer?"

"Please. Brought him lunch."

"How's he doing?"

"Fine if you don't count his blood pressure." He cages me in against the counter. "Did you accept?"

"Their offer?" I ask for clarification as I spin in his arms to face him. He blinks, his expression unreadable. "I asked for a more strategic position."

"Really?" His disbelief is mildly humorous. "But you love the field."

"I do." I nod and rub my fingers through his beard. "I did. I liked it more when you were in the field with me." It's a tiring life. It's not meant for forever. I've accomplished what I wanted and then some. I'll always want a career. Ideally in intelligence. But now, in my thirties, I find myself wanting more. I have Fisher and a robust chosen family with Arrow, but a strategic role opens up options. I pull his hand to my lips and press them to his knuckles. "But I wanted to talk to you about something."

"Yeah?"

"Well, tomorrow is my gynecologist appointment." He pulls back to better see me. His thumb strokes my throat, and I lean into his touch. "What would you think if I had her remove my IUD?"

His eyebrows narrow over his nose. "Seriously?"

The question is breathy, and if I'm hearing him correctly, hopeful.

"Yeah. I mean, it won't happen immediately—"

My feet leave the floor, and he grips me so tight my ribs constrict. He pulls back, and it's a look I recognize as him double-checking he read me right. "No more field work?"

"I like strategy."

He spins me in a circle, not kissing me, just looking at me in complete disbelief.

"It's not going to happen immediately," I say. "And, you know, I might choose later on to go back in the field. And if it's not something you want, I get it. It's just—"

His lips cover mine. And then he backs up, holding my face between his palms.

"I love you. So much. You know that?"

The dark blue irises I love so much glimmer beneath the light.

"You really want this?" He nods. "Why didn't you say anything?"

"I just...I want you to be happy."

"Well, husband of mine, what do you say we take our upcoming vacation, and see what happens without birth control?"

Once again, I'm in the air, only this time I'm slung over his shoulder, giggling, as he charges down the hall to our bedroom.

"Wait. It's still in."

"You know me. I'm all about the practice. The best things come to those who try, try, and persevere."

I bounce on our mattress, laughing. There's so much love. I see it. I hear it. And suddenly I'm not laughing at all.

I love my husband more than I ever thought possible. I love my life, and I love our future.

****

The Arrow Tactical Team continues with the Beauty trilogy, a modern twist on Grimm's Rapunzel.

Her sister vanished. Someone's trying to kill her. And the last person she'd choose to turn to is her only hope.

. . .

Alice Watson, a heart transplant survivor, is no stranger to life or death situations. But when her sister goes MIA and an assailant breaks into her house, Alice runs to the only person she knows who can help.

Knox Williams, a former SEAL and member of a black ops private security team, hasn't seen Alice since he graduated from the Naval Academy with her brother.

And while the attraction he felt for her then is still present, seeing Alice also brings back memories of the night her brother died. A night he'll forever hold himself responsible for.

Though his feelings are much deeper than guilt, Knox pushes them aside to keep his former friend and comrade's sister safe.

All clues point to Alice's sister, a scientist on the Cayman Islands, as the reason for Alice's current danger. It's clear whoever has her will do whatever it takes to silence Alice.

As Knox and Alice close in on the truth behind her sister's vanishing, they are plunged into mortal peril that tests their newfound relationship. Will they save her sister in time or will they become the next victims?

Releasing March 2024... Stolen Beauty

FROM THE AUTHOR...AKA IZZY

If you enjoyed the story, I hope you'll take a moment to leave a review. Five-star reviews truly do sell books, bringing me closer to the day when I might be able to do this full time. So I'm deeply grateful for them.

In case you are curious...

Better to See You is technically the first in the Arrow Series, but the Arrow series is a spin-off from the Twisted Vines series, which spun-off from the Haven Island series.

The Arrow Tactical team continues on in *Stolen Beauty*, Knox's story.

Her sister is missing. Someone's trying to kill her.

Knox is the last person she'd choose to turn to, but he's also her only hope.

ALSO BY ISABEL JOLIE

Standalone Romances

How to Survive a Holiday Fling (Oliver Duke and Kate)

Always Sunny (Ian Duke and Sandra)

The Romantics (Harrison and Zuri) - Releasing December, 2023

NOTES & GRATITUDE

Cloak of Red concludes what I think of as the "Wolf trilogy." It's not the end of the Arrow Tactical Series. I'm going to try something a little new and plan to do a minimum of three trilogies within the Arrow Tactical series. I like the Arrow Tactical family and I'm not ready to say goodbye to them forever, plus, they give me a platform to explore a number of different cases and modern retellings of human themes.

There are those who don't love first person, but it's almost always my favorite to read. I firmly believe it's a subjective thing. But, when it comes to writing a trilogy, I truly love the opportunity first person provides. To take one event and look at it from all these different angles. It's something I plan to continue to explore and play with.

When it comes to Cloak, there are a number of people I must thank. First, my husband, who I lovingly refer to as Mr. Jolie. He read the first draft and had me delete a ton of chapters. (PS - Look for deleted scenes) But, as usual, his feedback was spot on. Removing some of those chapters with Sophia's interactions with her father and brother made the whole story flow so much better.

I didn't hire a developmental editor for Cloak of Red, but I did hire Kimberly Hunt from Revision Division for a manuscript critique. I loved her input and insights and am grateful to her for her positive critique. She gave me confidence.

And along these lines thanks go to Lori Whitwam, the keeper of all the words and my editor since the beginning, and Karen

Cimms, my proofreader. Karen proofread all the books in the Wolf trilogy and I'm especially grateful for the time and care she takes. By the time she gets it, the errors are minimal, but I love knowing she's spent so much time pouring over it for any oversights.

And, as always, I have to thank my beta readers and ARC readers...and well, all my readers. There are so many books out there to read. **Thank you so much for choosing mine**.

ABOUT THE AUTHOR

Isabel Jolie, aka Izzy, lives on a lake, loves dogs of all stripes, and if she's not working, she can be found reading, often with a glass of wine. In prior lives, Izzy worked in marketing and advertising, in a variety of industries, such as financial services, entertainment, and technology. In this life, she loves daydreaming and writing contemporary romances with real, flawed characters and inner strength.

Sign-up for Izzy's newsletter to keep up-to-date on new releases, promotions and giveaways. (Pro-tip - She offers a free book on her home page...just scroll down after arriving at her site)

Or follow her on your favorite platform.

ALSO BY CAP DANIELS

BOOKS IN THIS SERIES
Book One: *The Russian's Pride*
Book Two: *The Russian's Greed*
Book Three: *The Russian's Gluttony*
Book Four: *The Russian's Lust*
Book Five: *The Russian's Sloth* (Winter 2022)

BOOKS IN THE CHASE FULTON NOVELS
Book One: *The Opening Chase*
Book Two: *The Broken Chase*
Book Three: *The Stronger Chase*
Book Four: *The Unending Chase*
Book Five: *The Distant Chase*
Book Six: *The Entangled Chase*
Book Seven: *The Devil's Chase*
Book Eight: *The Angel's Chase*
Book Nine: *The Forgotten Chase*
Book Ten: *The Emerald Chase*
Book Eleven: *The Polar Chase*
Book Twelve: *The Burning Chase*
Book Thirteen: *The Poison Chase*
Book Fourteen: *The Bitter Chase*
Book Fifteen: *The Blind Chase*
Book Sixteen: *The Smuggler's Chase*
Book Seventeen: *The Hollow Chase*
Book Eighteen: *The Sunken Chase*
Book Nineteen: *The Darker Chase* (Fall 2022)

OTHER BOOKS BY CAP DANIELS
Stand-alone Novels
We Were Brave

Novellas
The Chase Is On
I Am Gypsy

MW01258755

THE RUSSIAN'S LUST